AMBASSADOR 7: THE LAST FRONTIER

PATTY JANSEN

GET FREE EBOOKS

Visit pattyjansen.com
or scan the QR code below with your phone to get four series
starter ebooks for free!

1

———

MY FATHER'S KELPIE, Fred, was getting old. Where once he would have bounced along the beach, chasing seagulls, dipping in and out of the surf to bark at the dolphins that would come in close to the shore, he was now kind of limping along, finding it hard to keep up with retrieving his stick, especially if Thayu threw it. He would hobble after the stick stiff-legged, and would bring it back, carrying it in his mouth, where the hair around his snout had gone light grey. His ears would still twitch and perk up, but he no longer had the breath to bark much.

After three weeks at my father's house, Thayu was no longer afraid of him; and it was a good thing for me to see her playing with poor old Fred, even if afterwards he was so worn out that he spent the rest of the day sleeping on the rug in the living room in front of the heater.

Poor Fred had gotten a gruelling workout during our visit. The visit had been very nice, and, for once, most people had been respecting my vacation rather than inundating me with messages. I was almost beginning to wonder how things were going.

I had spoken to Dharma Yuwono a few times in the past three weeks. Dharma was smart, agile, from the Blue class, angry and keen to make things better for himself and his community. His priority was to get the Blue class interested in registering to vote and voting in the referendum, preferably *for* Earth to join *gamra*, without actually mentioning the referendum, because it hadn't been called yet.

Dharma had imposed a gruelling schedule on himself to travel to the major cities where influential Blue class groups of people resided: Delhi, Jakarta, Cairo, Bogotá, Lima, Caracas, Mexico City and Los Angeles, to name a few.

There were far more of the Blues than there were Whites, and a very high proportion of Blues had neither voted in previous elections nor even registered.

Dharma was putting in a lot of groundwork, travelling to the corners of his extensive community, speaking to people in poor parts of the world and giving his local contacts information to pass around. I'd gotten one message from him a couple of weeks ago with vids of rooms full of men and women showing off stamps on their hands and their registration confirmation on whatever devices they used for communication.

Dharma had also crafted a number of vids, from documents and recorded speeches—for those who couldn't read—that set out the reasons why the status quo wasn't working, what companies owned by the Pretoria Cartel were doing to their workers and why joining *gamra* would undermine the cycle of abuse.

We had one chance and this was it.

I'd also seen in the news that Robert Davidson's trial had ended a week ago with a most unsatisfactory fizzle. Judge Hermans had convicted him of being a leading cause of Gusamo Sahardjo's death, and he had been sentenced to house arrest for five years, to be reduced based on good behaviour.

I was not happy with that. I suspected few people were happy. Good behaviour! Men like Robert *bought* good behaviour. He'd be free to do whatever he wanted in no time, and no doubt we'd soon see him back in Barresh, up to his old tricks. If that happened I couldn't guarantee that none of the Thousand Island Pengali were going to stick a knife in him, unhappy as they had every right to be with this lame excuse for a justice system.

In an effort to ameliorate a bad situation, I'd sought to communicate with Robert. I had told him that Barresh would look more kindly on his presence if he let us know which contacts the Pretoria

Cartel used in Barresh. So far the lack of response had been deafening. He probably realised, just as well as I did, that I couldn't promise him any favours because they weren't mine to give.

Until Margarethe Ollund, President of Nations of Earth, announced the referendum and, in doing so, officially opened the voter hunting season—which was unlikely to happen until August—I'd done all I could do. I did think it was a bit strange that I'd heard nothing more from Margarethe about that process, but I assumed that she, like most other people, respected my holiday.

And over the last three weeks, we'd picked up a variety of tasks to help my father or Erith or the little community of twelve families who lived in Rocky Bay, along the coastal road that skirted Parekura Bay in the Bay of Islands. Nicha and Reida helped one of my father's neighbours put a new fence around his horse paddock. Eirani and Karana learned to make jam with berries and apples that Erith had grown, collected or traded. Devlin took an interest in the small community's power supplies: the solar installation, the windmills, the geo heat and gas installations. He spent days fine-tuning the electricity and gas hub so that different processes happened based on the sun, the wind, the rain and the fullness of the water or recycling tanks. He also helped put up a new satellite receiver.

Although we got busier, even in this very isolated pocket of the world, every morning Thayu and I made the time to walk on the beach and let ourselves be guided by Fred.

Right now, he had the stick in his mouth and had turned away from the water, usually a sign that he'd had enough. Which was just as well, because it was cold this morning. It would be a beautiful day later, but right now the mist hung over the headlands, cascading into the ocean like a waterfall made of cloud. I'd forgotten that the clouds did that.

"Let's go for breakfast," I said.

"Yes, I think he's tired." Thayu had jammed her hands deep in her pockets. Her cheeks were rosy. Her breath steamed in the chill air.

I took her arm. She smiled at me. She had fully recovered from her miscarriage and was ready to try again once we got back to Barresh and I could—oh joy—be poked with more needles.

Fred had put down his stick and was sniffing at a basket-like thing that had washed up on the beach overnight.

I called out, "Come on, Fred. Breakfast!"

He raised his head.

"What has he got there?" Thayu asked.

"No idea." It looked like some sort of cage. A craypot, maybe.

I went to have a look.

The thing was indeed like a craypot except it had floaters attached around the bottom with pieces of rough string. Well, no one was going to catch many lobsters when it floated on the surface like that. At the top of the cage, strung with a snap tie, hung a little box. I stuck my fingers through the wire of the cage. A slippery layer of algae covered the smooth surface.

"What is it?" Thayu asked.

"I don't know. It could be that the kids have been making rafts." It was badly enough made, except for that box.

I ran my nails over it, but couldn't find anywhere to open it. Maybe it wasn't a box. Maybe it was a solid piece of plastic, but I was curious.

By now, Fred was making impatient whining noises.

I yanked at the snap tie, but it wouldn't break.

"Wait." Thayu took the cage from me and pulled the snap tie loose. "Here." She gave the little black box to me.

I studied it, but the algae-covered plastic surface revealed no secrets about its purpose. I stuck it in the inner pocket of my jacket. I'd give it to Devlin to dissect.

It was time for breakfast.

Fred limped ahead of us between the rocks, across the dew-covered grassy field, where several rabbits made a hasty retreat, white tails bobbing.

We crossed the deserted road.

My father's house lay nestled at the bottom of a hill, where the lush green paddock met the forest. It was a low, single-storey building with a wide veranda and a rose garden at the front.

My father had owned the beach house since before I was born, and parts of the house had barely changed since then.

We used to spend Christmas here with the family. My mother, my grandparents, now all dead. Uncles and aunts and cousins, many of whom I hadn't seen in years, and who I wasn't sure wanted to see me anymore.

Cory Wilson, betrayer of Earth, that was how many of them saw me.

At the back of the house was a paddock with three horses, a camel and two llamas, a white one and a black one. All those animals were curiously standing along the fence, looking at the goings-on in the shed, where I spotted Deyu's silhouette through the window in the hay loft, tossing down bales of hay into the cart below with big, dusty *foomp*s. Deyu was growing more formidable by the day, and even through her jacket I could see her muscled shoulders. I had always suspected that in each high-level Coldi association, one of the women took hormonal supplements to develop into a fearsome fighter and that Deyu was destined to be that person for us.

Sharp and strong as she was, Deyu had a gentle character, too patient and observing for her young age.

She jumped down all the way from the loft, never mind the ladder, landing on the ground with an audible thud. She picked up one of the hay bales, tossed it over the fence as if it were an empty cardboard box and vaulted after it. The horses gathered around to nuzzle her pockets, pulling the fabric until she extracted the carrots she carried in there. She patted their hairy flanks and scratched between their twitching ears. Even the llamas came, and they were notoriously grumpy.

It was a wonder to see. Most Coldi people were apprehensive around animals, especially those that were taller than a person. Their home world Asto had no large vertebrate animals.

But it was as if Deyu had known that she would come to love animals, even before she had seen any. She seemed to have a rare and special talent. I mean, if I went in that paddock, those llamas would probably try to take a bite out of me.

But every morning, Deyu, who had grown up in the desolate stone and concrete jungles of the Eighth Circle of Athyl, would put on her overalls and go to the paddock. She would feed the animals and clean out their sheds, refresh their water and groom them. Erith had been teaching her how to ride a horse and Deyu loved every bit of it.

She had informed me that she thought a horse would be a great idea in Barresh, but I pointed out that it would probably be too hot and humid for horses. That was just aside from the fact that quarantine would have a heart attack if I proposed it. Besides, I didn't think anyone had successfully brought any animals across.

The large vertebrate animals on Ceren, the world of Barresh, were all dangerous enough for people to stay far away from them. In Barresh, they lived in the water. Beisili—plesiosaur-like creatures— and giant marsh eels were not suitable to be kept. All of them would enjoy people for breakfast.

Thayu waited at the door while I held Fred by the collar and used an old broom head to brush the sand off him before letting him inside the house.

While I was doing this, a white car came along the beach road. It slowed, and the single occupant—a man with blond hair, short down the sides and longer on top—turned his face in our direction.

I held up my hand in greeting, because that was what people did in this quiet part of the world. He didn't react and I didn't recognise either the man or the vehicle. Probably a tourist, although it wasn't the tourist season. He looked away.

The car sped up and disappeared in the direction of the peninsula, where, after another twenty minutes' drive, the road ended in a car park with a boat ramp surrounded by a few shops frequented by yachts. The yacht people usually didn't drive and the permanent population of that settlement was about ten in total.

I had a feeling I should know who this person was. Look at me —I was turning into my father, obsessed with what other people did in this tiny secluded corner of the world.

"Veyada will get some information on him," Thayu said.

My association liked being obsessive about what other people around us were up to. My father had even taken Sheydu and Devlin for tours along all the little dirt roads and explained the purpose of all the fields, buildings and paths. They had *wanted* to know, for the sake of security.

Thayu asked, "Anything about him that makes you uncomfortable?"

"Just the face. I don't think I've seen him before. But he doesn't seem the tourist type."

She chuckled. "How long ago was it that you told me off for being paranoid about people?"

I smiled at her, and she slapped me on the shoulder.

They would look at it, she said, in all the magical ways that my association looked at these things, with equipment that I didn't realise they'd brought and didn't want to know was here. Seriously, at times I thought my association was in the possession of a magical expanding suitcase. We hadn't brought all *that* much luggage, had we?

Fred, now without sand, followed us inside the house.

The air in the kitchen was warm and smelled like bacon and eggs and coffee. Just that smell brought memories back to me of when my grandmother used to stand at the same stove that still graced the kitchen.

Today, that position was taken by my housekeeper Eirani from Barresh, and she had a set of two burners going underneath the hot plate on which lay five eggs and a mountain of oysters, tomatoes, onions, mushrooms—those fancy yellow ones—and a bunch of sausages.

"It's almost ready, Muri," she said, wiping hair out of her face.

"Thank you, Eirani."

Every morning when we walked Fred, she would venture into the chicken coop to get the eggs. Eirani was *very* unsure about the chickens, but was fine as long as they didn't come too close and they didn't fly. But she understood eggs. Eggs in Barresh were of the soft-shelled lizard or fish variety, and you went to find them, or in her case, *buy* them.

The kitchen was full of chatter and laughter, all in Coldi, and that definitely did not fit with my memories of this place.

My father sat at his favourite spot at the kitchen table, on the bench with the cushions, leaning against the wall. Erith, my Damarcian stepmother, had completed a batch of blackberry jam yesterday and was writing out the labels, watched by Reida, who was both intrigued by the process of writing with ink and the lettering. He was a very practical young man who had never received much in the way of formal education, but he was smart and was fast catching up.

Erith put the jars in a neat row, with her long-fingered Damarcian hands, in which the thumb and index finger were much longer than the other fingers.

"Are you going to deliver these somewhere today?" Karana asked. She was attempting to feed Ayshada, who sat on her knees, but he was much more interested in a cup of tea.

It was alarming to see a child stick his hands in the scalding tea, but he was Coldi and it didn't harm him. In fact, he was now trying to put his face into the tea, but Karana put a stop to that.

"Three of these are for the neighbours," Erith said, indicating the jars. "But the others we can keep."

Much in this little community was traded between families, and she would give these jars to other families in return for hay for the animals or a dog-grooming session for Fred or a slab of eggs.

Eirani brought a plate of sizzling food to the table. She had added fried sliced eggplant to the mix. In the past few weeks, she and Karana had learned about growing vegetables. I'd been informed that the small yard at my apartment in Barresh would now be transformed into a vegetable garden. And that jam was a really good thing.

It seemed like taking Eirani on this trip had been one of my better decisions.

"Cold out there?" my father asked as I sat down.

"A bit."

We had this conversation every morning, and like every morning, Fred drank noisily from his bowl and went to the quiet of the living room.

I took a cup of tea from Eirani and sat, and it wasn't until then that I registered that the rest of my team were engrossed in something on a screen.

Veyada and Sheydu were watching something on a reader propped up against a fruit basket so that everyone could see it. Nicha was watching, too, but he had taken over Ayshada who was getting just a little bit too dangerous with the hot drinks, so he had to watch from a distance.

I got up, walked around the table and looked over Veyada's shoulder. "What are you all looking at?"

"We finally got this." He showed me the screen.

The screen displayed a written document. The header showed

that it came from the Athens Exchange and the sender was a Coldi person. A doctor, to be precise.

Ah, yes. The report on Jemiro.

At one time I would have said "poor Jemiro"; but, after speaking with the doctor at the Exchange when we were there, I'd wondered if Jemiro was even human and if he qualified for sympathy. I wanted to feel sorry for him, but wasn't sure if there had been anything for me to feel sorry *for*. Had been, yes, because the reconstructed body that looked like the person we knew as Jemiro had died two days after we brought him to the hospital at the Exchange, when his brain pretty much stopped performing all the body's vital functions.

More than anything, thinking about him filled me with a deep sense of disgust and betrayal. Disgust because these people who had made him and passed him to us had no respect for a family, even one as dysfunctional as Barresh's Pakiru family. Betrayal because someone had sent this not-person with our group while pretending that he was a normal human being, while acquiring our sympathy. I'd known that Jasper Carlson, who had recommended Jemiro to us, was up to some tricks, but this deeply disturbed me.

Neither Jasper nor any of his cronies had shown any interest when Jemiro's brain malfunctioned and he died or, should I say, stopped working, two days after we delivered him to the hospital.

The doctors had thought him an interesting case and had requested his body for investigation. I asked that they do it quickly and send the body to the Pakiru family so they could rebury the son they'd buried a month earlier—paid for by my account—and to send me a copy of the report. I'd almost forgotten that it was coming, preferring not to think of the whole sorry episode while we were on leave.

The document contained pages and pages of medical data, including scanned images of his head and other body parts. There were a lot of medical notes superimposed over the images, indicating how the body was cobbled together from various parts, probably because by the time they acquired the corpse—"acquired"? How about "stole"?—some of the organs were beyond repair.

His body included numerous bio-implants, designed to work with living tissue and take over the function of body parts. The report stated that, after the death of the original person, the intestines had decayed too far to function. This was why his stomach cavity contained a couple of larger implants. But the connection between them and the tissue had not been made properly, or rather, not enough of the dead intestine had been cut away to prevent the rot from spreading.

The report suggested that if he'd been properly conscious, as he certainly was when speaking to us, he would have been in insufferable pain. He'd never said anything. Had he been told not to?

That feeling of disgust about the whole episode crept up on me again. I was on leave. I didn't want to deal with this right now. I'd ask my team to go through it when we were back in Barresh, when I could brace myself for the utterly cruel and disgusting details that came too late for us to change the outcome. I skipped to the summary at the end.

The report said that by the time Jemiro came into the hospital his brain had already begun to shut down, and they could do nothing to reverse the process. In the back of my mind, I asked the question whether they even wanted to.

And then I wondered how many other not-people like Jemiro were walking around deceiving people into thinking that they were genuine employees.

Jasper Carlson's company had advertised that they could find a person for every job. Was this how they fulfilled all those contracts? In that case, there must be other people in Barresh who had run into the same issues with their "employees".

Was Jemiro a Tamerian or was he something else?

We hadn't yet found out how Tamerians were made, and whether they were made at all, or if, like the Coldi, they had been made once and left to their own devices and their own reproduction. I didn't think so, but no one could communicate much with Tamerians. They did the jobs people asked them to do. They were strong. They were formidable fighters, shooters and runners, but they had no social skills. Jemiro hadn't had those either. But he had been made out of a keihu body, not . . . whatever it was that Tamerians were made from, *if* they were made and not born.

While we were at the court, Lenka Trnkova had told us about the faceless assassins who had killed presidents and dissident leaders in Africa. Most of those had been African, but there had been others belonging to other races. *Earth* races. What were these people and did they all come from the same source?

I leafed through the rest of the report, unrest gnawing at me, knowing that when this holiday was over, I should contact someone to investigate what was going on at Tamer and how this related to Jasper Carlson's activities and why he'd tried to pass this person onto us.

The report concluded that the hospital had been powerless to stop Jemiro's death and that if the family consented, the report should be sent to all major medical facilities in *gamra* worlds. The report also said that neither I nor anyone else had a hand in his death and no criminal investigation was necessary.

Well, phew. That issue hadn't even crossed my mind.

Then at the very bottom, the Coldi doctor had scribbled a hand-written note that said, *Please feel free to contact me if you have any questions, although I understand that, in the current situation, your mind will be elsewhere.*

I looked at Thayu and she frowned back at me.

Your mind will be elsewhere . . . in the current situation. What situation?

I showed it to Nicha and then to Veyada and he showed it to Sheydu. They all sat up straight, showing mildly alarmed expressions.

What situation?

Thayu picked up her reader and scoured through the news.

"Something has happened, clearly," Nicha said.

But we couldn't see anything in the news feeds. In fact, the news had been really quiet. We had joked about that a few times this week. And my messages had not been half as numerous as before. I'd thought it was because people respected my time off, but come to think of it, when had they ever done that before?

A deep chill went over me.

I went to our bedroom, at the back of the house, that looked out over the mountains and the horse paddock.

I dug up my reader. I *had* made a point of switching it on at least once a day during this holiday and, even so, it was amazing how buried it would get under clothes and other things that we used throughout the day.

I switched it on while walking back to the kitchen, but nothing unusual showed in my messages. Certainly, if something had happened that justified the doctor making an offhand comment about *the current situation,* my messages should have exploded with questions. Because they always did.

Thayu gave me a strange look. I pushed the reader across the table to her. Her eyes moved as she looked at the screen.

She nodded. Said nothing, but her brow furrowed.

Nicha leaned over and she showed the screen to him, too. And then Sheydu and Veyada.

Quiet nods. Lips pressed together. No words were necessary. Somebody was partially blocking our communication and probably had been for the past three weeks.

The holiday was over.

2

———————

AFTER THAT DISTURBING discovery, we finished breakfast quickly.

Devlin and Veyada had already disappeared to their room to see if they could shed any light on the lack of communication or the nature of the block that we had shamefully, utterly and completely failed to notice.

Shit, shit, shit.

I joined them as soon as I could wolf down the eggs and bacon, sadly not appreciating Eirani's excellent cooking.

Devlin and Veyada sat in the room with the curtains closed, blue light illuminating their faces from below. When I was young, this used to be one of the kids' rooms where all the cousins used to sleep. The bunk beds that used to stand here were gone, replaced by five single beds, but the curtains with dinosaur prints still hung over the windows and the door that led into the back yard. Apparently, long before my parents bought the house, the room had replaced a lean-to shack that housed a chicken coop.

Veyada, Sheydu, Evi, Telaris and Devlin had called it their home for the past few weeks, complete with the dinosaur curtains, the set of shelves with old toys, the ping pong table—and watching games of ping pong between Veyada and Reida had turned out to be nothing short of amusing—and the cartoon murals.

I didn't see Telaris until I was already in the room. He sat in the very corner, on the Tommy the Space Pilot bedspread, fiddling with a frequency map on his screen. This was still a very normal guest bedroom. Normally, my association would set up all their equipment on a table in the middle and there would be screens and projectors everywhere. We hadn't even bothered setting up a communication hub. We were on holidays, damn it.

Veyada didn't meet my eyes. He took a deep breath and let it out again while staring at the screen.

I remained near the door and let them work for a while.

There was no need to deliberate on their failure to detect that we were being blocked. They were going to be beating themselves up over this a lot without my help. I had no doubt that I would have to field expressions of failure and offers to leave my association, and they would be uncomfortable with my refusal to be angry enough about it to let them leave. That was the Coldi way.

I'd have trouble getting some of them to change their mind, too. This was a serious business, especially for young people like Reida and Deyu, who were training and aspired to be the very best.

Damn. I should have known that there really was no such thing as a relaxing holiday as the head of a Coldi association, especially if you were not Coldi yourself and possessed none of the instincts that told Coldi people what to do and how to feel.

"We were led astray because we *have* been getting news and communication, but not all," Veyada said. He still didn't meet my eyes.

He was fairly prone to taking on too much guilt and I hated, *hated* that the confident man who had once been part of Ezhya's guards acted subservient to me. Veyada knew so much. I loved Thayu and Nicha, but if I had a diplomatic problem, Veyada's was the opinion I would consider the most.

"Find out where it's coming from and who might be involved," I said.

Serious nods. Very serious. This was deeply serious business. I needed to give them the opportunity to redeem themselves or they would start making stupid suggestions, such as leaving my household. I should address the issue later, when the dust had settled.

Telaris looked up. "I wonder what else we've missed." How many messages were waiting for us about truly important stuff?

I said, "We might go for a little trip once we find out how big this blocked area is."

"Any thought that it could be for another reason than us being here?" Telaris said.

"I can't see why."

My father came to the door, a frown on his face. I realised we had been pretty cryptic about what was going on, and was going to explain it, but he said, "Were you expecting a visitor?"

A visitor? "No. Why?"

"There is someone outside."

"At the door?"

"Not yet. In the driveway."

I went with him to the living room, where Erith was looking out the window.

The white car that we'd seen earlier had returned and had stopped in the house's driveway. The door was open and the occupant was coming out. With his grey suit, he looked like a real estate agent, but failing that, a lawyer or undercover cop. Nobody in this laid-back area wore jackets like that.

"Do you know him?" my father asked.

"Not at all. We did see him drive past when we were on the beach."

The man came up the path through the rose garden to the front door. This was telling, because no one ever used the front door of my father's house. While it was at the front of the house, you had to turn off the driveway and walk through the garden to get to it.

My father went to open it. I remained in the hallway around the corner, out of view of the front door.

Thayu and Veyada stood behind me, Thayu with her reader, Veyada with his hand on his jacket. I didn't *think* he carried weapons, but it wouldn't be the first time that he would have surprised me this way. Devlin waited further down the hallway with Evi.

A waft of cool air came in as my father opened the door.

"Mr Wilson?" The man's voice was clear. He sounded younger than he looked.

"Yes. How can I help you, young man?"

Never underestimate my father's capability of diplomacy. I probably would have told him I didn't buy from door-to-door salesmen.

"My name is Jarek Malicki and I work for Benton Gonzales International Lawyers. I would like to speak to your son." He spoke with the cultured accent that was typical of the Nations of Earth diplomats. International lawyers were mostly German.

"My son is on recreational leave," my father said.

"But I understand he is here? Please. It's quite important. He sent my client a message about a possible collaboration and I've been trying to contact him. He's a very hard man to get onto."

I frowned at Thayu. Did I send a message? His client? Wait—was he talking about Robert Davidson?

I glanced at Veyada. He nodded. Thayu, too.

I stepped out from around the corner. "I'm Cory Wilson."

My father turned around. The visitor smiled. Relieved?

His face cleared. "Ah, Mr Wilson, I was just asking your father about you. I'm so glad to see you. I'm Jarek Malicki, from Benton Gonzales International Lawyers."

Glad to see me?

From close up, he was a fairly thin man. His suit was clearly designed for cooler weather, and drops of sweat pearled on his forehead. It didn't look like it was a cheap suit either.

I said, "I hope you understand I'm on leave. I don't make a habit of letting work intrude on my sparse free time."

"I do understand, and I do apologise. I've come a long way especially to meet you." Yes, he was a bit whiny, but that was not why I distrusted him.

"You could have sent a message announcing your intention to visit."

"I could have, but the matter I'd like to discuss is too confidential for messages. I would have contacted an office if you had one, but this was the only address I had for you."

And I didn't feel comfortable with him coming to my father's house. I guessed finding out the address wouldn't have been too hard. My father didn't keep his address a secret. But I felt protective about him. My father was retired. Even when he still worked for Nations of Earth as station manager, he'd never been involved in high-level diplomatics and he didn't deserve to become involved in it now.

I said, "Well then. You were talking about a client of yours. Who are we talking about?"

"Robert Davidson. I understand you sent him a message inquiring about his cooperation in naming people in Barresh that he knows to have a relationship with the Pretoria Cartel."

"And the fact that you're here means that he's interested?"

"Interested, yes. But I need to explain his position to you. It's not quite as simple as it sounds."

I couldn't see, for the life of me, what was complicated about giving information, but I stepped back, repressing a sigh. "You better come in."

I preceded him into the hallway. There was no way that I would take him into the kitchen, but I could not let him stand at the door, either.

Thayu, Veyada and the others were smart enough to duck into doorways so that he couldn't see we had an audience, although he would probably know who else was here. The time I'd seen him this morning might not have been the first that he came past the house.

We went to my father's study, just to the left of the front door.

After retiring, my father had little desire to keep up with the highly-strung world of politics and diplomacy, and the farm was his priority.

Therefore, the study had been relegated to the smallest room in the house save the toilet. When I was little the room used to hold nothing except a wardrobe with coats and other spare clothing, because there wasn't much room for anything else.

The wardrobe was gone, replaced by a desk with the home hub and computer on one side and a bookshelf on the other. The bookshelf held pictures and other memorabilia of his working life: pictures of meetings with important people, like then president of Nations of Earth Pedro Gonzales, and his meeting with Joyelin Akhtari, who had been part of the furniture at *gamra* for so long in her position as Chief Secretary. I remembered that first meeting well. It had been at Midway Space Station and I'd been ten and I'd been more concerned with recapturing my classmate's pet rabbit-tooh than the most powerful woman in all the inhabited worlds.

Of course she had now also lost her position in the aftermath of the turmoil over the old Aghyrian ship and whether or not the Aghyrians in Barresh knew about it.

The top shelf also held a picture of the three of us, my father, mother, and me as a little boy, on the beach outside with our previous dog Mitty.

It was all deeply personal, and I felt reluctant to have this man in here and to let him look over all these sections of my life. I let him sit in the room's only chair, which had its back to the shelves and faced the computer screen—dark, because the computer switched off after half an hour of disuse.

I leaned against the doorpost, as there was no room for anyone else to sit. It also made me look like a headmaster berating a naughty student. I wasn't sure that this was the message I wanted to give him, but my feelings about this situation were definitely not all positive.

Both Thayu and Veyada had come into view of the door.

Jarek looked at them, his eyes widening briefly.

I gave him a nod. "Please, do tell me why you're here."

"You wrote to us asking my client for information. My client is happy to talk to you about his contacts off-world."

"Is he?" Just like that, huh? No response and then all of a sudden he sends someone across the world.

He reached for his reader. Veyada and Thayu, both in the hallway behind me, stiffened and reached inside their jackets.

Jarek looked up. "Whoa. No need to be so nervous." He held his hands flat on the table. That was a position that was shown in the Nations of Earth anti-attack and safety manual. I remembered getting that training myself.

I looked pointedly at his hands.

He withdrew them, not sure if he got why I picked up on it.

He continued, "I understand if you're suspicious, but I was only going to show you the letter." He looked pointedly at the pocket in his jacket.

"Just show me the document, then."

Veyada and Thayu relaxed. Jarek blew out a breath.

He extracted his reader from his pocket and turned it on. After flicking through a few pages, he turned the screen to me. It displayed a handwritten document. The writing was messy, as if the writer was unused to writing on a pad. The letter was only two paragraphs long.

I read aloud so that Veyada and Thayu and the others in the hallway could hear it.

Mr. Wilson,

I have now received several of your messages regarding my contacts in Barresh. I understand that if I were ever to return to Barresh, I would need to present some form of compensation for grievances held against me by both kehu and Pingali tribes.

Real classy, misspelling keihu and Pengali. Keihu were not a tribe, either. That showed how much respect he had for those groups.

My business interests in Barresh are important enough to me that I am prepared to talk to you and reveal my contacts there. I have sent Mr Malicki, my lawyer's legal assistant, to instruct you on how to contact me. As you will be aware, I was placed on house arrest and cannot travel anywhere. Mr. Malicki will assist you. He was trained in international law and worked at the Nations of Earth court before going into private practice. He is registered with the International Law Association. You can check out his details there. He is a trustworthy person.

I glanced at Thayu when I finished. She glanced back. Suspicious. We weren't wearing feeders, but I didn't need a feeder to see that. When someone needed to point out that someone else was trustworthy, this was not usually a good sign.

I met Jarek Malicki's eyes. "What leads him to this change of mind? I wrote to him several times, but did not receive a reply."

"He wanted to reply, but he needed his lawyers to clear it for him."

"*Wanted* to reply?" I could not imagine Robert Davidson wanting to do any such thing.

"He feels sorry for his actions in Barresh and wants to make up for it."

Sorry for his actions? Sorry for himself more like. "Mr Malicki, please don't waste my time. I know Mr Davidson just as well as you do, and he would not be *sorry* for any of his actions. He might need to come back to Barresh, because he's got unfinished business or money parked there, but *sorry*, no. Tell me what Mr Davidson's conditions for giving me this information are and I might think about it. I want to stress that while it would be nice to have his information, it is not of vital importance to me, so it had better be good, or he had better not ask too much."

A short but uneasy silence followed.

I didn't know what he had expected from me. That I would roll over and tell him that I'd do anything for this information?

He asked in a soft voice, "Then why did you write?"

"I asked Mr Davidson purely out of an opportunistic mindset, knowing that he might apply for some favours in return for some names. There are *some,* limited, favours I could give him, things that are in the realm of travel bonuses. I could provide accommodation. I could arrange security—which he's going to need if he will ever visit again. But please stop trying to appeal to me for sympathy, because he won't get it."

"I told you, he's sorry for what he did. Genuinely sorry. He spent a long time in custody and had a lot of opportunity to think about it."

"And my name is Santa Claus."

Another uneasy silence.

I asked, "How long have you known him? Did you know him before you got this unenviable job?"

"Well, no . . ." he wiped sweat off his upper lip.

"In all the interactions I had with Robert and the stories I've heard about his business ethics, I very much doubt that he even understands the pain he inflicted on people, let alone feels sorry for them. Robert Davidson serves Robert Davidson, no one else. But let's just say we both understand this and go into the discussion from that point of view, what can he bring for me that I don't already know and that is not going to cost me something I cannot or am unwilling to give? Money is one of those things. I do not pay for information."

"Oh no, I understand that."

There had been a number of recent scandals involving bribery of that type.

"All right then." I crossed my arms over my chest. From the

corner of my eye, I spotted Thayu and Veyada in the corridor, listening to every word.

He started haltingly, "As you know, Mr. Davidson is a member of the Pretoria Cartel—"

"Let's establish this first: he *is* or he *was* a member of the Cartel?"

"That's immaterial."

"No, it is not. If he *was* a member, he'd be inclined to give me information that harms the current members. Also you may like to know that I am in contact with Minke Kluysters about a matter of business." A bit of bluff. The man—considered to be one of the Cartel's leaders—had asked me to help him establish an office in Barresh, and I'd indirectly told him to perform an anatomically impossible act on himself, but because I'd never formally told him as much, I suspected that if I came back with an attractive proposal, the door was still open.

"Mr Kluysters told me that he is no longer interested in getting this office." His blue eyes met mine. So, there was a bit more grit to this man than appeared from first impressions. Not that I believed him, but we were all bluffing here.

The game was on.

"All right. Now what exactly is it that Mr Davidson wants me to do in return for this information?"

"He'll tell you, but he wants to meet you, but since he's under house arrest by order of the court, he'll pay for you and up to two companions to travel to him."

"To South Africa?"

"That's where he is."

"And who is to say that I'll be safe travelling there?" From what I understood, Robert's property was quite remote and the territory was hostile, in the hands of the free landholders who made up the Pretoria Cartel.

"That's what the companions are for. You can take guards. Really, Mr. Wilson, I've been there several times and it's safe. I would think that you have faced much more dangerous situations. Mr. Davidson will send a driver to Pretoria to pick you up and take you to the property. The van is very nice with comfortable seats and a minibar. The driver will handle any problems, but none have ever presented themselves when I travelled there."

We'd see about that. "And I get to take two people?"

"Well, he's facing a lot of court costs, and cost is a consideration."

For a man who owned many mines and city renovation projects? I was more inclined to believe that the number restriction existed so that he could control me and prevent me from leaving when I wanted, or from investigating places where I wanted to go rather than where his minders wanted me to go.

When I'd been silent for a while, he asked, "So, can I make the arrangements?" He sounded much too keen.

"I'd still like to get an idea of the type of information he can give me and if it's going to be worth my time."

"It will be worth it. Take it from me."

"And what conditions will be attached to the information?"

"I'm very sorry, Mr. Wilson. Mr. Robertson instructed me explicitly not to talk about that."

"So I'm supposed to travel across the world for some unknown information—"

"That you asked for."

"Maybe I did, but I don't play games. I'm not going to see him unless I get more details about how useful it is likely to be. It's a long way to South Africa, and I'm officially on holidays."

"I can guarantee that it will be very useful."

"I think I prefer to be the judge of that."

His face worked. He put his hands on the armrests of the chair. "Well, if you're going to be like that . . ."

"What else did you expect? That I would commit to coming with you without knowing what type of thing I'm going to be told and what sort of situation I'm being led into? Anyone with an inkling of experience in the diplomatic circuit will know better than that." Come to think of it, why didn't *he* know better?

"I'll have to talk to Mr. Robertson about what information I can share. It's night in South Africa, so I'll have to come back tomorrow."

He got up from the chair and I accompanied him out of the door. Pearls of sweat glistened on his upper lip.

He walked down the path back to the car, lonely and kind of forlorn.

"What do you think?" I asked Thayu and Nicha, who had come up behind me.

"He is a strange fellow," Nicha said. "He is either very smart or is kept deliberately dumb. Why would he come here and not tell us anything? That seems like a waste of money."

"Because he knows someone is listening?" Sheydu said from further in the hallway.

That brought me back to what we had been doing when he turned up: checking our communication and wondering what was being blocked, how, why and by whom. And wondering if perhaps Jarek Malicki came here because he knew about it.

"He'll probably be back," I said. "He's probably been told to hang around until we give in." It might all be a game, including his statement that he needed to talk to Robert.

Sheydu said, "I'm not sure that he is just a runner."

Thayu shook her head. "I don't think so either. He's a strange man. That's all I can say."

Through the window, I could see Jarek walking through the rose garden back to the car.

"It would be worth trying to find out more about him."

"We already did that," Nicha said, holding up his reader.

Seriously, this was why I loved my association.

"He checks out," Nicha continued. "He's a lawyer, as he said. He has worked for the Nations of Earth court, but now he works for private clients. Robert Davidson is listed as his client."

Somehow, I thought about the last time my team had checked out someone and their information had been consistent with their promises. That had been Jemiro, and his information had turned out to be fabricated.

"Someone is playing a game with us," I said, to no one in particular.

"Yup," Veyada said. "We have to prove that we're better at it than they are."

Sheydu, Thayu, Nicha, Devlin, Evi, Telaris, Reida and Deyu all exchanged serious nods and looks. Because the first thing that would occur to a human—notifying authorities so that they could stop the game being played—did not even enter their minds.

Outside, Jarek took a look at the house as he got into the car and drove off, in the western direction, to the main road across the peninsula.

Yes, there was a good chance that he would be back, and I had no idea what I could offer him if he did. I had nothing Robert would want, and nothing I was happy for him to have.

Robert was already in the only place where he was safe: his own house, surrounded by his own vigilante. If he left his property, he wasn't safe. The Cartel probably operated in Barresh, and he wasn't safe there either. He definitely wasn't safe from the Thousand Island tribe if he ever came back.

If he had pissed off the members of the Pretoria Cartel, there didn't seem to be any places where he could flee. They were everywhere.

I stared at the idyllic setting of the bay and the beach and the green headland and the yachts that lay offshore and the blue sky. It didn't feel so safe anymore.

3

____

WE MET IN THE KITCHEN, a gathering of serious faces.

"The fun is over," I said. "We urgently need to find out who these watchers are and what's going on in regards to a communication block, how far this extends, and what technology they use to do this."

Veyada nodded. Sheydu, too. Yes, absolutely.

"We also need to find out if this Jarek Malicki guy has anything to do with whoever is listening and blocking and whether he knows about it. We need to know where they are based, how far the block extends and whether they're recording our conversations."

"Yeah," Sheydu said. "We need to map their priority profiles and tag their signatures, create profiles for each and make frequency maps."

"I'll get started," Devlin said. He rose and looked at me. "Can we use the back room?"

"Why ever not?" They slept there.

"We'll need to unplug a few things and create our own dead zone to minimise interference."

"I'm sure it will be fine."

Sheydu, Devlin, Thayu and Telaris went off to do these things, whatever it all meant. One did not have to go very deep to find that my team's knowledge of security speak was much better than mine. That was why I had them.

The rest of us remained in the kitchen to make a plan.

It was likely that we were being watched, so outwardly we wanted to do things that fitted within our daily pattern of the past three weeks so as not to make the watchers suspicious, because first we needed to know where they were watching: from the land, from the sea or, heaven forbid, using satellites from orbit. *That* thought rattled me and brought me right back to the image that Amarru had shown me, with parts of the Earth, in South Africa and the eastern American coast, excluded from the normal communication networks and receiving information from off-planet.

Had we stumbled into a similar enclave without noticing? I mean, our feeders didn't work here, but they never had. This far from the Exchange, I would have been surprised if they did work. There were few Coldi people in New Zealand and there was no need for coverage.

I asked my father if he had ever heard of unusual activity in this area.

He said, "I can't tell. There are so many bays and farms where someone can hide if they want to. The dive boats come in from all over, from overseas even."

I was thinking more about electronic unusualness, but I guessed my father had ceased to think in those terms. He would not understand the concept of selective transmission blocking and "unusual" for him meant people sneaking around the back of the horse paddock or hiding things in secret caves in secluded bays.

I decided not to worry him any more than necessary.

By this time, the "setting up" in the back room was completed. I went to have a look. They had dragged a table to the middle of the room and filled it with equipment I didn't know we had. Devlin explained that they were devices to listen in on multiple frequencies and seek out and zoom in on those where information was being transferred. It all depended on pattern recognition, a skill in which Coldi possessed true excellence.

"We only need to find a good place for the receiver," Veyada said. "I was thinking we can hook up a repeater somewhere on the hillside and then maybe we can tap into the satellite dish at the top of the hill."

That dish was not something a normal person would notice, but it sat by the side of the road next to the community's power station.

"I can take you there," Erith said.

It was part of Erith's daily task to check and maintain the small community's energy sources. The energy park with a solar generator and a couple of windmills sat at the top of the hill behind my father's house. Erith would go there to check up on the plant, as she usually did a few times a week.

"I can go with you," I said.

Of course, when I went, Thayu and Nicha wanted to come. Thayu received various items of equipment from Veyada to use on the dish's control panel while he, Evi and Sheydu scaled the hill and found somewhere to put the repeater.

Deyu offered to take the horses for a walk along the coastal track, as she often did, and bring equipment. She'd keep going until she noticed a change that indicated that she had left the restricted zone. Reida said he'd go with her, even if he was not nearly as confident with the horses.

Devlin said he would stay in the house to coordinate everyone's communication. "Use your short-range receivers to keep in contact with each other."

Yes, he had grown so much in confidence during this trip.

"And we'll just look after the little one and make bread for everyone," Eirani said. She and Karana had already started on the bread for lunch.

While everyone filed out of the kitchen, my father came up to me. "Is there anything you want me to do?" In the semidarkness of the hallway, the light from the kitchen hit his face sideways, showing up the wrinkles and uneven skin on his face.

"Apart from keeping yourself safe, not really." I breathed out heavily. "I'm sorry about this." I wanted to say that it was probably nothing serious, but he would know it wasn't true, and I knew it, too. "Keep an eye on the Vine and tell me when people are reporting unusual activities." This was the local communication message hub.

He put a hand on my shoulder. "Sorry I can't provide better

security for you, son. You seem to have gained status and I have not kept up."

I remembered seeing his surprised face when we had arrived. I didn't think he'd realised how many of us were in the group. I didn't think he'd quite realised that I had acquired some of *Ezhya Palayi's* ex-bodyguards. Although Veyada and Sheydu had acclimatised and didn't look so intimidating to me anymore, they probably still did to an outsider.

"No, Dad, we provide our own security. I would never ask that from you."

"I know, but . . ." He shrugged.

I felt guilty. My father and Erith had been living a relaxed life for the past few years, away from the high stress and the friction points between Earth and *gamra,* away from the need to have personal security.

I told him, "Don't worry. My people will look after it."

He put a hand on my arm. "I would just prefer that you didn't get involved. You've tangled with the Pretoria Cartel. They're nasty people who won't give up until they have what they want, and they have the power and money to get it. Believe me, I've dealt with the type."

"So what should I do? Sit here and let them take control of us? I don't think you ever did that, either."

He sighed. He knew that was true, and I knew it, too. "Sometimes I wish you were a lot more like your mother and less like me. I was challenging relatively minor players when I was director at Midway station. You're playing with the big guys. I'm worried that one day you'll come to a sticky end, son."

"There's no need to worry." But I'd come close enough a few times already.

He shook his head. He pointed at his hair. "See this?" His hair had gone completely grey in the few years I hadn't seen him.

"That's from worrying. You're the only family I have. Remember that."

I *did* remember and thought of him a lot, even when I was in Barresh. He wouldn't know that, though. Like a typical father to son and son to father, we rarely shared our feelings. I looked into his eyes, still sharp but with so many wrinkles. "Is anything wrong, Dad?"

"Not really, except that I worry."

There was some sort of issue, I could feel it and would need to talk to him about it, but my team were all in Devlin's room already talking about their plans, and I really had to be there.

And damn, I remembered this feeling of being torn in different directions from my engagement with Eva. *She* wanted me to have dinner parties with her and her friends. My work required me to be elsewhere. Wherever I was and whatever I did, I always felt guilty about not giving enough, either to my job or to my family. *That* was one thing that living in Barresh, with my association, had freed me from. My home life in Barresh *was* my work life and they didn't compete.

I went into the bedroom and collected the device that would tell Devlin where I was.

"It's as much to eliminate false positives from our scan as it is to actually tell me where you are," he said while handing me the small, button-like transmitter.

Telaris was also in the room. I watched them for a while until Erith had collected all her jars and was ready to go. I was thinking about what my father had said. It was true that I hadn't been here for a long time. The last time was when Thayu and I had held a ceremony in place of a wedding. I'd had to check whether that was five or six years ago.

Yes if she wanted a child, we should probably get on with it, because by all means it didn't look like it would be easy.

I went with Thayu and Nicha to the kitchen, where Erith was packing the jars of jam into a crate.

"I'd promised to bring these around," she said. She was wearing a woollen checked jacket of the type that locals wore, jeans and gumboots. Until you noticed her hands with the uneven fingers or her black-rimmed yellow irises, she could be any farmer or horse keeper.

We all rugged up against the wind that was always cold up there. Nicha offered to carry the crate, and we left the house, walking down the driveway and then to the road that ran along the foreshore.

The small settlement of Rocky Bay had two vans for general use, which were parked on a piece of land surrounding the charging station on the foreshore. Both vehicles were plugged into the hub. A flock of kereru pigeons were foraging in the grass in the park between the power box and the beach. A few birds lifted their heads, but most took little notice of us.

I smiled.

"More memories?" Thayu asked.

"I used to stalk these birds when I came out here as a little boy. I would lie behind the grass clumps and attempt to catch the birds. They look fat and clumsy, but they're quite fast, so I never succeeded."

"Wait until Ayshada discovers them," Nicha said.

True. We'd already had to pry a duck from his hands.

Erith unplugged one of the vehicles. Nicha put the jam jars in the back.

The settlement had only one sealed road. It came from the western headland down to the beach and park in front of my father's house and up through the woods to the eastern headland.

Various driveways and dirt roads went off the main road. Erith steered the car in the westerly direction and turned off the main road when we were halfway up the hill.

A narrow dirt road ran in between two fields, one with cows, the other with a crop of corn. The road wound around the hillside to a farmhouse that overlooked the bay. The couple who lived here were both war veterans in their seventies, Erith told us along the way. Because the woman had received some type of augmentation treatment during her service, she had never been able to have children.

"They're the grandparents of this community. They run the school network, they organise deliveries for the town, they organise the clinic, and they make pretty good cheese."

Cheese was, indeed, what we'd come to get. The husband, Jack, came out of the front door. He carried a round yellow wheel of cheese and was followed by a little baby goat, jumping up as if it was trying to get something out of his pocket.

He ignored the goat and walked to the car, where he placed the cheese on top of the hessian bag that he'd told Erith to spread out.

"There." He rubbed his hands. "Cold this morning. You should come inside. Melanie has something you might like."

The little goat was bleating and jumping.

Jack noticed Thayu looking at it.

He grinned. "Oh, that's an orphan. Melanie has been bottle-feeding it. I was just about to feed it when you came. I got the bottle in my pocket. Here." He took it out and pushed it in Thayu's hands.

Now the goat jumped at her. She gave me a helpless look.

I picked up the little hairy body, and held it so that it could reach the teat of the bottle. The goat latched on and I dumped the whole lot into Thayu's hands. She gave me a wide-eyed look.

We followed Jack into the house, where Melanie was in the kitchen.

A bucket on the table held spiky crayfish, so spiky I couldn't even see how many.

"I got these in the pots this morning when I went out on the boat," she said. "Pick one, seeing as your mates like fish."

Veyada had been out on the boat with her. He liked crayfish.

Nicha looked into the bucket. It seemed that picking out one of the crayfish was his task. His opinion had been going back and forth on the subject of eating fish or chicken. I suspected that he liked both, but wanted to show solidarity with Thayu, who steadfastly refused to eat them. And besides being his sister, she was his *zhayma* in our association, so who else was going to stick with her?

He lifted a crayfish out of the bucket by one of its spikes. Melanie put another hessian bag on the table for him to set it on.

Thayu pulled a face.

"They're good ones this time," she said. "We weren't the only ones out there getting them. Some city folk on a boat had no idea. They were floating the pots on the water."

I looked at Nicha. I knew Thayu had trouble understanding her strong accent.

I asked, "City folk? What were they doing?"

"They were putting out craypots but with floaters attached."

"Where?"

"Out near the point. They were in a hired boat."

"And where did these craypots float?" I remembered the thing we'd found on the beach in the morning, that I'd assumed was a creation of a child. I had completely forgotten the plastic box in my pocket that Thayu had removed from the cage. I felt cold.

She shrugged. "I don't know. With the wind, I guess."

When we were back at the car, I asked Thayu, "Do you remember that thing we found on the beach this morning?"

"I was thinking about that, too."

"Can we check the beach before we go up to the power station?" I asked Erith.

So we went down to the beach, but the tide had come up and the craypot was nowhere to be seen.

"Or maybe someone removed it," Thayu said.

"Someone like Jarek Malicki?"

We met each other's eyes, Thayu from over the top of her knitted shawl. It was sunny, but the wind was quite chilly.

She said, "Did you give that thing to Devlin?"

"Not yet. I forgot. It's still in my jacket." Which hung over the chair in our bedroom.

"Maybe we should go to see if we can collect the rest of the contraption."

I nodded. It had looked primitive and cobbled together, but the little cube in my pocket could be something important—like a repeater or transmitter.

Shit.

I'd have to look at it when we got home.

From the beach, we took the vehicle up the eastern headland, through the forest with its tree ferns lining the road.

At the top of the hill, a group of solar panels sat in a semicircle facing north, waiting for the sun to come out. The power generating honours were being done by a couple of windmills further up the headland. Also, an underground waste-disposal system generated gas. A small van was parked here and a man I knew stood at the gas outlet, filling large bottles for cooking. It was Morgan Peters, who was also a mechanic and electrician. The community was almost completely self-sufficient. They had a nurse, but no doctor, although a doctor lived in the next bay.

Erith parked the van next to the electrician's. He waved at us.

While Erith went around checking and wiping the solar panels,

Nicha and Thayu crouched at the bottom of the satellite dish and set out their equipment. To the casual passersby—of which there were almost none—it would look like they were doing maintenance on the panels. In reality they used the power station's satellite antenna to connect to the house so that Devlin could scour the area.

I let them be, unfamiliar as I was with the technology.

They knelt around a couple of interconnected boxes. Thayu kept changing the settings; Nicha sent details through to Devlin, who created maps that he sent back to us. There was nothing for me to do except wait.

Erith finished her work, too, and we sat on a rock in the sun, overlooking the grassy paddock, the forest and the bay. I apologised to her for bringing this kind of trouble to their secluded spot, and she said not to worry about it.

"Trouble comes and goes anyway. If it's not this, it's something else. Your father gets protective of this place. You have to understand that it's the only existing place he still has where Emily used to be a part of his life. Her parents died; he lost contact with her brother."

Emily, my mother. Those grandparents and my uncle had always been more distant from us anyway. "Do you feel you're still living in her shadow?"

"I used to, but not anymore. I guess I'm too different."

I chuckled. "Really?" Then I added, "But what about you? Don't you ever feel terribly cut off from Damarq living in this remote part of the world?"

She shrugged.

From the first, she'd been coy and distant about her family. I had heard from my father that she didn't get along with them, and none of them had ever shown up at any family event, including her wedding. Apparently she had a brother who sent her nasty comments when she and my father looked after a Coldi foster child for a few years while I was at university. Erith's family were, I understood, aristocrats, and the idea of her *working* on a *farm* was abhorrent to them.

"Have you ever been back at all since you married my father?"

"I've had no desire. Too many bad memories, you know . . . You probably understand."

I didn't think I understood, because my memories from this place were good, and it would always have a special place in my heart.

"Think of Thayu," she said, and we both looked at where Thayu and Nicha sat in the grass with their equipment. "Do you think she'll ever go back to that hyper-competitive world of the Asto military spy division? I don't think so. For one, she'd have to leave you and she won't do that. But it's also a nasty world which, once you've left, reveals its true nature. When you live there, you think that the things that happen and nasty things people say to each other are normal, and you first need to leave to see that they're not. That's what I feel like. When I as much as think about going to Damarq, I feel ill. I remember my family's house and the scent of warm oil and how we had to line up to have our hands and feet covered in it before going to bed, stinking of oil and all that. And how I was never allowed to go outside because my skin would blemish. Our house was beautiful, but it was a prison."

She held up her hands. They were typical hands of a sixty-year-old woman: with wrinkles and blemishes, and although the shape of her hands was unusual, with the very long thumb and index finger, they were otherwise very normal hands. Come to think of it, I'd always found that Damarcians had this waxy, highly cultured look about them. They were never dirty or sweaty. Erith was more human because she *was* those things sometimes.

She sighed. "So yeah, I've changed too much and there is nothing there for me. The good things, however few they are, live in my memory."

But I saw through her words that, like this place for me, Damarq would always be part of her. My father had never been there, and maybe it would be a good idea for the two of them to visit. As memory tourists, not to call on unwilling and uninterested relatives. They need not even tell anyone about the visit.

Thayu and Nicha had finished whatever they'd been doing. Nicha got up with his reader and pointed at landmarks while studying maps on the reader.

Erith and I joined them.

From the grassy knoll that held the power station, we could see over the entire bay: the beach, the road, the charging station, the park and the rose garden in front of my father's house, though not the house itself, because it lay hidden behind the trees. The view to the north stretched across the bay dotted with islands. A number of sailing boats lay moored offshore and around the point, where there was another secluded beach and safe anchorage. None of the boats were moving and none were out near the point where Melanie would go fishing.

The sky was blue with big clouds that cast shadows over the bay. Wherever the sun hit the water, the waves sparkled.

"What have you found out?" I asked.

Nicha said, "There is a type of partial communication block that seems to cover almost all of the bay. It goes inland and back to the shore over there, and then at least out to that island over there." He pointed. "It looks like there are repeaters at several places in the water."

Damn it. Those floating craypots.

"The disrupting signals are particularly strong around that boat over there." He pointed at a white speck on the water, one of the boats anchored furthest away from the beach, but quite close to my father's boat.

"Does it mean that there is some kind of transmitting equipment on that yacht?"

"Either on the boat or somewhere in the water."

"It looks like we may need to go fishing later today."

4

—————

W E WENT BACK to my father's house, where we found everyone in the kitchen, which smelled of coffee and freshly baked bread. Deyu and Reida had also returned and sat at the kitchen table.

Eirani was applying a bandage to Reida's shin. He sat with one foot on a chair, his trouser leg rolled up, looking put out. He had a number of gashes across his skin.

"What happened?" I asked.

"The horse didn't like Reida," Karana said. She bit her lip from trying to keep a straight face.

"He got thrown into the blackberries," my father said from the stove, where he was making tea.

Reida glared at Karana and then at Deyu, who was still wearing her riding gear as if it were her second skin. Reida had been struggling a little recently. Traditionally, he'd been the tough one, but his position with us entailed a certain accountability that made all his skills—breaking into things and wooing girls—useless. He *was* working very hard in his training and his interest in security devices was genuine, but sometimes I wondered if he got homesick for the physicality of his previous life: trying to survive in the harsh world of Athyl's Outer Circle and dealing with gang warfare, a punishing climate and poverty. Sheydu had taken both the youngsters under her wing, but I made a mental note to check out if he was all right, because he had not quite blossomed as Deyu had.

Erith went to retrieve her special first aid kit from the cupboard in the hall. She pulled out a bottle that contained Coldi-grade disinfectant and gave it to Eirani. "Use that. Those blackberry thorns can be very nasty."

I had learned that Coldi skin could display allergic reactions to some Earth plants and early treatment was vital.

The fluid in the bottle was oily and spread a scent like turpentine. Ugh.

While this was going on, Thayu and Deyu compared maps.

Reida and Deyu's maps had turned out very similar to ours. Most of the blocking frequency transmission was coming from a yacht out in the bay. Several repeater stations floated closer to the shore.

I finally retrieved the cube from the pocket of my jacket and gave it to Devlin.

He frowned at it and I told him where I had found it. He inspected the surface, trying to find a place to open it. Nicha, next to him passed his scanner over the thing. The lines on the screen wriggled.

"Do you think this is one of the repeaters?" I asked.

"Could be," Devlin said. "It would help us if we could get this thing open."

"Give it to me." Reida held his hand out. He studied the cube, and then got up from the table, hobbling and wincing the first few steps.

While he was gone, presumably to the workshop, we made another plan for this afternoon.

We'd go out on my father's boat, which lay anchored off the beach, and use that as base to investigate the frequency hotspots with the dinghy. We drew up maps and made lists of items to bring.

Eirani and Karana had produced fresh bread for lunch and we all sat around the table.

Thayu brought up the contact details Jarek Malicki had given us and, through our new connection to the satellite dish on the top of the hill, we could track where he had been. According to the data, he had left my father's house, turned left, *not* stopped at the beach, and gone in the direction of the main road that ran about ten kilometres south of the settlement. But then he had stopped not far off, and no movement had been logged for the last two hours.

Strange.

"What's the bet he's thrown the reader out the window?" Nicha asked.

"After giving me the contact details?"

That didn't make sense, they agreed with me.

"What is there that he could be investigating?" I asked my father, who sat with us and was listening to all the conversations.

He took the reader from Thayu, looked at the screen and frowned. "Nothing. Just paddocks."

So while my father and Erith brought out the life vests and other boating gear, Thayu, Nicha and I went to get the van from the charging station to check out the spot.

The road to the west snaked up the hill between sheep paddocks and crested the ridge from where you had a view over the bay.

When we came over the hill, we could see the white car sitting by the side of the road. I slowed the van, while Thayu scanned the area for hot spots that would indicate the presence of a person.

She shook her head. "There is no one here."

I pulled up next to the car.

We got out and walked around.

The doors were locked, and there were no signs of damage or a struggle. We looked in through the windows. A small cloth backpack lay on the front seat.

Nicha offered to force open the door, but Thayu established that the bag contained no electronic devices. "We don't have a strong reason to damage the vehicle, so we better not do it."

She was always much more cautious, and that suited me, because Sheydu would already have smashed the window, with all the trouble that might entail.

We found no obvious tracks leading away from the vehicle, but walked down the farm road for a bit anyway, looking for footprints. The track stopped at a gate and a paddock where cows grazed. The grass was lush and tall and gave no sign that anyone had walked through recently.

"Strange," Nicha said, squinting against the sunlight.

I agreed. Very strange.

We could do nothing except return to the house. The rest of the team had carted everything we needed to the beach. They'd brought life vests for everyone, even if some of them looked like they'd been hanging in the shed for years, the boat's radio and beacon, flasks with drinks and boxes with food, and the engine's battery—which was really heavy.

I met Devlin on the beach. He showed me the inside of the plastic cube which Reida had cut open. Inside the housing sat a little electronic device. Devlin shook it out onto my hand.

A tiny little circuit board with a couple of thin wires attached.

"That is the antenna," he said. "It attaches to longer wires encased in the housing."

"So this is a listening device?"

"It's used to repeat the signal that comes from the boat. There are others all over the bay. I presume they're tied down with a rope and something heavy at the bottom. This one must have come loose accidentally."

From where we stood, that boat was barely visible behind my father's boat and a couple others.

My father helped us take the stuff out to the boat with the dinghy. He climbed the little ladder onto the deck and took the cover off the stairs into the cabin, muttering at the amount of seagull shit on the deck. He helped Devlin hoist his receiver to the top of the mast and helped him connect all the equipment. Then Veyada took my father back to the beach. He offered to stay, but I didn't want him to become entangled in whatever was going on. His house was the safest place to be.

From the deck, the suspicious yacht was a lot closer, with barely a hundred metres of water between us. We were still within the bay. The water was calm enough that we could see the patches of coral underneath. I used to snorkel here as a boy and thought it was normal to see the colourful fish that tourists travelled long distances for.

The team went into the cabin below deck and set up scanning equipment which established that the yacht indeed contained the main blocking equipment.

I studied it through binoculars. The name of the boat was *King-*

fisher, and Nicha established that it was registered with a rental company that hired yachts for parties and holidays.

By this time, Veyada had come back with the dinghy. He climbed the ladder onto the deck and the first thing he said was, "They're watching."

He glanced at the bay, where another dinghy was making its way across the calm water. Coming in our direction. It was quite a distance away, but through my binoculars I could see that there were at least three people inside.

I said, "Hmm. What should we do?"

"Watch them back. See what happens. Get somewhere they can't see us."

We clambered down the ladder into the boat's cabin. With all the equipment on the table, it was crowded in there, especially for Evi and Telaris, who could only stand straight in the middle of the cabin, away from the storage cupboards that circled the ceiling.

Veyada stayed at the top of the ladder.

"They've turned to the beach," he reported. "There are three men in the boat. They don't look like Tamerians."

The latter didn't mean anything. Jemiro had not looked like a typical Tamerian either, not the ones we saw in Barresh: solidly-built, with a characteristically heavy brow. But he'd had his brain tampered with like a Tamerian. "Are they talking to each other?" A strange question only someone familiar with Tamerians would ask.

"No."

That was a worry. Because Tamerians didn't talk much even when spoken to. They might not even understand a normal person's speech, like Puck in Barresh.

Veyada said, "They're at the beach now. One of them has gotten out of the boat and is walking across the sand. He appears to be looking for something."

"What's the bet he's looking for that thing we found this morning?"

"We can guess, but where is the cage? Is it still on the beach?"

"We didn't see it when we went to check. I'm guessing the tide took it back out."

We waited a while.

Then Veyada said, "He's going back to the boat. He has found nothing. They're pushing off."

We waited some more. I could hear the bow waves slapping against the side of the boat as the dinghy came past us.

Then Veyada said, "Ha. Now one of them has taken out a fishing rod. Oh, bugger, they're throwing out the anchor. It looks like they're staying there for a while."

"How far are they?"

"They're near the rocks on the other side of the bay."

I formed a mental picture of the bay. The rocks where the water was deep and clear and where Melanie would set out her crab pots were about five hundred metres away. It was also a spot popular with snorkelers.

"So what do we do?" Nicha asked.

"We can go fishing, too," Veyada said. His voice sounded hopeful.

Out of our group, Nicha, Veyada and I were most proficient with boats and least afraid of water. Evi and Telaris were not that bad either, but we decided not to put more people in our dinghy than they had in their dinghy, especially because Evi and Telaris were big and heavy. Veyada and I carried the fishing rods and cray-pots from the deck to the ladder and handed them to Nicha who put them into the dinghy.

Then we climbed in ourselves.

Against the glare of sunlight, I could barely see the other dinghy.

Veyada kneeled on the bench. He set out his scanning equip-ment against the side of the boat and propped his reader screen against the anchor box. It displayed a map of the area with trans-mission activity spots surrounding our boat, their yacht, their dinghy and the houses along the beach.

"Where to?" I asked him, while turning on the engine.

He glanced over the bay in the direction of the rented yacht. "Could you justify going in that direction? I want to see if I can get a passcode signature so we can decode it and listen in to what they're transmitting."

"I could go to the reef behind it, past the yacht. That would make sense if we were going fishing."

I gunned the engine and we pulled away from my father's boat. Thayu met my eyes between the bars of the deck railing. The expression in her eyes was concerned. Yes, I knew she didn't like open water or boats. She didn't like *me* going out onto the ocean. In the Coldi ways her mind operated, she would have preferred to be on the dinghy herself, because doing stuff kept her fears at bay.

We turned around my father's yacht, into the breeze. Small waves slapped against the sides of the dinghy. The breeze was picking up, and most of the clouds had gone. It would have been a nice day to go sailing.

The other yacht looked deserted from as close as I dared to pass it. The sails were folded, the door to the cabin closed, as far as I could see. There was a small window in the side of the cabin from which the occupants would probably be watching us.

I glanced at Veyada's screen, which showed little activity. He switched to infrared and it showed a couple of lighter spots inside the yacht.

He nodded at the screen. "There are three or four people inside."

We passed the yacht at a distance of fifty metres or so, and went over to the reef at the headland, where Nicha threw out the anchor and we put together our fishing gear.

Nothing happened for quite some time. We watched the yacht, the three people in the other dinghy watched us, my team in my father's yacht pretended to be enjoying themselves with drinks on the deck, and the others in the rented yacht remained below the deck. We didn't catch any fish either.

And then all of a sudden, Nicha shouted and there was a splash from something big hitting the water. Someone had jumped off the other yacht and was in the water, swimming in our direction.

The men in the other dinghy were fast hauling up the anchor, but they were way over on the other side of the bay, closer to the beach.

Veyada jumped to do the same. He pulled hard at the anchor chain. The dinghy came loose. I gunned the engine.

We were much closer to the man in the water than the other dinghy, but now three men had come to the deck of the yacht, and one of them pointed a weapon—

—And he was hit in the chest by a flash. He fell backwards. His two companions scrambled into the cabin.

Sheydu stood on the deck of my father's boat with her gun in her left hand.

Nicha yelled, "Careful!"

He lunged over to me and pushed my arm that held the rudder. The dinghy swerved to the left before the rudder flew from my grip. It clanged into the side of the boat, almost upsetting Veyada.

Something hit the water where we had just been.

What the hell? Were they shooting at us?

Sheydu yelled at them to drop their weapons. Thayu was also on the deck of my father's boat, as were Deyu and Reida, all of them armed.

Veyada jumped up while yanking his gun from under his jacket. He braced himself. I ducked between the benches, and felt the charge go off. Once, twice.

Meanwhile, the swimmer had come much closer to us. Nicha and Veyada dropped to their knees and I steered the dinghy in his direction.

He called out, "Help me, help me, please."

The swimmer was no other than Jarek Malicki. Veyada reached out and pulled him into the dinghy while the fight continued between the other two groups.

The other dinghy had reached the rented yacht. The three men aboard clambered up the ladder. I couldn't see the stricken person on the deck anymore, but they were now pulling up their anchor.

Jarek lay in the bottom of our dinghy, panting. His suit clung to him with water.

He cried, "Please, get me out of here."

His face was bruised and blood ran from a cut in his lip down his chin. He was shivering.

I turned the dinghy around. Thayu yelled at us from my father's boat, but her words distorted in the breeze. As it turned out, the other yacht had started their engine and was coming towards us.

I steered to the side of my father's boat and around the stern, where Reida caught the rope that Nicha tossed to him and hauled us in. Seriously, life was so much easier with the strength of Coldi people.

The dinghy clonked into the side of the boat.

Veyada pushed Jarek up the ladder and jumped up himself; then he hauled up Nicha and me.

Sheydu had donned her armour and was strapping her small gun to her arm. "Get down, get down!"

We scrambled into the cabin and crowded at the bottom of the ladder.

We waited.

People shouted outside.

Alarming thunks and thumps on the deck made the boat shudder. What the hell were they doing? This was my father's boat and I didn't want anything to happen to it.

I scrambled up to look.

Sheydu had, in full pirate style, thrown the second, lightweight, anchor to the other yacht, where it had stuck behind the railing, and Deyu was hauling the other boat in.

Seriously, how many old pirate movies had they watched while I was at the court with Abri?

A man on the other boat was trying to untangle the chain and the anchor. He was pale-skinned, with short light hair—not Tamerian at all.

Deyu pulled in the last metres of chain. Reida used his foot to stop the two boats crashing into each other. He and Deyu jumped onto the other deck.

The blond-haired man straightened just in time for Deyu to sock him in the face and throw him over the side.

There was now only one man aboard.

But before Deyu reached him, he pointed a gun at his head and fired. His head jerked backwards in a splatter of blood. As if in slow motion, he fell backwards, overboard.

Damn, I could really do without that.

Reida disappeared down the ladder into the cabin. He came out a moment later. "All safe."

I felt sick.

My legs still shaky, I climbed up on the deck and jumped to the other boat. There was a smudge of blood on the deck. I took care not to touch it so that we could analyse it later, although I wasn't quite sure how we could identify Tamerians. I must ask Lilona Shrakar at the hospital in Barresh.

"Have a look in the cabin," Reida said.

I stuck my head into the cabin door and, whoa, there was a lot of equipment in there. On the table in the middle, on the benches and the overhead shelves. Wires and cords everywhere, linking pieces of equipment like spider silk. Most of the equipment was of a type I had never seen. The cases were made from a greenish metal, with control pads of a rubbery, semitransparent material with unfamiliar markings. I didn't dare touch anything because it might be recorded. I didn't see anything familiar. Even the cords were unusually thin.

"Whoa!" Thayu said, coming down the ladder after me. "What is this? Where does it come from?"

She crouched at the table, studying the equipment without touching it. She waved her scanner over the table, probably to determine which of the pieces of equipment was on. The lines on her screen jumped.

I moved out of her way.

By the look of the number of empty containers in the kitchen the men had been living here for some time, probably the same amount of time that we had been at my father's house. The bench was clean and neat, the plates neatly stacked away in the cupboards. The two sleeping cabins in the bow were also neat, the beds made, clothes packed away with military precision. This reminded me of living for two weeks in the cramped confines of an Asto military ship, where everything had to be stowed or tethered at all times, in case the ship needed to move quickly. What if all these various forms of Tamerians—if they were Tamerians—were members of a private army?

That was a chilling thought.

The overhead storage area contained the men's bags. They were of a cheap, Earth-based brand, quite new, although one bag had marks on the outside from scraping against something in transit.

Inside the bags I found nothing that identified their owners. Just male clothes and toiletries. Even those were of a cheaper kind. I looked for—and found—shaving gear, so at least some of the men were locals, even if the equipment in the main cabin clearly was not.

The brands of washing gel and toothpaste were all global. According to the small print on the tube, it had been distributed through a centre in Germany. It did not necessarily mean that it was bought there, although it did seem likely it was bought in Europe. It still didn't mean anything.

I went to check the small print on all the toiletry items. The deodorant came from South Africa. The shaving canisters from Turkey. But I noticed something else: all the stuff was out of date, including a packet of—unused—painkillers. And all the bags contained a bundle of exactly the same type of cheap socks: those knitted black ones that lost shape after a few wears.

I thought I could see the signs: these men had been supplied with this stuff specifically to hide their identities. I looked through all the pockets of the bags, and found no papers. What form of identification had they used to hire this boat?

I found a number of the hire company, but when I tried it, no one replied. It was the middle of the afternoon, and the company was in Paihia, normally a busy tourist town where a lot of dive charter boats left. They would *not* leave an office unstaffed at this time of the day.

It was very odd.

I tried to remember if we'd had trouble reaching people, but the truth was, I hadn't tried to reach that many people because I was on leave. Some people had been reaching *me*, but were those all the messages that had been sent? I had assumed that if something really important happened, someone would contact us. We had lines of communication with Nations of Earth and the Exchange. Either of those should have notified us.

If they weren't being blocked.

I backed out of the cramped sleeping cabin into the equally cramped main cabin.

"Find anything?" I asked Thayu, who sat on her knees at the end of the table, studying a panel with blinking lights.

"I don't understand where this was made," she said. "There are little signs printed on these panels, but I don't recognise them, and I don't know what type of technology this is based on."

That, coming from Thayu's mouth, was a pretty disturbing confession.

"Aghyrian?" Nicha said, his voice dark. He stood at the bottom of the ladder into the cabin.

"That would be the logical conclusion, but I don't know," Thayu said. "It doesn't look Aghyrian to me."

"It doesn't look ancient Aghyrian," Nicha said.

We all looked at each other. One of these days, that behemoth Aghyrian ship with its near-immortal arsehole of a captain was going to turn up somewhere to make our lives difficult. It could be that they were doing this already. Or maybe not.

"We should ask our prisoner what he knows," Nicha said.

"Do you think he knows?" I asked. Was Jarek a prisoner? Was he a victim or an actor?

They both looked at me. Nicha snorted. "He'd know more than we do."

I said, "They kept him prisoner here. He might have just blundered into something that he didn't know about." After all, Robert had fallen out with the Cartel, so it would be unlikely for his lawyers to be informed about what the Cartel's spies were doing. And it was likely that these men were hired by the Cartel.

"They would have had to stand by the side of the road to stop his vehicle. They must have been very keen at stopping it."

True. Jarek would have been on his way to his accommodation, likely in Paihia as well, or in the bay-side resorts along the way.

Why had they stopped him? Because they wanted to stop me from going to Paihia, outside the communication block area? Because Jarek had some information they needed?

Had he come here independently? He wouldn't have had the car otherwise, would he?

There were far too many questions.

Thayu said, "He is going to know a lot more than we do. Yes, I think he could provide us with useful information."

However they'd get that information out of him was a second matter, and one that chilled me. I didn't like the thought of Jarek being taken back to my father's house. I didn't *think* any people in my association would go as far as mistreatment and, heaven forbid, torture, but I couldn't be certain. The Coldi mind had all kinds of unexpected dark corners. I couldn't make them promise me they'd treat him humanely either, or at least not without looking weak, and there was also the issue that my association felt that they'd failed me and were probably doubly keen to make up for it.

I asked Thayu if she wanted to take all the equipment. She said she had already taken scans that would tell her a lot, and explained that if we wanted to remove the devices from the cabin, we needed to tow the boat to shore. "This technology will all be set up to run automatically. Once we disconnect and disable everything, *someone* will get a notification, will send reinforcements and the fight will be on."

"Won't they already notice that they're not being sent regular reports of whatever those guys were doing?"

"Maybe, but we still have some time before they are sure that something is wrong. I'd prefer not to touch the equipment at this point."

"But what can we do? We have a couple of dead bodies out there. People will notice and the police will turn up. There will be a lot of questions." This was not Asto where if a person in First Circle said that someone had wronged them, it was accepted as truth and as valid reason for a murder squad, or where matters of law were sorted out between clans or between individuals. And where dead bodies were seen as collateral damage.

The police would find me here, and the whole thing would blow up to the highest level of politics and get back to Nations of Earth, and be another argument for the *We don't want aliens* camp.

And yet these men were not from off-world. But this technology was.

I thought of Amarru's projection and the large zones on Earth where the Exchange had lost coverage. I thought of the lines of communication into space. A shadow Exchange, that's what criminals and shady organisations had wanted for years. The notion of a secondary Exchange that was not controlled by authorities was of immense value to people with secrets to hide. The current system was almost watertight, definitely when it concerned the travel of people.

Never mind the holiday. Once we disabled this equipment, I was going to go public and contact both Amarru and Margarethe immediately.

I came up onto the deck to find that not only did we have an audience in the form of a bunch of locals on the beach, but the police had already arrived with three cars, one of which towed a trailer and a rubber dinghy which they were in the process of reversing down the beach. I counted at least ten people in uniform.

Well, that was going to take some explaining.

Veyada and Sheydu stood on the deck, giving the gathering on the beach a bewildered look.

"We're governed by local law," I told them. "We have no options but to answer their questions."

"These men weren't governed by local law," Sheydu said, glancing at the dinghy, where Deyu had been so industrious as to collect the dead. There were four men, and all of them were Earth humans. Two Africans, one Middle-Eastern type and the blond man. They were in their late twenties or thirties and I had never seen any of them.

Reida said, "We came to investigate, they attacked us. They took a prisoner. He tried to escape and they tried to kill him. We defended ourselves and the prisoner. Is there anything we did wrong?"

Well, they had used their Asto-produced guns for which they probably did not have local licences and I doubted any of the local police would have seen before.

I now regretted never having asked about why Sheydu and the others thought they could get away with bringing their weapons, but knowing Sheydu's disdain for bureaucracy and inefficiency, I had always been hesitant to do so. I'd already had to hear so much grumbling from her, and she was right: the presence of their guns *had* been a very good thing for us many times, which was why I'd let it slide, but we were on Earth, and there were laws about weapons. Amarru had once suggested to me that authorities were willing to turn a blind eye in the case of guards of visiting dignitaries—that would be me—as long as the weapons weren't used. I guess we failed on that front.

The police officers had launched the dinghy which was now coming in our direction, so we waited until they reached us, cut the engine and floated to my father's boat. One man noticed the other dinghy with the bodies. He nodded at it and his colleagues acknowledged.

"A bit of a mess you've got here, Mr Wilson," he said, in a typical dry tone. He seemed to be the officer in charge of the group. He glanced sideways at Sheydu.

Oh, there was going to be some trouble.

He climbed from the dinghy onto the hired yacht and shook my hand. His nametag said Dan.

I explained to him what had happened. I showed him the equipment downstairs in the dark and stuffy cabin. He didn't say much while I spoke, but he studied the equipment on the table, frowning.

A colleague came down the ladder.

"Look at this," Dan said, nodding at the table.

The other officer studied the interlinked equipment. "I'm guessing this breaks several of your *gamra* import rules, Mr Wilson."

"My team doesn't recognise any of this kind of equipment either, but we think it's specialised transmission-blocking gear. Have you had any communication issues?"

At the same time, one officer said, "No," and the other said, "We've had some issues back at the station."

The first one said, "But I don't think that it could have anything to do with . . ."

Then they looked at each other, a look of comprehension passed between them.

"How long has this been going on for you?" I asked.

"A few weeks."

"Three?"

"About that, why?"

"That's how long I've been here. This boat must have been moored in this area for that long."

"We'll contact the rental company."

"I tried that. They're not replying."

"You must have struck them at a bad time. They're a big and busy company."

"Who would always have someone at the main desk to answer calls, right?"

"Yes."

"The number is here. Try it."

He did. There was no reply. I saw that on his face before he disconnected. His attention went back to the equipment on the table, frowning. "But I can contact the guys on the beach, and I have no trouble getting onto the station."

"This setup blocks very specific information. Very sophisticated. We're not familiar with it."

"Do you know any of the men outside and who they're affiliated with?"

"I don't know them, but we rescued a man who was being kept prisoner by them. He visited me this morning. He's at the other boat."

So we went to my father's boat.

My team had provided Jarek with a blanket against the chill wind, but he still looked cold, miserable and worn out. The bruise on his face had swollen.

As it turned out, the officers had been in the area to investigate an abandoned car by the side of the road—Jarek's—and they had no clue about what had happened there either.

Jarek said that he was on his way to his hotel when he'd been stopped by a man walking along the road. He'd asked if the man needed help, and while the car was stopped, two others came up and dragged him out. The next thing he remembered was waking up in one of the sleeping cabins in the yacht. He'd managed to escape when three of the men went in the dinghy and he was left in the care of a single man.

"Do you know who these people are?" I asked him.

He shook his head. He didn't meet my eyes.

"Who do you *think* they work for?"

He shrugged. "That's anyone's guess."

"I don't think so. I think you know very well. Is it the Pretoria Cartel? Is it enemies of the Pretoria Cartel? Is it any of the members individually? Where did they get this tech?"

"Oh, that's made in a factory in Kenya."

"Oh, rubbish. Have you even seen it?"

"Yeah, there is a factory that makes this stuff."

"In *Kenya?*"

"Why does that surprise you so much?"

I spread my hands. *Because it doesn't look like Earth technology.* But I couldn't say that for sure. And the icons on the panels could just be unfamiliar because they were unfamiliar to me. With the advent of on-demand manufacturing even the concept of a factory was much reduced compared to the behemoths of the previous century. You could make a few copies of anything and make it look like any kind of alien design you wanted.

"So who do *you* work for?" I asked Jarek.

"I work for Robert Davidson. I already told you. I knew nothing of all this, or why people were shadowing you. First thing I knew was when they stopped the car. To me, it seems like you're the type of person who can be expected to be followed."

Sadly, he was right about that. I'd come to expect to be shielded from this sort of activity at Barresh, but on Earth, my team did not have the means or knowledge to protect us to the same extent. I had not deemed it necessary. I had been wrong, and I was at fault for putting all of us in danger, including my father and Erith. "Then what did they ask of you once they brought you to the boat?"

He chuckled nervously. "Ask? They didn't ask anything. Once you left, they were going to pull up anchor, kill me, and dump me in the water. You don't argue with those guys. They got their orders and they will follow them. They don't speak to prisoners. They don't negotiate."

That started to sound familiar, like *Tamerians*. "What sort of men are they?"

He shrugged. "Hired guns? Plenty of people who will do stuff for money. They have zero power to negotiate."

"And where do these hired guns come from?"

"I don't know! I'm a lawyer, not a criminal."

"Then tell me this: is this the sort of thing Robert Davidson wanted to talk to us about?"

"I don't know. He knows things about the Cartel that I can only guess. He hasn't told me any of it. He says he can give you information that you'll find very useful, but that you'll need to visit him to appreciate."

I bet the Cartel would like that. "I guess he may have changed his mind given the current situation."

"I don't know. I haven't spoken to him for a number of days."

We weren't getting anywhere. More and more, I suspected that he genuinely didn't know anything. I wasn't sure that he was a proper lawyer either. But he might have an important clue to what was going on.

The police officers had called for reinforcements to deal with the yacht and the bodies and those were now arriving at the beach-front. They said they needed to question Jarek. I asked Dan quietly if he could see a way to keep Jarek in custody or at least make sure that he stayed in a place that was well-protected and where we could be sure to find him.

"Sorry, Mr Wilson, we can't hold him without reason, and we have no valid reason to hold him."

"Not even for his own protection?"

"Only if there is a demonstrable risk to him."

"He was just kidnapped, is that not demonstrable risk?"

"We have no proof that these people will do the same thing again. In fact, they probably won't because they're dead."

From his perspective, he was right, but several aspects of this set my senses crawling.

Jarek had come to me with an offer. He had come in person while he could have sent a message. He had claimed not to know that I was being watched or who was watching.

Either he was genuine and not very smart, and he had just coincidentally blundered into the situation, or he was playing tricks and acting dumb. His offer could be real, or it could be a trap.

Of course my mind started playing tricks on me, and I saw conspiracies everywhere. Then I noticed that Sheydu and Thayu looked impatient as well.

We were on a boat in the middle of the bay, exposed as hell, unable to get out quickly. Sheydu had searched for explosives and found none, but we were vulnerable here in hundreds of ways.

"Let's go back to shore."

Their serious nods showed that they shared my concern.

5

WE GATHERED THE GEAR we had brought to my father's boat and handed it down to Nicha in the dinghy. I locked the cabin and put the cover over the deck while the police officers went to their boat and the other members of my team got into the dinghy.

The police were stringing out ropes to bring the dinghy with the bodies to shore. They were also going to bring the yacht closer to shore and at some point would take all the electronic gear off and investigate it. They had already floated the anchor and had attached a rope from their rubber dinghy to the post on the deck. Jarek sat in the police dinghy, ready to be taken to the station, looking cold and miserable.

I lowered myself from the ladder into our dinghy, which Veyada then steered across the calm water of the bay. Not too fast, because we were heavy and a stiff breeze had come up which produced choppy little waves in the bay.

"What do you all think?" I asked as soon as I was sure we were out of earshot from the police.

"I think something smells," Sheydu said in her typical blunt tone. "That guy who came to visit us this morning *has* to know more of this. I think he was baiting us, either to distract us, to get information out of us or to lead us into a trap."

"Yeah," Nicha said.

Thayu agreed.

Veyada said, "There is definitely something strange going on." Sometimes it was hard to believe that Veyada was Sheydu's son. Their characters couldn't be more different. She was blunt, he was cautious, even in the way he steered the dinghy, always alert, always expecting trouble and expecting to have to circumnavigate it.

"Let's just put all our thoughts together." I was sitting on the back bench, closest to Veyada, and most of them needed to turn around to see me. "Tell me what you think is going on and what you think is strange."

"What these people are all doing here, for starters," Sheydu said. "I get that they're trying to block us, but why go through all this effort?"

"Have you been able to find out what sort of event the doctor might have referred to on the report about Jemiro that we got this morning?" I asked her.

"No. I doubt he was talking about a major disaster or anything of the kind."

"Maybe they are showing off the capabilities of Tamerians because they're still trying to convince us of the value of them," Reida said. "You know, as people who will just do what you say with no questions asked. Like Jemiro: translate this, translate that. He never spoke a word to us."

"These were no Tamerians," Nicha said. "They're locals. Tamerians are stocky and broad and have dark hair and a severe face."

Thayu said, "I think those men are still Tamerians of some sort, even if they're not real Tamerians."

"Like Jemiro?" Deyu asked. "He was some sort of Tamerian?"

At some point, *Tamerian* had started to mean more than someone from the ice world of Tamer. It meant someone whose mind or mind and body had been artificially manipulated. And yes, in this way, Jemiro was a Tamerian.

Jemiro was another piece in the mystery.

Jasper Carlson had offered us Jemiro, and was obviously convinced that tailoring people for jobs was the way to go. They might have been designed as disposable people, even. Thinking about the shell that we'd known as Jemiro made me feel sick, but the thought of disposable people made me feel even sicker.

And then people on Earth said that *Coldi* were barbaric? Coldi would not do such a thing. For one, if they couldn't form social bonds with a person, they didn't want to associate with the person. Secondly, they had enough people themselves, people who were brilliant at a wide range of things.

"One thing bothers me: these people here don't appear to have any special abilities," Nicha said. "They're not very strong, or shoot well—I mean—none of them came even close to hitting any of us."

Sheydu snorted. "What abilities do Tamerians have, other than the ones they're taught? Unless you count the abilities to blindly follow orders, which they obviously do have, never mind that they can't communicate. The ability to follow orders is absent from a lot of the people here. They don't see the benefit of what a leader says and they go off and do their own thing, and they are rarely punished for it. That is why this is such a chaotic society. They all *say* they work for a common good, but when you really ask about it, everyone is looking for what's in it that benefits *them*."

That was such an amazingly correct observation, and one only a Coldi person could make. *They* had a pathological need to follow their superiors in whatever associations they were in. They saw the association as a unit that should benefit from their actions, not the other way around.

I asked, "What should we do about this invitation to visit Robert Davidson?"

"I don't think this Jarek character is going to be available to take us there," Devlin said, glancing at the police dinghy, which was still behind us.

Veyada steered the dinghy to the middle of the beach, where, heavily laden as we were, we could still come quite close to the shore without anyone having to get out and wade through waist-deep cold water.

Quite a number of people remained on the beach, including my father's neighbours. When we arrived, they all wanted to know what was going on, and whose the other boat was.

I felt guilty about having brought this world of violence and distrust into their community. These were good, trusting people.

I tried to explain as best as I could without alarming them. But a couple of men were dead and that alone was alarming. They had seen it. *Children* had seen dead bodies in a dinghy.

The fact that these dead men weren't "real" people alarmed them even more. Even the people of Rocky Bay had heard of the faceless assassins who had murdered heads of state in faraway countries. Why had they come to their safe and secluded part of the world?

I didn't know what to tell them. Because I was here? But that seemed like I had a high opinion of myself.

I'd met most of these people for the first time in the past two weeks, and they had accepted me. The least I could do was answer their questions as well as I could.

We were standing on the beach, surrounded by the locals when there was a strange moment of silence. The air vibrated.

Whoa!

I turned around.

Something out in the bay went *thump* and again, *thump*. I could feel it though the soles of my shoes.

People on the beach gasped.

A boy yelled, "Look, look!"

As if slow motion, the sides of the rented yacht blew outwards and out of the water. A spout of water gushed up, rising from the bay like a fountain. It sprayed outwards, over the nearby police dinghy and the officers in it. The dinghy rose and tipped sideways. A few of the occupants fell out.

My father's boat copped a big splash, too. It rocked violently from side to side, the mast swinging.

Then the remains of the rented yacht, and the dinghy still containing the bodies, sank below the surface, leaving a big wave in their wake.

Sheydu gaped. I knew that she had searched the rented yacht for explosives and found none.

These people had smarter equipment than we had.

There were people in the water, yelling. I recognised Jarek Malicki with his life vest, hanging onto the side of the rubber dinghy. The police officers had also fallen out, and one climbed back in, but the dinghy was full of water.

The people on the beach sprang into action. "We got to go and help them," someone said, and a few people ran to drag another dinghy into the water.

As we stood there, as the locals fired up the engine, as the police were bailing water out of their inflatable, as my father's boat still rocked with the wave from the explosions, my reader burst into life with a cacophony of all the possible alarms that could go off.

What the hell.

I shut the noise down, but then it beeped, and then again and again. And then it let out a constant stream of beeps.

I pulled it out of my pocket, expecting to see something about the explosion, a message of glee or a threat, but it was a screen full of notifications about meetings and agenda items to be added . . . and more scrolled over the screen as they came in.

I'd stopped working for Nations of Earth years ago. I used to get this stuff—until I figured out how to turn it off—but I hadn't received any of it since at least two years before I went to Barresh.

And still the stuff was flowing over my screen. Thousands and thousands of messages.

Sheydu stood with her hand over her ear on the side where she wore her feeder which she had connected up to her devices. Nicha had pulled out his reader as well.

The messages on my screen flowed and flowed.

In between the automated notifications that I shouldn't be getting, I spotted some other subjects.

Cory, are you there? from my officer at the Exchange who was in Brazil at the moment.

A bit later, *Cory, did you get my message?*

Mr Wilson, do you have some time? From someone at a commercial office.

Another person asked, *Given the current situation, could we get some advice?*

And yet another, *Biotechnical industry seeks off-world contacts.*

I always got lots of messages, questions and meet requests from those people when I was here. Many wanted to do business with *gamra*. Few went ahead with it, but the interest was always there, until they realised the extent of the bureaucratic hoops that needed to be jumped.

As soon as I visited Earth, those types of requests exploded.

I had thought that it was odd that I hadn't received anything for so long. But I'd assumed that for once, my liaison office at the Exchange respected the fact that I was here on a holiday, and that they would contact me when something was up.

Clearly I'd been wrong.

Not only hadn't they contacted me, it seemed that, judging by the headlines, there had been some sort of chaos.

And I even found a message from the Exchange saying, *Urgent discussion needed*.

The message was a few days old, and it mentioned that Amarru wanted to speak with me, if a secure line was available.

Thayu and I looked at each other.

Sheydu said, "That boat that just blew up? It was maintaining a communication filter. It let through just enough that we weren't getting suspicious, but it kept out the majority of news."

I checked the news and barely recognised the world we had left, where Robert Davidson's trial, sporting events and industry news had occupied the key positions. Headlines screamed, *Chaos!* and *Return to War* and *Magolis collapses, others teetering on the brink*.

What?

Magolis was one of the leading international financial institutions. What had happened?

I skimmed the first paragraphs of the article.

It seemed that about two weeks ago, a number of worldwide financial computer systems had gone down when the security of their core sensitive systems was breached. More specifically: someone had gotten into the accounting sections. How long they'd been in there was unclear, but systems had shut down when bots started to transfer money out. Ironically, the money was being transferred to other sections of government. Who the money went to appeared random. There was a story of a small local district in Spain that suddenly found millions in their accounts for no apparent reason. The term Robin Hood bandits was coined, but there were also some larger corporations who had received untraced transfers. It was just not as obvious for them to spot the irregularities.

But, as a result, people and, more importantly, major companies no longer trusted the banks that used the system in question and withdrew their money. The sudden influx of a lot of money into other banks sent the automated investment systems into a roller-coaster and then a tailspin, until people intervened and stopped all trade. By this time, a lot of the damage was already done.

Magolis Finance was hardest hit, because they developed the system.

But when people started investigating, it didn't take long for other breaches in security to come out.

News services were screaming foul, led by the ever-colourful Flash Newspoint with the headline, *Governments Lied: Your data was never secure.* The article went on to accuse banks of making up numbers and hiding breaches in security which, according to the service, had started two years ago but probably went back much further than that.

Because all money was digital, there was no safe place to put it. No mattresses or treasure chests in the back yard.

And who had done all this, or why? There was a lot speculation on that subject, but to me, the patterns were clear. It had been quite a while since the conflict in Kazakhstan where the Coldi Zhori clan mafia had helped rebels with off-Earth arms. The clan had been thoroughly investigated; some members had fled, some gone to prison, and many had found honest lives, most of them in Africa. The criminal elements in the clan had gone underground. People had expected them to resurface at some point. I had always said that they would not fight with weapons again. They would take their attacks to the vast computer networks. This was it.

I sat on the sand, scrolling through the headlines from around the world.

Many banks, especially across Europe and much of Asia, closed their services in an attempt to halt the escalating panic. Then people found their money frozen and could not buy anything. Shops closed because no one came to buy. Shopping centres lay deserted, at the mercy of bands of looters.

A crazy market in physical assets sprang up. Gold, jewellery, real estate, boats, collectibles like old furniture, books and old technology.

People went into the streets protesting against Coldi. Coldi leaders, including Amarru, came out saying that this had nothing to do with anyone under their power.

All within two weeks.

Sheltered from this news, it seemed this little enclave was the only place in the world where people were not panicking.

This meant that the people on the beach, as they stood watching the activity in the bay, and watching the police go out in someone else's dinghy to assist the first one, were all blissfully unaware of what was happening, and maybe only now would be getting the same messages I was also getting.

I didn't understand.

What was the point for people from the Pretoria Cartel of going through all this effort to hide world news from us?

While Veyada and Deyu carried the dinghy up the beach, I looked for, but didn't see, my father or Erith. Locals were now asking me questions and some even joked about security, because that was what people here did: if they were uncertain or nervous about something, they made a joke.

We put the dinghy in its usual place above the high tide line, covered it up, grabbed our bags and crossed the road to the house.

We found my father and Erith in the office, sitting at the house hub and looking at a projection of a news clip. My father looked up at me.

I started, "Did you notice . . ."

And he put his finger to his lips. "Watch this."

There was no room in the tiny office, so Thayu, Nicha and I remained standing at the door, with Veyada and Sheydu in the corridor looking over our shoulders and the others behind them.

Ayshada was yelling for his dad in the kitchen.

I recognised the hall in the projection. I recognised the dais and the symbol of Nations of Earth on the wall behind it. This was in the big assembly hall at the Nations of Earth complex.

To applause and cheering, Margarethe came to the dais. She gestured for silence, touched the surface screen on the dais to turn on the projection of her notes that only she could see in front of her. I'd done this and stood in that same position. She did not normally speak from this position, because she had a desk on the main floor that had a built-in microphone.

She started speaking.

"In recent weeks, our world has been the backdrop to a level of violence and unrest we haven't seen since the end of the last war. Criminal elements have threatened to upset our banking system. They almost succeeded. We have seen large-scale panic, runs on financial institutions, protest, looting and general civil disobedience that has required the despatch of several units of Nations of Earth peacekeeping troops. I am happy to say that unrest has now been quelled, including in the refugee camps near Cairo."

She looked around the audience.

"However, I could not neglect to mention that a lot of people have suffered and are still suffering. Some community services have still not been fixed. Some areas are without supplies. Power installations have been damaged and shops are still closed. Most importantly, while the unrest has been stopped, the underlying issues have not been addressed. These are the same issues that have dogged our administration, and indeed the previous administration, and the administration before that."

She paused for effect.

"Forgive me for taking you through a little history lesson. Twelve years ago, the world saw an unusually costly and vicious conflict in Kazakhstan. Joint regional troops were sent to quell an uprising of rebels, and they were met with a brutality such as has not been seen since the Pakistan war. They were slaughtered. Peacekeeping troops. The rebels had been aided by the Coldi Zhori mafia and used off-world weapons hitherto unseen on Earth. Despite heavy losses, our troops eventually prevailed, bringing peace to the region. The mafia leaders were brought to justice or were killed. Their families fled. We always knew that they would be back. This is that time."

"Shit," Nicha said, in Isla.

I nodded. Nicha had lived in London during that time.

We had all known that it was unlikely that we'd seen the last of the hardline Zhori, the very earliest Coldi refugees on Earth, who had always distanced themselves from the Exchange and lived underground in remote communities. We knew they were active in Africa. Many had started businesses and led honest lives, but we also knew that the criminal elements were still active.

Margarethe looked straight at the camera. "It is time that we face this issue. It's time that we stop tolerating the mess that allows these people to stay where they are and conduct their criminal activities. It is time that we take action. I have called this special public meeting of the assembly with the view of unifying the people on Earth, with the view of tackling the most important issue that is the root cause of the problems: the fact that we cannot deal with the Zhori mafia directly without upsetting the *gamra* assembly, which will find its way back to our friends at the Exchange, putting them in a difficult situation. We've been skirting around this issue, not fixing it, avoiding it. But I have made a decision. In six weeks' time, all member countries will vote in a referendum on the most important decision we are likely to make in our lifetimes: whether Earth will move forward and officially join the entities of *gamra*."

A veritable tumult broke out in the assembly hall.

I looked from Thayu to Nicha, to my father, to Erith and Veyada.

What the hell?

My father said, "Hadn't she told you that she wouldn't call the referendum until August?"

"She did." I still saw Margarethe sitting there in the dark in the bus. "I don't understand why she did this now."

Veyada's expression was dark. "My guess is that she saw no other option."

"When did this happen?" I asked.

"Two weeks ago," my father said.

And I'd known nothing of it?

Shit.

Then I realised: that was why we'd been blocked. *Someone* had known that Margarethe had this plan. They also realised that I possessed power to influence the outcome and figured that Margarethe had planned for me to be part of the campaign. Maybe that was why she'd called it early, so that I could help.

Lucky that we discovered this now, but meanwhile, two valuable weeks had been taken off the time we had to help Margarethe push through the yes vote.

We had four weeks to make a difference. Four weeks to change the world.

6

W E MET IN THE KITCHEN, a gathering of solemn faces.

For those who hadn't seen it the first time because the office was too small to fit everyone, I replayed Margarethe's speech. Ayshada sat on Nicha's lap, babbling through it, despite Nicha's efforts to shut him up. His was the only cheerful voice in the room.

At his age, he didn't understand. I doubted Deyu and Reida understood either. In the past two years since joining my association, they had come to know *gamra* as a vitally important, peaceful organisation. Why would any society not want to join that?

I'd explained the politics, but discussing Earth politics with a Coldi person from Asto was like trying to explain a telephone to someone with telepathic abilities: they didn't see the need for things like political parties or campaigns, because associations sorted out all that, right?

I'd explained, but they didn't grasp the concept of campaigning and why I even should be able to make a difference to Margarethe's vote. In a Coldi society, *everyone* could trace their loyalties back to Ezhya Palayi. His loyalty web spread from his immediate surroundings to the furthest corner of the Outer Circle. When, for some reason, there was a break in this chain, the whole network became unsettled. He was like the queen bee: without the queen, there was no hive. That also meant that Coldi people psychologically could not vote between two people for which was to become their leader because, in their minds, there was no choice.

Nicha might understand the system of elections, because he had lived on Earth, but the others were struggling.

"Winning an election is about perception. It's about what people think you can do for them. It's about exposing the negatives of the plans of the other parties."

I often thought on my feet, and that last sentence made me realise just how true this was. The fact that Margarethe had almost lost the election earlier in the year had come about through a fairly weak campaign in which she had chosen not to expose the influence of the Pretoria Cartel behind the other candidates. I had no idea why she or her campaign manager had made this decision, but it had been a mistake. As we had seen outside the courtroom, people had been hurt by the Cartel's members and their businesses. They had expected at least acknowledgement of those facts.

And so Margarethe had faced a lot of discontent and I hadn't quite understood it either until Dharma told me about this.

People had been unhappy with the way their issues had been ignored. These were people in Africa—where voter registration was the lowest—already hit hard by drought and war. They had wanted help against the big corporations that were buying up their governments, their land and resources. All they saw was the closed faces of institutions that had systematically ignored them for hundreds of years. And by extrapolation, they thought that *gamra* would add another layer of bureaucracy that could go on ignoring them. They had turned off, because they were convinced that no one would listen to them.

We needed to *show* them how they could make a difference. Show them what Sudan could do with their solar glider industry—technology illegally imported from Indrahui. Show them the huge numbers of Zhori Coldi living amongst them, especially in the hottest and poorest parts of Africa. Show them how these people had brought business into the poor communities. Show them their power.

There was hope, if only the roadblocks could be busted.

I had already done my bit: talked to the off-Earth community, and concluded they were overwhelmingly going to vote in favour. I was feeling smug about that, but the battle would not be fought in that community or in the hallowed halls of the Nations of Earth assembly. It would be fought in the poor regions of the world, and especially in Africa.

And that line of thought brought me to the only conclusion of what I could do to help. Dharma was already doing his best to get as many people as possible to register to vote. I had not realised fully how important his contribution was.

As for what we could do: we could give people a reason to vote *for*.

We had the means—weapons—and the evidence—Jemiro's report—to show the world what Margarethe's opponents were up to. If we could prove that they were messing with sick and dying people on Earth as well—and the indications were that this indeed happened—then we had a strong case. We'd looked into Charlie Awaba's story and had found that the story of his sick brother's disappearance had happened right under the noses of the Pretoria Cartel, in a nearby village. Charlie no longer lived there, but his family still did, and the building where he had seen people being treated with helmets emitting electric waves was also still there.

Meanwhile, around the table, my team were still discussing possible reasons why Margarethe would have called the referendum early.

I put my hands on the table as if I was about to get up. Everyone in the room looked at me, a circle of gold-flecked Coldi eyes and dark keihu ones.

"It doesn't matter when or why she called the referendum. There is no point discussing it. We can't change the fact that the referendum has been called and that because of this communication block, we have lost two valuable weeks. There is one thing we can do: make sure that she wins, because I couldn't bear the alternative. If this referendum doesn't go through, it will be at least another ten years before the time is right to try again, and the world will have changed completely by then. This is the one chance we have."

They all looked at me.

Sheydu said to Veyada next to her, "I thought talking sense was your job. Where have you been with your sharp tongue?"

I loved it how Veyada blushed when he got embarrassed, and this obviously related to a lot more than Veyada's tongue. Maybe he'd been a little less sharp the last few weeks, but we'd been on leave, so that was excusable.

But on the other hand, that female lawyer Mereeni had stayed in Athens and Sheydu was clearly teasing him with the officially secret relationship between her son and Mereeni. I *had* noticed that he had been writing a lot of messages.

I continued, "We can help expose the true nature of the Pretoria Cartel not just to the people in power at Nations of Earth, but to all those people Dharma is signing up to vote. When *they* see how other people, like them, poor people, people without a voice, are being hurt, then they will know that they can make a difference by voting. For the strongest effect, we ideally need to expose something that creates a scandal on the doorstep of the Pretoria Cartel. We have, between us and Amarru and the lawyer Lenka Trnkova at the Nations of Earth court, a wealth of information that *could* blow away any opposition against *gamra,* if we present it well. We have, with Dharma Yuwono and his network, the means to distribute this information all over the world, and get it to places where politics doesn't normally reach. The White population's vote is one third of all eligible voters. Many of the Blues are not registered. What we're going to do is prove the Cartel's foul dealings, make our findings public and then let the whole world know about it. Then Dharma and his people are getting these people to vote."

"All in four weeks?" said my father at the door in Isla. He understood Coldi well enough.

"Four weeks is all we have. It will be crazy, but we don't have much time."

My father said, "You should give a speech in the assembly, son."

"Agree, but first we need something to give the speech about."

"I was kind of joking."

"But I wasn't. If we do nothing, these stooges for the Pretoria Cartel will sow fear in the population. They will say that 'aliens' will take their land and their houses. If we don't provide other information, many people won't vote and the no vote will win. They can't be allowed to win. Earth will suffer. *Gamra* will suffer. The people will suffer, especially those that are suffering already. We need to hit the Cartel where they are most vulnerable: by telling the truth."

"But what can you do? The Pretoria Cartel is a widespread organisation. There are many members and branches."

"We're going to find Charlie's brother Jacko Awaba. I'm sure the world has heard stories like his before; but, without further evidence, the allegations never went anywhere, because they were never taken seriously. We are going to find out where the Earth's 'Tamerians' come from. We are going to collect evidence, take pictures and any kind of information. We're going to turn it into a huge report that we will distribute as widely as we can."

"A huge report? In four weeks?"

"Well, maybe not a huge report, but we'll find something damning."

"Do you have any evidence, and any idea where to find this evidence?"

"As a matter of fact, we do."

"Does that mean we're going to talk to Robert?" Nicha asked. He was bouncing Ayshada on his knee.

"If Jarek told the truth and he really does want to see you," Thayu said, her voice dark.

I said, "No. We're not going to talk to Robert. This is what they expect us to do. We're not going to waste time talking to someone who has petty grievances with the Pretoria Cartel. We're going to talk to the boss. I'm going to Minke Kluysters."

Nicha and Veyada frowned at me. "You?"

"He told me he wanted an office in Barresh. I'm going to tell him I'll reveal to him in person how he can get one. And then I'll have a chat with him."

Veyada said, "You're expecting him to just tell you what his companies are doing?"

"Of course not. But he wanted an office in Barresh, and he's a businessman. So he will be interested in what I have to say about commercial opportunities in Barresh. I'm not going to mention anything about Tamerians or missing people. I'm going there to make him curious. And by keeping him curious, we will ensure that he wants to keep talking to us. He's a businessman with different political opinions, not a villain."

And this, ultimately, was something that Coldi completely understood. *Keep your enemies in your association* might even be a proverb. If it wasn't, it should be.

Sheydu sniffed. "And I'm guessing that while we're there, we might as well do some of our own investigating?"

"You might be correct."

She grinned. She liked that.

"But he lives in a remote area that's controlled by the Cartel," Nicha said. "Without invitation, we're likely to get shot."

"I don't want an invitation. If he invites us, he'll be sending minders. We don't want those. We'll get an invitation when we're there. After we finished at the court, I had a look at this region. The properties owned by Minke Kluysters and Robert Davidson are next to each other and both back onto a private game reserve. The reserve is open for limited numbers of visitors and holidaymakers. It has tourist accommodation and caters for hunting trips. We're going hunting."

"You checked that out?" Thayu said. "Since when are you doing our job?"

"This is my world. I want the referendum to succeed. We go to the reserve, we worry about an invitation to see Minke Kluysters when we're there."

Sheydu gave a single nod.

Veyada nodded. "I'll scout out a few people." He rose.

Thayu instructed Deyu and Reida to start packing. Everyone sprang into action.

We had a plan.

My father stopped me at the door. "I don't know if there is anything I can do, son, but you're welcome to keep using my house as a communication hub for that hare-brained mission of yours." He shook his head. "Going straight into the den of the lion."

"It's what we do best. I don't think we can use the house. I would, but this business with those men today puts you into too much danger. I want you to be safe."

"Then what are you going to use as a safe base?"

"We'll figure out something." It was likely that we would coordinate our team using Asto's military satellites—those ones that no one was supposed to know about. I didn't like it, but we didn't have much choice.

We still had a lot to deal with before we could go.

With all communication channels open again, I sent messages off to Margarethe and Dharma Yuwono.

Margarethe was probably in bed, but being in a closer time zone, Dharma replied immediately and I spoke to him briefly.

He was in Kenya, having already visited his hometown of Jakarta and other sections of Asia. He had been wondering about us, but had not had the time to worry. He'd been working very hard on getting as many Blues to sign up for the referendum voting as he could. It was a silent campaign, he said, and explained that this involved creating a chain of recommendations through people's personal contacts, rather than visible advertising through the usual media that could be targeted through counter attacks.

I told him to keep going, and made a note to ask my team how they could get secret messages to him, detailing our plans.

Amarru had sent me some of the more obnoxious "No" ads that she had come across.

Most of them focused on fears that joining *gamra* would be bad for business and therefore jobs. Also that it would create a second elite of people who could afford to travel off world.

I'd argue that elite already existed, and that the people who put their faces on those campaigns benefited from that elite by being part of it, and therefore didn't want it to end.

More than ever, I realised that getting Blues to vote was going to be the key to winning the referendum.

I sent a very short and businesslike message to Minke Kluysters, saying that "in the light of recent events" I might have some good news for him.

While I was tending to the communication, my team packed.

The police came to the house for interviews. They took each of us into their van for that purpose, separately, but Nicha translated where necessary. I imagined Sheydu's statement would be quite interesting. *When someone shoots at me, I shoot back. They might miss, but I don't.*

Ayshada decided in the middle of this that he wanted to go to the beach, and we thought that, with the police and dead bodies still out there, that was not such a good idea. He rewarded us with a full-scale tantrum.

A sharp and brief shower burst when it was my turn to speak to the police, and I ran through the rose garden to the van. I sat on the back bench while facing an officer.

He wanted to know if I knew Jarek Malicki and whether I recognised any of the dead. They showed me pictures of their faces. I'd never seen any of them before.

I asked, "Are you going to do autopsies on these men?"

"Only if there is a question about the cause of death. It seems pretty straightforward to me. But the coroner will have to decide."

"If I raise a question for the coroner, will it be done?"

He flicked up his eyebrows. "Why? Do you have any information that could help us?"

"Do an autopsy. You will find it very interesting. You don't have any other information on these men, right?"

"What if we did?"

"But you don't."

He frowned at me. "I don't understand. Why is a autopsy going to change anything?"

"Do it." I reached for my pocket but realised my reader was in the house—at their request. "I will send you an autopsy report for a man suspiciously like the ones who were killed. He came with us to the Nations of Earth court. We only took him at the last minute when Nations of Earth wanted us to get another interpreter at very short notice. It's extremely hard to find a certified interpreter for Pengali at the best of times, but one popped up just as we were about to give up. We hired this man, but during the entire trip, he barely spoke to us. He barely answered questions and reacted strangely to a lot of things. After a few days with us, he suffered some sort of breakdown when he insulted one of our delegation and she threatened him, and he fell apart after that. His mental state deteriorated rapidly, he deteriorated physically. He died about two weeks later, and we have the autopsy. It turned out he was never really human at all, but a reconstituted human, made up with electronic parts fulfilling functions in his body where the organs were gone. The problem was that they didn't do a very good job on him."

A deep frown. "What do you mean? He was like a zombie?"

"A bit like that, yes. Someone who has been recreated to produce a person who can only do a particular task, but doesn't ask questions. One of the characteristics of these people is that they don't talk much."

The officer glanced aside, to where the rain squall turned the water of the bay lead grey. "And you're saying that these men might be the same?"

"Might be. No one will know until you do an autopsy. It will be interesting. Contact me with the results."

He said it was ultimately not his decision, and then wouldn't tell me what they were going to do with Jarek Malicki, but I guessed he would have to face more intense questioning and would probably be here for at least another day.

When I got back into the house, everyone had packed up.

I looked over the pile of stuff in the hallway, hating it how work always came between me and my family. We'd planned to stay at least another week, and I hadn't seen my father for so long. He and Erith were both getting older and I didn't know how many times I'd still see either of them in good health.

"Let me at least take all of you to Auckland," my father said.

Nicha had been able to get us places on the suborbital and I knew I wouldn't be happy until we were at the Exchange. It was a long way from here and many things could still go wrong. From there, we'd send Eirani and Karana home with Ayshada. I'd debated sending Devlin with them, but he'd acquired a lot of skills in the last few weeks that might come in handy.

My father went to get the settlement's bus, the same he'd used to pick us up.

We said goodbye to Erith in the garden. I hated to go and I hated leaving them like this.

Of course I could come back, but who knew when that was going to happen? It looked like we would stay on Earth until the referendum. Maybe I should make some time to come back here for some more sailing and sitting around the fire at night.

We left the settlement along the winding coastal road. It was afternoon and the light was already turning golden. I was staring out the window at the forest and the bays. Thayu sat next to me. Neither of us were wearing feeders, but she tended to know what I was thinking anyway. She put her hand over mine. She didn't need to say that she was sorry.

There was nothing anyone could do. I'd outgrown the places where I'd lived as a boy, and I'd outgrown my family. I cared deeply for them, but my presence only brought them into the limelight with the associated danger.

"Next time we will go and see the places where *you* grew up," I said.

That would take some organising, because, while the climate on most of Asto might have become milder and it even rained regularly in some places now, Beratha was still frightfully hot.

"Will you attend the ceremony to join the Domiri clan?"

"I think I will. Unless you don't want me to." I understood that it was a big honour to be asked to attend by the clan leader, her father.

"I do." And then she looked out the window at the scenery of undulating fields.

Thayu rarely made emotional statements. Usually, they were cryptic remarks so vaguely related to something she desperately wanted that only someone who knew her very well could decipher the meaning. Clearly, she wanted this.

"All right, we will organise it when we come back."

Her beautiful smile warmed me. The glittering in her eyes even more so.

On the seat in front of us, Sheydu was studying something on her reader. I tried to look over her shoulder, but all she had on the screen was a huge block of hexadecimal code.

I had no idea what she could see in all that, but Coldi always looked at patterns. They looked for balance. They could read this code. They often saw things that no one else understood because they thought so differently.

She straightened suddenly. "Someone is following."

How did she know that? I looked out the van's rear window, but saw nothing except an empty road that wound between paddocks, copses of trees and fields. In the distance, I could still see a glimpse of the bay.

Sheydu showed her screen to me. It now displayed a map of the road with the occasional farm or driveway. A little red blinking dot crossed the fields behind us.

I was going to say that this could never be a pursuer because there was no road in the location of the dot, but then I realised: someone was following through the air.

I peered out the back window into the sky. Afternoon sunlight hit the clouds, edging them with gold. A couple of seagulls flew against a patch of blue sky.

"There," Thayu said.

She pointed, but I still saw nothing.

I called through the cabin, "Dad, can we stop for a moment?"

My father stopped the bus in the first place he could: a turnoff to a dirt road between two paddocks.

Thayu and Sheydu got out, and then Evi, who carried a bag over his shoulder with a particularly suspicious longitudinal shape inside, about the length of his arm.

He ran to the back of the vehicle, crouched and slid the fabric off what was indeed a gun. He turned the power on and took the protector off the display. A small orange light flashed.

He raised the gun, supporting the butt on his shoulder, the barrel following whatever he was seeing and that I was very much not seeing.

The muscles in his arm tightened. The gun discharged with a soft *pop*.

You couldn't see charge gun discharges in daylight, so the first I noticed was a tiny flash, and then a small puff of smoke exploded in the sky. Something fell down into the cornfield.

"Drone," Nicha said.

Evi looked pleased with himself. As did all Indrahui, he really had amazing eyesight.

Deyu and Reida vaulted the fence and ran through the cornfield. A van came past, slowing down to ask if we were all right. Fortunately the farmer didn't say anything about my non-Earthly companions and their battle gear outfit, but I told everyone to get back into the bus just in case.

"Did you find anything?" my father asked. He sounded a bit worried.

He sat behind the wheel in the bus, where it was getting quite warm and where Eirani and Karana were looking out the window with wide eyes.

I realised how Eirani saw us come and go, but the closest she got to anything we did with weapons was tell Sheydu, "Please take those things off the table." And Sheydu would scowl and pack up all her explosives, guns and detonators and take them to wherever in my apartment Sheydu kept those things.

I said to my father, "A drone was following us. Evi shot it down."

Deyu and Reida ran through the green corn field outside, both of them carrying mangled pieces of plastic and electronics that they stuffed into a bag.

"You have really pissed these people off, haven't you?"

"I don't think it's about anything we did yet. It's about something we might do." How true that was. They had wanted to restrict my movements since I arrived at the Exchange. "And we're going to do it regardless."

Deyu and Reida came back into the bus with the pieces of the wrecked drone, molten plastic and twisted metal. Reida pulled open the equipment housing. My team gathered around, wondering aloud about where to find the data node.

My father shut the door of the bus and we continued on.

Sheydu and Veyada held the pieces of the drone on their laps; Deyu and Reida knelt facing backwards and leaning over the backrest of their seats. Thayu crouched in the aisle, Evi stood behind her and Nicha, and Devlin and Telaris looked over the back of Veyada and Sheydu's seats.

They located the data unit. They established that it had been damaged and would need equipment they didn't have with us to read.

"I don't like any of this," Thayu said when she returned to our seat. "This seems so far outside of what is common on this world that I think we have to act quickly. I think we should risk no more locals, whether they are related to you or not. These are not locals we're up against so local rules don't apply."

Sheydu snorted. "These *police* have a habit of slowing us down too much with their questions and laborious processes. If you don't mind, we should ignore them from now on."

"What do you suggest then?" I asked. "We are already on our way to the Exchange. Do you have information I don't have?"

I expected Sheydu to reply with a blunt statement, but it was Nicha who replied instead. "I think the situation justifies contacting someone from the register."

This was the Coldi register that held all the Coldi people on Earth so that wherever you were, there was always one person to help you in time of need.

I'd used it a few times before, but had never been easy about it. Because, in essence, it meant betraying my own people. Contacting the register meant you wanted no one else to know and you had nowhere else to turn.

"I don't see how anyone can help us get to the Exchange any faster. We're on an island. Athens is on the other side of the world. We'd still have to use the suborbital we've already booked." I realised it *was* a risk, using a public form of transport, because it was a funnel point where we could be traced, a point that required our ID to be registered.

"Do we?" Veyada's expression was dead serious.

"Well . . ." The rule was that any off-Earth traffic could only take off and land at the Exchange, except for medical emergencies. Of course, there *were* illegal off-Earth ships that went to places on Earth that were not the Exchange. Those were still Exchange-sanctioned because otherwise they would never come to Earth through the network in the first place. On the one hand, the Exchange was doing its best to appease the Earth authorities, but, on the other, they were constantly testing those rules.

I didn't know much about those ships, where they were, whose they were and why they were not at the Exchange. Thayu's and Nicha's father Asha Domiri came here outside the Exchange, and I was sure exceptions could be made for the right kind of people. Was I such a person?

Veyada said, "We get someone from the register. They come to pick us up."

Nicha nodded, slowly.

"Can they still take us to the Exchange?"

"I don't think we'd want to go to the Exchange."

"We don't?" I was under the impression that we were going to

Athens to liaise with Amarru as much as to drop off Eirani, Karana and Ayshada so that they could return home safely.

Thayu said, "These people are sent by someone with more advanced tech than we have. They know where we are, and have followed us and listened to us for the past three weeks. They sought to influence us so that we didn't realise the turmoil that's been going on in the rest of this world. We now managed to break their block. They will know that we did this. Any time we lose, they will use to catch up to us."

I asked, "How can we get around them?"

"We have to go straight to Minke Kluysters."

"In South Africa? With all of us? That's madness."

She said, "We'll keep the non-essential people in a safe place. But we need to act quickly because we may not have that much time before they discover where we've gone."

"They might already be looking out for us in key positions." Such as the airport and customs in Athens.

"Amarru says that their route there is safe."

And Amarru knew everything.

While the van travelled along the windy road, we discussed the logistics. According to Veyada, someone was going to pick us up from a nearby field. I was amazed at how quickly they could be here. I'd never taken much notice of any Coldi in New Zealand—except to notice there weren't many. But, also, maybe Amarru had sent some people to shadow us, in case we needed them. I wouldn't put that beyond her either.

My team spread all the weapons on the floor and divided them up so that each person in my association qualified to use a gun had a weapon within reach. That included everyone except the domestic staff.

Karana, who was rarely privy to our discussions, listened with wide eyes. Eirani heard a bit more of it usually, and she shook her head. However that was not an uncommon reaction for Eirani, who preferred that we all came to eat our breakfasts, lunches and dinners on time. I hoped they could stay safe.

I had my own gun and Thayu insisted that I strap it on.

Veyada went to speak to my father about the changed direction.

I couldn't hear what they said, but a moment later, the bus stopped and turned around.

A bit further back, we took a turnoff that was a narrow and bumpy dirt road. It went in between some paddocks for a bit, then past a dilapidated shed and up a hill through forest. Here, the track became progressively worse the further up the hill we went.

At the end, we came to a gate to a hilltop paddock that fell away to blue sky and golden clouds. A rickety fence ran along the ridge. It looked like the end of the world.

My father stopped the bus and Veyada got out to open the gate. The grass was lush and green but the cows in the paddock were more interested in some mysterious shimmering thing with a hazy outline that stood at the highest point of the paddock.

Even though I knew it was there, it was hard to see the Asto-built craft. Those craft ran a current through the surface, which deflected the light and warped reflections. It made the air shimmer.

If you knew where it was and what it looked like, you could see the craft; also, the grass blew to one side with the air streaming from the engines.

As soon as we had come through the paddock's gate, a pair of Coldi people appeared from behind the craft.

The pair, both in Pilot's Guild uniform, were male and female, I thought; on occasion I still found it hard to tell the difference between Coldi men and women, especially when they dressed in similar clothing.

They presented themselves with polite bows and deferent glances.

"Come inside, Delegate."

We were back in *gamra* territory.

"So that's it, then?" my father said behind me. "I don't have to take you to Auckland?"

"No, thank you. We've got it organised."

My team set about unloading the bus. Goodbyes and thank you were said, and then it was just me and him.

He squinted at the blurry shape in the paddock. I presumed my father had seen Asto-produced craft. Maybe he hadn't. I didn't know. I'd offer him a ride if we weren't in so much of a hurry. In fact . . .

I gave him a hug. "I promise I'll do my utmost best to come back after the election and finish the last week of our holiday."

He patted me on the shoulder. "Don't worry about me, son. You've got big fish to fry."

"No, Dad. I promise."

"That would be nice."

The other members of my team had already boarded the craft. I left him standing forlorn and lonely at the gate to the paddock, with the empty bus, surrounded by curious cows.

7

———

THE INSIDE OF THE CRAFT was sleek and modern, the Asto style of design achingly familiar to me. I stepped from the world of my past into the world of my present, waving to my father at the door. I wasn't sure if he could see me.

While the craft took off, we settled in soft couches and found drinks in the cupboards. I didn't know why, but I always had the feeling that my team was more subdued when we were on Earth, as if they were afraid to upset old relationships I had with people we met, relationships they didn't understand.

Laughter and banter filled the cabin. Display sheets with maps came out.

Eirani was in her element preparing drinks. The kitchenette contained a jug with hot water, filters and powder to make *manazhu* and, not much later, we all had steaming cups of the bitter and dark green liquid that even Devlin had come to appreciate.

Eirani still thought it smelled vile and as usual didn't hesitate to let us know.

We had long since left the coast of New Zealand behind and were now flying over the ocean. Since we were flying over the south pole and it was winter, light would be low. Already, the ocean below hid in hazy murk and the sun had vanished in orange-tinged haze.

We sat on the floor surrounding Thayu's maps.

As I had expected, Devlin and Evi had researched the area of the wild game park in South Africa and had established routes to it from the safe landing spot where the craft would drop us off. A contact was also in place who would come to pick us up.

"So you actually have a register contact under the noses of the Cartel?" I said. That had to be the heist of the century.

"More than one. Wait until you see who else is there," Devlin said. "The Exchange knows that the Cartel has a stronghold in the area, and there have been Exchange spies for quite a while."

Damn, my team appeared to have prepared for this already.

I asked, "So where are we going? To the park or some other place nearby?"

"No, we're going straight into the park. You're down in the guest list as an important guest. We have someone who works in the park."

I'd also noticed how Devlin had started talking about *we* along the same lines as my association. Not that I had ever doubted his loyalty as my employee, but he now aligned his personal aims with ours.

"What about Eirani and Karana and Ayshada, though? I don't want to bring them into any danger." Especially Ayshada.

"They will continue on to their safe waiting spot and stay there until we've done what we came to do. A guide with a vehicle waiting for us will take us to the park. Anyone not necessary for the operation can remain on board the craft."

I glanced at him, thinking of the frumpy youth I'd inherited when I first moved into my apartment in Barresh, the apartment I'd been keenly aware wasn't mine, and I had no money for paying rent.

Did anyone know how to operate the hub, I'd asked the slightly terrified staff in the office downstairs.

Devlin had raised his hand, looking mortified.

Today's Devlin was a strapping young man. He'd eschewed the keihu tendency for long lunches and getting soft around the waist. He wore his curly hair in a Coldi-style ponytail. The legs of the feeder glittered through his hair behind his ear.

And, for some reason, this trip had propelled him into utter highly competent professionalism.

"Do we know anything about this guide who is going to meet us?" Sheydu asked.

"Amarru vouches for her," Evi said.

And that was all we needed to know. I thought Devlin knew, but it didn't matter.

We established possible routes to take and discussed at which point we would contact Minke Kluysters. Not too early, because he would send "guides" to control our movements.

Not too late, because he would be nervous and feel ambushed. He would already know that *someone important* would be visiting the park next to his home.

I said, "All right, so that is the official part of the trip sorted out. What about the addresses we were given by Charlie and Lenka?"

Devlin said, "Some are in the area. Some are elsewhere. We hope that while we're at the park, we'll be able to break into their systems and siphon off information."

That was always a good start. Information was the lifeblood of this spying business.

"You look tense," Thayu said, when I sat next to her.

"I'm not sure how much I like this, even if it was my idea."

"Don't worry. *We* like it. This—travelling secretly, using our contacts, breaking into systems, finding things—is what we were trained to do at the academy. Me, Veyada, Sheydu, Nicha. You know why Amarru has all these people with vehicles on standby wherever we are, in case we need them? That is why. Because we're trained and we're the best team she has."

Cory Wilson, fake human figurehead for a Coldi spying unit, how was that?

Granted, things had been like that for a long time, and I didn't mind it. Coldi leaders spied and allowed spies to look into their business. It was one of the curious quirks of Coldi society that kept both sides honest.

Ayshada had enough of sitting still. He ran around, even if Karana told him to sit and tried to strap him in. He wormed his way from under the seatbelt and ran in circles along the aisle that looped around the seats.

Nicha got fed up with it. He picked up his son and took him through the security door to the pilots' compartment. I followed them.

Cocooned off from our fairly noisy group, the pilots sat in their little glass bubble in the semidarkness.

The muted sounds and soft blinking lights and the rush of air along the outside of the ship mesmerised Ayshada. His big dark eyes reflected the dots of blue and yellow lights at the controls.

He pointed and said, "Ta." Whatever that meant.

The chief pilot turned around. I glimpsed the screen in front of him, which showed a coastline. The line of light spots in the view out the window matched the shape. It was the rugged coastline of eastern Antarctica, dotted with small towns. I had the impression that they were mostly seasonal fishing and mining settlements, but obviously someone was out there in the middle of the long and dark winter.

The pilot explained to me and Nicha that they took this route because it was far from the commercial suborbital routes.

He said it would be a while still before we arrived, and back in the other compartment, I sought out one of the couches against the back wall of the craft and fell asleep to the background noise of the low hum of the engines.

———

I woke up when Thayu shook my shoulder.

It was dark outside, and after I'd sat up trying to remember where I was and how I'd gotten here, I realised that the engines weren't humming anymore and therefore we were on the ground.

I could have guessed that any arrival by stealth involved darkness. It was how the Exchange liked it.

Telaris opened the door to the craft. Someone outside said something I couldn't hear. Telaris replied in Indrahui. I guessed it made sense to have Indrahui working here. They could very superficially pass for Africans.

I grabbed the bag that contained my reader and a few personal items.

Telaris was already in the luggage store retrieving all our bags.

"Karana and Eirani stay with the craft," Veyada reminded him. Ayshada would be staying, too, and he was out cold, with his little face scrunched into one of the benches.

"I hope he won't give you too much trouble," Nicha said to Karana.

We were ready to go. Apparently a vehicle was waiting somewhere in the darkness, where the air smelled earthy and had a nip of cold.

I had expected to be in a field of some sort, but the craft had entered a large hall which had probably been built as a farm shed. On the concrete floor, by the glow of a few fluorescent lights, stood a pile of crates. At the bottom of the craft's ramp waited a Coldi woman.

Well, I presumed she was a woman, judging by the way she held her hands behind her back and leaned on one leg while holding her hip out to balance herself.

I walked down the ramp, meeting her on the floor of the hall. Yes, a woman indeed. Like most Coldi women, she was stocky, with broad shoulders and hips. Her thighs were as thick as my waist, and I didn't think there was a lot of fat in them. She wore trousers made from some tough work gear material, and a leather jacket with many pockets. A little insignia with a symbol was affixed to the chest of the jacket. It was too dark to see what it represented. Her skin was dark and sun-beaten, and her hands callused.

"I'm Cory Wilson," I said.

"You don't say."

As was common with Coldi, I was the only one she'd speak to initially, because I led my association.

"Get all your stuff in the truck. We got a distance still to go."

Two vehicles stood at the entrance to the shed. One was a minibus, the other a small delivery truck. My team carried all the gear from the aircraft's luggage compartment to the truck, where a second woman, equally tough and also Coldi, had emerged.

We handed her our bags and got into the bus. Nicha was last on board. He had to say goodbye to Ayshada, who had just woken up and was cranky. He wanted to come with us, and Karana was having trouble controlling him. I glanced at Thayu while we sat in our seats in the bus waiting for Nicha to come. It was hard on him. He loved that little man.

We hadn't expected to see any dangerous situations on this trip. I guessed we should have known that dangerous situations always eventuated, but would the solution really be to leave the poor kid at home all the time we went out? No, certainly.

"Poor Nicha," I said.

Thayu said, "He loves that kid. It's been good for them to be together. They spend far too much time apart already."

While high-placed Coldi families—like those where she had grown up—used nannies, the parent responsible for the child also frequently worked from home. I didn't think her father, as high-ranking military officer, had a lot of time to share, but I did think Thayu deeply cherished the time he had made for her. She never said so in so many words, but I thought that her sharp senses had been honed by him. She had once told me that he'd wanted her to become the best spy on Asto and, although she no longer did spy work for the Inner Circle, I had found that those who did regarded her highly.

Finally Nicha was able to leave. Eirani and Karana looked lonely and forlorn at the top of the ramp, Karana holding Ayshada who was wiping his face with the back of his hand, probably after having been told by Nicha that he could have something he wanted if he behaved.

"Wonder where they are going?" I said.

"There is a safe house in Cape Town," Veyada said from the seat in front of us. "That's outside the communication black zone. They'll be looked after well."

The safe house owner was likely to be Coldi and fortunately Eirani, at least, spoke it well.

The driver came into the bus and positioned herself at the top of the steps.

"Now, listen, all of you."

My team fell quiet.

Our guide leaned against the back of the driver's seat, her arms crossed over her chest. Her eyes went over our group. After the long flight, we probably appeared less organised than we would have liked.

"I'm a park ranger of the Witbok Reserve. Everyone in this area refers to me as Jenny."

I wondered what her real name was. I could see no sign of earrings, and many Coldi on Earth didn't wear them anymore.

"I'm going to take you into the reserve. It's a place where tourists come—rich tourists—so you can pass as one of our clients going on a hunting safari. The reserve is a large area of shrub land and grass. There are some rivers and water points, but we'll stay away from those because that is where the tourists are. There is a small resort where you can stay and freshen up. I understand that you are here to see Minke Kluysters. Up until this point, you'll look just like tourists. Act like tourists and they won't make any inquiries about who you are. These are nervous people and you don't want to spook them, because they'll take drastic action when you do. You are in their territory, and Minke's word is law around here. Expect to be messed with once they find out who you are."

"What about bugs?" Sheydu asked.

"There are bugs, but discretion is one of the advertising strengths of the game reserve. They can't be caught listening to their own guests. These are high-profile people they cater for here."

"Do they only receive Cartel guests?"

"No, although the reserve is owned by a consortium of local business owners, Kluysters and Davidson amongst them, who enjoy hunting, and hunting is a group activity in the Cartel. They let the tourists in to qualify for certain grants and pass certain inspections."

"I thought the Cartel had started their own state here?"

"They voted for it, but it never went ahead. The push relied on permission from the government and traditional landowners. They were not going to agree, so after a few violent clashes, they just bought the land. All the owners have land adjacent to the reserve. Don't, however, think that you can get in that way. Once you have your appointment, he will send a car to pick you up."

She slid behind the wheel, shut the door and we plunged into the night. The shed was surrounded by a desiccated lawn and, surrounding that, a tall electric fence.

There was an impressively large wildlife grid in the road at this point.

Deyu, behind me, remarked that she had seen these near my father's farm, but she didn't see any cows here.

"I don't think it's to keep the cows in. It's to keep the other animals out."

"Animals?"

"Yeah, antelope, zebra. Would there be elephants and giraffes?"

"It's a *game* reserve," Jenny said, in a *what do you think* kind of tone. Yes, there were elephants and giraffes, obviously.

After driving carefully across the grid, the bus kept going into what was, even for me, thoroughly unfamiliar country.

The road was narrow, bumpy and dusty. Low trees grew on both sides, many of them without leaves.

"Look at the prickles on those trees," Deyu said.

She had become acquainted with the concept of thorns in my father's rose garden. In Barresh, the vegetation was too lush for thorns, and on Asto, plants protected themselves from being eaten by being extremely poisonous. There was nothing on Asto that would be deterred by thorns anyway. Worms, slugs and snails just crawled around them.

Not too much later, we came to a taller fence with vicious spikes on top. There was no grid, but a big, forbidding gate rolled aside at our approach. The bus went through and waited on the other side until the gate had rolled shut again. And then there was only the dusty road and shrubs for a long time.

We dozed a bit. My team obviously trusted "Jenny", although she still hadn't told us her real name.

I was terrible at sleeping on public transport, so I went up front to Jenny, her craggy and sun-browned face lit from below by the dashboard lights.

The bus' headlights lit the road ahead: straight, flat and flanked on both sides by featureless scrub. The occasional pair of red dots indicated the eyes of small animals. Sometimes she would slow down a bit for larger creatures: antelope or wild dogs.

She glanced sideways at me a few times, as if waiting for me to speak, or wondering if she should speak first.

I'd met these type of Coldi before: probably second or third generation immigrants, deeply embedded in Earth societies with no ties off-world. A lot of them lived in Africa; others were still in Greece, although these people would argue that Athens and the Exchange had been taken over by the conformist crowd: people who still had ties with Asto and *gamra*. As such, these Coldi, like Jenny, might not be unequivocally supportive of the push for Earth to join *gamra,* because it might upset their lives. It might give authorities the tools to pursue them for things done in the past that they preferred to forget.

Although the fact that Jenny was on the Coldi register meant that she was at least somewhat friendly to our cause, right?

I had to grab this chance to talk to her. Amarru did nothing without purpose. The fact that she had picked Jenny to drive us meant something, I was sure of that.

So I asked her, "You work here permanently?"

"Permanent as it gets." She did not take her eyes off the road.

For a while, I thought she was not going to say any more, but then she added, "Jobs are not easy to get around here."

No, probably not, especially not if you were Coldi. "How did you manage to get work at the park? I mean, they're all anti-*gamra*?"

"They hired me because I'm a mechanic. There's also not that many of those around here. At least not that are any good. They didn't ask me what I thought of *gamra* when they hired."

"But you did put your name on the register." Because one's entry was voluntary. It meant *I'm here, willing to help if a person related to the Exchange gets into trouble.*

"Seemed the right thing to do. Didn't think I'd ever get someone, let alone you and your party."

"The register doesn't pay you, right?"

"Nope. But we're all Amarru's people," she said, with sideways glance at Thayu and Nicha, both of whom were asleep.

"I'm Amarru's, too. We're all on the same side."

"I don't know. There's a lot of folk out here who would rather see you gone. You bring all the people they don't want to see around here. You're friendly with Ezhya Palayi, and most Coldi folk around here would rather die than let him into their safe areas."

"That's also something *gamra* membership will prevent. *Gamra* is not Asto, and Asto can't interfere in another member entity's world under *gamra* law."

She snorted. "Laws are full of noble words. Do they mean anything?"

"I think so. Obviously, you think so, too, or otherwise you wouldn't be here."

She snorted again. "Just don't think of our clan as your *friends,* because we're not."

She was Zhori, I was sure of it. "Then why are you here?"

"Membership of *gamra* is marginally more palatable than letting these idiots keep running the place." She gestured at the darkness outside the window. "But we will talk to *gamra* through Amarru, and Amarru only. We are part of this world, and want nothing to do with Asto and your friends."

"I'm happy with that."

"Good."

We fell quiet. My eyes felt gritty for the lack of sleep, and my brain was too foggy to keep thinking up new things to talk about. Jenny did not raise any issues either. She seemed the taciturn type, and to be honest I wasn't sure how much I could trust her.

About half an hour later, another fence loomed up in the glow of the headlights. It opened at the approach of the vehicle. The truck with our luggage had caught up and was behind us.

On the other side of the fence, a much better road curved over a slight rise. Little lights along the roadside came on through motion sensors. The grass looked green and well-watered. A couple of wallabies scrambled to their feet and hopped away.

What? Wrong continent.

On the other side of the hill, the road ended in a circle. A low building—dark and lifeless—lay on the other side, where the land fell away. A bridge connected the road to the entrance through a garden with several slender white-trunked gum trees, which towered over the building's low roof.

Jenny stopped the bus. "Here we are."

Everyone in the bus had woken up. I had not slept of course, and was the first to step into the crisp night air.

The driver of the truck had opened the back and unloaded our bags onto a trolley, as well as several boxes with various items of food. Jenny pushed the trolley over the wooden bridge, stopping to unlock the door to the building.

She flicked on the light. Ouch, that hurt my eyes.

Inside the building, we came out in a hall that flowed into a kitchen with adjacent living area. The far wall was all glass, giving access to a balcony. A couple of couches surrounded a low table, wood blocks—probably fake—lay stacked up in an open fireplace. A large screen took up most of the wall to the left. The kitchen was huge, with wood-covered benches and every appliance that you could wish for.

"Wow," Reida said, feeling the softness of the couch with his hand. "These people have a lot of money."

"Bedrooms are that way." Jenny pointed to a hallway that veered off to the right, while taking our bags off the trolley.

Thayu and I grabbed ours.

Jenny said, "I'll leave you to freshen up and rest. Bartholomew will be around in the morning to cook breakfast. It's safe to walk around in the garden, although be careful not to feed the monkeys. Stay inside the perimeter fence. It's definitely not safe outside."

"Not safe?" Thayu said.

"There are lions. Lots of them."

Oh, right.

We were all tired and didn't spend much time looking around the house. There were four bedrooms and Thayu and I got a room by ourselves. It had a large window on the far side, where I could see into the crown of trees but beyond that it was too dark.

The bed was large and comfortable. Within minutes after a quick shower in a luxurious bathroom that also had a floor-to-ceiling window looking out into the dark bush, we were asleep.

———

I woke up with an annoying beam of sunlight hitting my face.

Well, argh. I heaved myself up on one elbow.

The bed stood in a large room with rugs spread out over the wooden floor. The ceiling sloped high overhead, with dark wooden beams against the pale limestone walls.

The light came from the window, filtered through the treetops in little dappled spots. We'd forgotten to close the curtains last night. But then again, there was no need. All we could see was trees.

The sound of voices drifted from elsewhere in the building, as well as the smell of cooking. I was hungry.

Thayu woke up with a "Hmmm?" and then got out of the bed. She turned around and squinted into the light.

"Fancy place, this," she said.

She was not wrong.

I went into the bathroom where having a pee while in full view of a huge window felt slightly disconcerting, even if the birds out there were unlikely to be interested. Even if someone stood outside, they'd be at least a floor down, possibly more, because the ground fell quite steeply.

Thayu came in. I didn't miss her glance at the ceiling. Checking for bugs was engrained in her habits.

"Found anything interesting?" I was sure that she had given the bedroom a check-over while I'd been out of the room.

"No. Jenny said there were no bugs. I don't think there are."

"There are other ways of listening in."

Yes, there were. They were watching.

We got dressed and left the room.

We had well and truly slept, because the rest of the doors in the hallway were already open. Through one—Sheydu and Veyada's room, I thought—I spotted a tangle of electronic equipment on the floor, most of it on, with lines of text scrolling over an untended screen and lights blinking. While we'd been asleep, they'd gone straight to work.

In the living area, we found Veyada and Devlin already seated on one of the couches.

There was also a man cooking breakfast at the stove in the kitchen. He stood with his back to me. A crate which contained loaves of bread, milk and eggs stood on the kitchen counter.

"I take it you're Bartholomew?"

He turned around. He was a fairly stocky man with straight blond hair that hung to his shoulders. He wore it loose, and it tickled the collar of his uniform, where he wore a badge that said "Bart".

He was "Bart" as much as "Jenny" was Jenny.

I'd seen this man before, briefly, when getting onto a train after having fled an attack on my plane in Rotterdam. I'd met him when going into one of Amarru's train carriages that looked like cargo containers, but were little secure apartments for people who needed to travel in stealth.

This man was Klaus Messner, German, top-level spy for the Exchange.

A lot of things were starting to make sense. "Jenny" was his wife, because I knew he had a Coldi partner. Melissa Heyworth was his stepsister.

I sat at the kitchen bench. "Fancy meeting you here." Of course there weren't any bugs here, because he'd make sure there were none.

"I could say the same."

"It looks like you've been here for a while."

"Since the end of the court case. My wife has been here a bit longer."

"Jenny."

He laughed.

"Is it important for me to know her Coldi name?" What I really meant was her clan, which I felt pretty sure was Zhori. But I wondered if Klaus would confirm it.

His gaze lingered on my Domiri earrings. "Probably." But he didn't say what it was. "Hmmm, Domiri surprises me. You don't come across as the military type. Seeing your occupation, I would have considered you a candidate for Azimi clan."

I chuckled. "So that I can get into more trouble with them?" Whenever I'd struck someone petty or vindictive, they had usually belonged to the Azimi clan.

He raised his chin. "Oh, well, in that case, Domiri makes sense."

"Asha Domiri invited me. He's my father-in-law."

Another nod. "He's not a bad leader. Harsh, but fair. He'll listen to anyone who doesn't waste his time, even those not usually in his influence."

I guessed that was an apt description of Thayu and Nicha's father. I had wondered why he'd seemed fixated on me, but, like Ezhya, he was very much a person who would throw someone in the deep end and watch how they swam. The "someone" being me.

Klaus put down the spatula with which he'd been turning bacon and mushrooms, and pulled a little pendant on a gold chain from under his shirt. It held a gemstone, and the intricate design of the setting was very much Asto-style. It looked like an heirloom, old and passed through the generations.

The gemstone was pale orange. A table existed with all the stone types and colours and clans they belonged to, and this was one I'd never seen before or noticed on the table.

"That's Zhori, right?"

"You got it. Zhori are like the Ezmi of Earth."

Almost all members of the Ezmi clan lived on Hedron. They had fled there en masse about a hundred years ago and were now doing very well.

I said, "I think the Zhori out-do the Ezmi at being rogues." While the Ezmi clan was sometimes referred to as bandits, especially by those in high positions on Asto, they had never done anything worthy of warnings or military responses, preferring to sell stuff instead.

"Our clan merely 'use resources'."

"Yeah—right. My name is Santa Claus. Many of them are convicted criminals."

He chuckled. "I see you're straight-laced as a Domiri, too. No one ever questioned the motives of the so-called Zhori mafia. No one wondered about where they could go once the Asto establishment they initially fled from years ago started to invade Athens and they were scared to show their faces in all the Coldi communities on Earth. For what? Standing up for the rights of their oppressed friends? It's good to see you brainwashed with that bullshit. I can show you Kazakhstan. I can show you the children with the arms skinny as sticks. I can show you the villages and fields abandoned when the water dried up. I was there. The Zhori clan fought for those people because some of us lived there and we saw our livelihood threatened. Yet the story that Zhori sold weapons is the one everyone hears."

"They *did* sell weapons."

"Were they expected to defend themselves with their empty hands?"

Guess not. But for most of my professional life, I'd heard the cannon that the Zhori mafia had become involved in the conflict to enrich themselves through the sale of illegal weapons. Not even the Exchange had expanded on who these Zhori were and what motivated them. I guessed it was because the overwhelming issue that affected the Exchange was security and the relationships between Earth and *gamra,* and the personal circumstances of the Zhori clan came a distant secondary to those concerns.

I still wasn't quite sure what to make of this man. I had expected him to be . . . more loyal, I guessed was the word I was looking for. I went to the kitchen bench and poured myself some coffee. "I surmise that cooking tourists breakfast isn't really what you do around here?"

It was quite chilly. The air was dry. I clamped my hands around the warm mug. Wasn't strange how, when you met someone you'd always wanted to talk to, you rarely knew what to say?

"This area is an Exchange black zone," he said.

"Amarru showed me."

"She sent us to investigate about three months ago, because we fit the bill of what constitutes an acceptable applicant for the Cartel. We applied for jobs in the resort independently. The Cartel thinks I'm a straight-laced good German white boy. You noticed how they employ no Africans here?"

"I haven't had time to notice. We arrived late last night. We didn't see anyone except your wife."

"You would have noticed if you had time, because they don't. This is not a friendly or danger-free area."

"And the fact that your wife is Coldi was no objection?"

"Ah, it would have been had she been from the establishment clans on Asto. But she is not, and around here, that makes a major difference. She was born in Sudan and grew up in Johannesburg. According to Kluysters and Co, the Africans are lazy and always looking to do less work and scam more. They are happy to employ Zhori because they don't ask questions, even if I can vouch for the fact that they're more likely to scam than the Africans."

This was all getting very tangled.

I guessed the Zhori mafia and the Pretoria Cartel had some shared aims, because definitely not all of the Zhori were friendly with the Exchange. They saw the Exchange as a mouthpiece for the rigid society of Asto, in which the Palayi, Azimi, Lingui, Vonayi and yes, Domiri, clans dominated. The fact that Amarru was Palayi didn't help that situation.

I said, "It must be dangerous to work here while also working for Amarru."

"No more dangerous than being out in New Zealand without any protection." He scooped two eggs out of the frying pan. He set the plate on the serving bench.

"No protection? I had my association with me. Armed and all."

"Out here and I imagine there as well, that sticks out like a sore finger. Protection is from those who can give it, not those who are too high-profile and only attract attention to themselves."

What? Did he just insult my team?

Veyada came to get his eggs, completely unperturbed by the insult.

I still felt I couldn't let it ride.

"You know," I said, my voice low. "I had looked forward to our meeting."

"Me, too. I should have realised that the diplomatic life makes for a particular type of windbag."

What?

I took a deep breath, blood roaring in my ears, contemplating what would happen if I told him to fuck off, and then I realised: we were humans using Coldi bluntness on each other.

I met his grey eyes.

He was about my age. His hair was light-coloured like mine. He had a short beard. His face was weathered, but friendly. Zhori, not a clan I had ever had any dealings with, but one that was going to be extremely important to our cause.

One corner of his mouth moved up. Damn it. He'd tricked me into treating this very Coldi-style interaction with the human part of my brain.

I chuckled. "I almost fell for it."

He laughed, too. "I was wondering how long it would take you to work it out." He handed me a plate with cooked mushrooms, two eggs and a few strips of bacon. "Your breakfast, sir."

"Windbag."

"Sir Windbag."

We laughed.

I sat down at the table, still chuckling. That was brilliant. I almost fell in the trap. In Coldi society, it was perfectly fine to say these sorts of things to someone's face. It was only when you took them into a human context that they became rude.

Most of the others had also come in for breakfast.

Klaus distributed plates and eggs. Veyada might have developed a taste for fish, but all of my association drew the line at bacon, so I, Evi and Telaris and Devlin were the only ones eating that.

"So what is the plan?" I asked. "I've been told that you will be our guide."

"I'll take you to meet Minke Kluysters after breakfast. He'll likely want to see only you." His eyes met mine. "He's not terribly fond of receiving groups at the house."

"Does he come here often?"

"His property borders the reserve, so it's easy for him. He invites business contacts to stay here at this villa. He sometimes visits, but he doesn't often leave the house."

A shout came from the room at the very end of the hallway.

Thayu and I looked at each other. "That sounded like Deyu." She and Reida had not yet come to breakfast.

Several people got up from the table.

I strode to the end of the hallway where the door to Deyu and Reida's room stood open.

Deyu was inside, pointing at the window. Reida stood at the door, an alarmed look on his face.

On other side of the glass, between the treetops, looking into the room, was the head of a giraffe. Its blue tongue looped its snout while licking something off the top of its nose. It gazed curiously into the room.

"What is *that*?" Deyu's voice usually increased in pitch when she was alarmed.

"Oh, that's Benny," Klaus said. "He wants his carrot."

8

———————

KLAUS WENT BACK to the kitchen and came back a moment later with a carrot. He gave it to Deyu, who, assured that the giraffe was not going to eat her, stood in front of the window, trying to mimic the giraffe's tongue movements as it pulled leaves off the trees.

"It has a blue tongue, like you," she said, looking at Telaris.

"Be glad I am not a giraffe."

Klaus told Deyu to open the window. The giraffe waited patiently, and took the carrot from her when she held it out, again by looping its tongue around it. She let out an uncharacteristic squeal.

Her face was bright with joy. I knew I would have to do something at home to satisfy her love of animals. On occasion, I'd already wracked my brain about which animals in Barresh would be suitable as pets, and I'd come up with *not too many*. Barresh's large creatures were aquatic and the slightly less large ones were not generally considered suitable as pets. People would sometimes feed the bat-like meili and in the past they'd even been used in the way one would use messenger pigeons, but they were very much wild creatures.

Once Benny had been supplied with a carrot, he wandered off, chewing. It turned out that he was not the only giraffe in amongst the trees. A small group of them waited down the hill. Deyu's eyes shone. She wondered if one could ride a giraffe.

Klaus said, "You can't. They're wild animals. They're unpredictable and can be dangerous."

"Like llamas," she said, obviously thinking of my father's animals.

When we were all in the kitchen, Klaus explained what would happen today.

"You have sent a request for a meeting with Minke Kluysters about an office in Barresh." He looked at me. "Mr Kluysters is intrigued, and will see you. The invitation applies only to you."

"Well, then he can't go," Sheydu said. "He's a *gamra* delegate and *gamra* delegates travel with security." She had been silent and broody since arriving here. She didn't like being out of her element and I guessed she felt very much out of her element here. She also disliked being told what to do and where she could go, especially by someone who was from a much inferior clan than hers.

Some unspoken communication passed between her and Veyada with hand signals that I didn't recognise.

"I will take two guards as far as he will let me," I said.

Klaus said, "That will be to the gate house. They will need to wait there."

"That's fine." In the past, many good things had come out of leaving my companions at the door. They noticed different things than I did. They could scout out the security arrangements.

"I suggest that you not take the Indrahui. I'm sure he can tell the difference between them and Africans, but his guards may not. They've got blanket approval to harass anyone who looks like an African."

"Am I supposed to come out of this alive?"

Klaus said, "While I can't vouch for the honesty of what's being said while you're at his house, I absolutely vouch for your safety. Above all, Mr. Kluysters is one hundred percent proper. One thing I have to say for the guy—much as he has a bad name, he is true to his word and easy to get on with. I tell you that you *will* be safe, and you will. If something happens to you on this trip, it won't be while you're at his house. I guarantee that."

Sheydu crossed her arms over her chest. Oh no, she wasn't

happy.

"Once you have spoken to him, you should probably leave as soon as possible, depending on the outcome of your meeting. The game reserve is used by all his associates, and they are known to play tricks on visitors. They're all gun enthusiasts and have a lot of military grade stuff that can make your life very uncomfortable."

"I understand."

He said he had a few other jobs to do, and he would be back later in the morning. He packed up the breakfast things, leaving us with a big pot of tea, and put everything in his trolley. When he was about to wheel it out of the kitchen, he gestured at me: *Come.* He used the Coldi security hand signal.

He had been so formal this morning that I was sure that we were being watched, so I said to no one in particular, "I'm going to get dressed for the meeting."

I rose and followed him into the hallway. There, he gestured again: *That way.*

I followed him to the front door, but he stopped me just inside the hall.

He bent towards me, enveloping me in a scent of cooking and soap. He whispered, "If I don't get the opportunity to see you again and you feel unsafe here, and you well may, there are a number of trucks in a maintenance shed about twenty kilometres from here. You will see it marked on the map. It doesn't look like much, but there is an underground storage compartment where you can find all kinds of supplies that you'll find very useful."

I was going to ask a question, but he turned around and strode to his van.

I watched him go, upsetting a group of wallabies grazing by the side of the road. The big fence rolled aside for him; he went through and the fence shut again.

Interesting.

I went back inside.

My team were in the living room. They had pulled out all the maps and satellite images of this area, and Sheydu was drawing with a stylus on the table, which resulted in lines appearing on a map displayed on Veyada's reader screen, which stood propped up against the teapot.

I squinted at it. It displayed the map of the game park, showing the roads and adjacent properties, some of which were almost as big as the park. Sheydu had marked our locality. A road ran from the gate to a ring road which went around the game park, including the park's main entrance. The shed that Klaus had spoken about was at the very end of another road that zigzagged between some waterholes and creeks. There was a second, smaller, entrance to the game park.

The main road ran outside the game park, and it went to the north-west, into a small town. This was where Sheydu's line led. There was a single-runway airstrip on the outskirts of the town.

"That's Charlie Awaba's hometown," Veyada said. "This shed is where he last saw his brother."

I nodded. I hadn't seen it on the map like this before, but I knew it was close.

"How did you want to check that out?" I asked. "We're in the middle of a highly supervised area and we have no transport." Even if we had a vehicle, the towns were full of people who would report news for payment, people who needed a few lousy cents for reporting that foreigners had come to town and bought lunch at the cafe. They'd kind of notice people busting out of the reserve and trying to hitch a ride on the main road. I very much doubted that we could just rock up in town and not be noticed.

"We have ways," Sheydu said. "If they can use flying bugs, we can use them, too."

Deyu gestured to me, and I followed her to her and Reida's room. Reida sat on the floor with a piece of equipment consisting of a structure with three prongs, each about the length of my forearm. I recognised the plastic and metal casing of the drone they had shot down in New Zealand.

"It works," he said and threw the thing into the air.

As soon as it was airborne, a jet engine came on with a buzz, and the contraption stabilised in the air. Reida grabbed his reader and tracked his finger across a square displayed on the screen. The drone moved through the room. Ah, the square was a map of the room.

"You made that from the mangled pieces of that drone Evi shot to pieces? I'm impressed."

"People should never leave their garbage lying about," he said, obviously pleased with himself. I was reminded that Reida was very much a hands-on person. He had little patience for diplomacy or computer systems.

Sheydu, standing in the doorway, said, "See, we don't need to go anywhere to check out the area."

"Still, be careful."

I went to our room and got ready. What did one wear when visiting an obscenely rich business magnate whom you were trying to fool into believing you were serious about the offers you were going to make?

I didn't want to go in *gamra* blues, because this was about Earth; it was not an official *gamra* visit. I would ask Eirani, but she had gone on to a safe place—hopefully, somewhere nice. She could not advise me.

The matter was not made easier by the fact that many of my more formal clothes were more than a little rumpled after having sat in the bottom of my bags ever since leaving the court.

I looked, but failed to locate ironing equipment, so that was out.

In the end, I chose a keihu-style loose outfit that I might wear on a trip into town in Barresh. Even though it was winter, the air was quite warm during the day.

Thayu and I discussed listening devices, which she spread out on the bed in my room. Apparently, Sheydu had a selection of stick-on transmitters that sat like a feeder on the skin. You could wear them under clothing and no one would notice. Thayu affixed one of the patches to the back of my right thigh, away from my arms and belt where I might wear weapons, or at least that's what she explained. Where those weapons were going to come from, I wasn't sure. I wasn't going to carry arms, and I'm sure that if I did, my weapons would be removed anyway. I didn't like her using that particular patch of skin because it was a place where I had not yet found the time to make appointments for permanent hair removal treatments. I'd spent enough time on my face, chest and arms already. The hair on my thighs was light-coloured and not terribly thick, but there was a fair bit of it, but Thayu assured me that the denseness of hair didn't mean that the patch wouldn't stick well.

Great. Just what I feared.

I put on my trousers over the patch, and Thayu hooked up a tiny transmitter to my belt loop.

Sheydu was in the hallway testing the reception.

"It will probably cut out when you're at the house," she said, as she was overseeing all these activities. "I can't imagine that a man like that wouldn't have watertight security and communication blocking. But if you're in trouble, get out of the house, and it will work outside. The range of this thing is not very big, but is enough to reach here."

And they were going to send drones into town. They might attract more undesirable attention than I would.

We were having an early lunch when a white van came to the front of the house. I could see it through the door, which we had left open to let the breeze through. The man who came out wasn't Klaus, but a stiff-looking military type who looked uncomfortable in civilian clothing. He came into the kitchen, greeting us with a nod. "You may like to keep the door shut, sir."

"It's quite cool inside. We were trying to get some warm air through."

"You have to watch the monkeys, sir. Once they're in, it's hard to get them out. They make a mess."

All right, I could see that. "Thank you."

We were in that strange situation where everyone was super nice and polite to each other on the surface, never mind the underlying feelings.

I shut the door after we left.

The driver of the car told us in clear terms that Thayu and Veyada would have to stay outside the house's gates. They understood. We knew.

The van looked surprisingly sturdy. I figured its exterior was made from armoured material—whichever was the latest fashion. The dark windows obscured any other occupants, of which, when the door opened, there turned out to be two, armed guards in military style grey uniforms, both young white men with stiff expressions. Militia or ex-military.

The van was of a similar type used at Nations of Earth, where the passengers faced each other.

This seating arrangement left me, Thayu and Veyada facing the guards.

They studied us, only their eyes moving.

We returned their gazes.

One had a weather-beaten freckled face that bore a few nicks from shaving. The other had a bronzed face but blond hair, an angular jaw and hard blue eyes. He looked like he went to the gym a lot.

I might have started a conversation about the weather, whether it might rain or something, but the sky was clear blue with not a cloud to be seen. It was not a chatty kind of situation, and I didn't feel like talking about tourist things.

The gym guy opposite me couldn't keep his eyes off Thayu. His gaze went over her muscled arms, hidden under a tight-fitting top that included a layer of insulating material. Her vest contained a layer of armour. She wore her gun in the bracket underneath, on the right-hand side. I knew because I had seen her put it on. He stared at her legs, his gaze moving up and lingering at her crotch.

I'd never felt particularly protective of her—she was very capable of protecting herself—but his gaze made the blood roar in my ears. How dare he?

Thayu herself was characteristically unperturbed by his attention. She didn't cross her legs or move them together as a woman from Earth would. She stared back at the radio equipment he carried at the side of his belt. Utterly professional, as always.

I looked out the window.

The landscape was pale under a cloudless sky. Many of the trees were leafless and the grass between them dead and dusty. Compared to New Zealand, the landscape was desolate. The only animals we spotted were a herd of antelope crossing the road.

The driver slowed down until the animals had passed.

He said, "I can take you past the waterholes on the way back. They all hang out there during the day. It's a pretty place. No one ever hunts there, and they come there with their young."

I felt sorry not to have taken Deyu, but Veyada had much more experience in matters of security.

I asked a bit more about the tourists—about whom the driver

didn't reveal too much, but Klaus had already told us were rich busi-nessmen—and we talked about the weather.

Then we ran out of things to say.

After about fifteen minutes, we came to the reserve's boundary fence. I didn't think this was the same place where we had entered, even though it had been dark last night. I didn't remember having come through the thick thorny scrub on the other side.

We waited until the fence opened, went through and stopped around the corner, at a low building hidden amongst the trees.

A surly guard with a gun sat on a bench outside, and got up as soon as we arrived. Another man came out of a door. Both wore militia-style grey uniforms with a small badge on their chest

"Your friends get out here," the driver said. "We'll continue on to the house, and we'll pick them up on the way back."

The blond guard opened the door. While Thayu and Veyada got up and left the car, he made the mistake of patting Thayu on the backside. She whirled around, grabbed him by the front of his jacket and slammed him into the back of the seat.

Veyada flew up, and had his gun in his hand in a split second. The other guard grabbed his weapon too late, as it connected with Veyada's hand and fell, with a clatter, on the pavement just outside the open door.

"Whoa!" I called. "Stop it, stop it."

Silence.

Everyone looked at each other. The gym guy's eyes were wide.

"You do not touch me," Thayu hissed in his face before releasing the grip on his uniform. He sank to the bench. Veyada put his weapon away, while the other man scrambled for the gun that had fallen underneath the van.

Thayu had spoken Coldi, but I presumed no translation was necessary. The guard wiped his face, avoiding my eyes. I knew the type. Nothing embarrassed these macho types more than being manhandled by a woman.

"I think my wife would like an apology," I said. Let's rub it in a bit more.

He looked up at me. "Oh . . . I didn't know . . . I'm sorry. I didn't mean . . . It was just a joke."

"It was not funny, and not professional. I don't think Mr Kluysters would be happy to hear of this."

He shook his head. "I'm sorry. I didn't know she was your wife." His face had gone red.

"It would not have been funny had she not been my wife either."

He looked down. His face worked.

I considered calling off the visit, but I didn't think the transgression was serious enough to waste the time and effort we had made to be here, and, perhaps more importantly, risk the efforts of whatever Sheydu and the others were doing while I was here.

The man had been thoroughly embarrassed and his apology was genuine. No, I didn't think Minke Kluysters was the type of man who would appreciate his staff insulting visitors he hoped to woo for his business projects.

But this attitude towards women, and Coldi women in particular, was a reminder, if ever I needed one, that we were in hostile territory, and that Mr. Kluysters might be friendly, but he could not have been further from being a "friend".

Thayu and Veyada had left the van and the two of them settled on a bench outside the overhang of the guard building's veranda. Both held their hands close to their weapons, while eying the guards.

Not happy.

I had to trust that nothing would happen while I was gone, but it was a lousy situation.

From the back bench in the van, I met Thayu's eyes. Her expression bordered on desperate. *Don't go.* I struggled not to give in to that very Coldi instinct. They didn't let association leaders do dangerous things by themselves. But this was a place where only I could go.

The driver shut the door, enclosing me in a bubble of tension, with the hapless guard still opposite me. The red had faded from his face, but he still didn't meet my eyes.

The driver climbed behind the wheel, and we started moving again. Thayu and Veyada slid from view, still looking unhappy. I hoped the guards would not provoke them too much, because I could not vouch for the results. Fortunately, neither Thayu nor Veyada were easily provoked. Fortunately, when they *were* provoked, they were amongst the deadliest in my association.

9

———

THE CAR HIT A PAVED ROAD with neat rows of bushes along the sides. It was a kind of absurd scene: African scrub seen from over the top of a garden hedge.

Then the scene opened up for an immaculate lawn—a golf course, I realised—with a creek through the lowest point. The grass was blindingly green, standing out against the surrounding countryside, brown and leafless because of the season.

A man on a ride-on mower moved over the grass.

The road wound around the golf course, past a lake with a variety of water birds.

The house came into view when we crested the hill on the other side of the golf course. It was a low, spreading affair, with wide verandas and French doors that opened onto them, surrounded by a flower garden and immaculate lawn. It lay on a hilltop with a view of the low hills and plains of the reserve. A gyrocopter stood in a shed in a field to the right of the driveway.

The car swept into a broad circular driveway and stopped in front of the steps going up to the house, in the shade of an awning.

A man came out the door to open the car door for me. With his neatly pressed white trousers and red shirt, he was clearly a member of the domestic staff.

"Mr Wilson, welcome to the estate." He bowed and gestured me into the house.

I stepped into a huge marble-lined hall with a grand sweeping staircase.

The doorman shut the front door behind me and crossed the hall. "This way, please, Mr Wilson."

I followed him into a palatial room two storeys high with book-cases along the walls.

A giant window in the opposite wall looked out over low rolling hills of wilderness, with taller hills in the hazy blue distance.

"Mr Kluysters will be with you soon," the doorman said. "Feel free to pour a drink."

He left me alone in the giant room. I padded across the soft carpet past the leather couches and bookshelves containing ancient volumes. The window was made of thick glass, probably insulated, and a waft of cool air coming down in front of it betrayed the location of the air-conditioning vent.

Another immaculate lawn sloped to a tennis court with another house. Behind that was the view of the reserve that I had seen before. It seemed like there was no fence between the lawn and the bush, yet I was sure there had to be some sort of barrier.

"Sit down," said a familiar voice behind me.

I turned around.

I had seen Minke Kluysters before, on a vid screen, while we were at the trial at Nations of Earth.

In the flesh, he looked the same: well-groomed, dressed in a smart casual shirt and trousers, with salt-and-pepper hair, a straight nose, clear brown eyes and short beard.

I guessed him to be somewhere in his late fifties. He was well-toned, a strapping man, looking much fitter than I felt—and I should really do something about that, because Eirani's delicious cooking was getting to me.

He shook my hand, his grip warm and firm, and gestured for me to sit down.

We sat at a set of couches arranged so that one could look out the window.

"I was just admiring the view," I said.

"That's the reserve down there," he said. "The elephants some-times come up to the boundary."

"How do they stay out? I don't see a fence."

"I don't like fences. It cramps the mind and spoils the view. A trench runs around the garden that they can't cross. Did you know that elephants can't jump? We jump by lifting our heels and pushing off with our toes. Elephants perpetually walk on their toes already. Their feet have no way of pushing off. Mind you, they run quickly enough. Have you seen any elephants yet?"

"No, but we saw a giraffe."

"There are plenty of giraffes. I bet it was good old Benny coming in for his carrot."

A woman came in carrying a tray with a teapot, two cups and a plate of biscuits. She set it on the table between us, put cups in front of each of us, poured tea and left again.

We drank for a while and ate biscuits and mused about how nice everything was.

Then he put his cup down with a sense of finality. "I could sit here forever and never think about business, but unfortunately, that is not going to get anything done. You're here to talk about establishing a business office in Barresh. Let's talk about that. I asked you about this before. Obviously, now that the referendum has been called, the situation has changed a bit."

The way he said it made me wonder: had he, too, known of Margarethe's plans?

"If the yes vote passes, there will be absolutely no problems, and I would be happy to assist you." That would meet with approval from my team since it fell under the Coldi habit of keeping one's enemies close.

"That is assuming the yes vote wins." Spoken oh, so innocently.

"True. If the no vote wins, there may be a problem."

He sniffed. "I don't really like those types of problems."

"The people will vote. We have to work with the outcome, regardless of whether we like it."

"Do we?"

"Yes, we do."

He gave me a calculated "ah" type of expression.

The subcurrents were thick in this conversation. He was still gauging whether I'd be prepared to do something illegal, and I absolutely would not. Not for him at least. Not for any type of money.

"The yes vote won't win." It almost sounded like a warning.

"You seem certain of that."

"One can never be certain until it happens, but I am pretty certain. After all, why would people vote for joining an organisation that will have a say in how their world runs?"

"Only for as much as it concerns off-world travel and any other interactions between Earth and other *gamra* worlds."

"You believe that will solve all the trouble?"

"Not all of it."

"A lot of it, then."

"Yes, it will."

"Where have our problems come from, then? I remember one person, someone who even justified the use of alien military force on Earth, who came from Indrahui. Is that a *gamra* world?"

"They have probationary status." Just the same as Earth, and I was sure that he knew this.

"If that's good enough to blast them out of existence from orbit, then I'm sure probationary status gives Earth enough of your kind of protection."

The remark rankled, *Your kind of protection* being wholly sarcastic. "I am sure that you know that Romi Tanakan, who was the war lord targeted in that attack, was one of *gamra*'s most wanted criminals. Desperate situations sometimes require desperate measures."

"Like blasting him from orbit." He gave a little smile.

"He was already dead. The blast destroyed his facility that included illegally imported biological material that was a contamination hazard." I didn't know what he was trying to do. Provoke me into saying something that he could use against me, probably.

He continued, "Let's consider another problem: Kazakhstan. How could that have been avoided, knowing that the people who were fighting were Earth citizens, and some of the Zhori clan happened to be amongst them?"

"They used illegal weapons."

He laughed. "They would have used *any* weapons. The point was not the weapons they used, it was the reason they fought. Nations of Earth were too ineffectual to stop it, as usual. And involvement from *gamra* in that conflict would not have made the slightest difference in the world."

"It would, because they would have sent proper help so that the first defeat of the Nations of Earth forces would never have been as devastating as it was."

"And that is precisely what I don't like. Alien soldiers on Earth."

"Recruited locals. That's how it would work, and that's how it works on other worlds. *Gamra* employs locals to uphold laws as they pertain to traffic to and from *gamra* worlds. They would *not* be from elsewhere."

He didn't reply. Maybe he had expected to win this argument or at least to be able to argue me into silence. Maybe he wasn't used to someone arguing back. Maybe, and that was more likely, he just didn't know enough to argue back.

A few moments of uneasy silence followed.

"I don't think you came to discuss this," he said after a while, his voice stiff. Did I imagine it, or did he sound a bit miffed?

"I think I did, because you expressed interest in setting up a business in Barresh, and there is no way that can happen unless the yes vote wins. I understand that you control a fair number of people—"

"I don't control anyone. People are making their decisions based on economic circumstances. I have no desire to control anyone."

Ha, ha, ha. "Circumstances which you control, since you bought out many governments."

A sharp look. Was this supposed to have been a secret? If so, a poorly kept one.

"You can control or at least influence how people vote in a great many of these countries. If you want this office—and I see a good deal of benefit in mutual commercial relationships—then encourage the people to vote yes. It's as simple as that."

Again, a sharp look. Oh, this was a shrewd man, because a dumber man would have started yelling about how wrong I was.

He leaned forward, elbows on his knees, and spoke slowly. "Say I did this—not saying I can or will, but let's just say I could and did— and the yes votes passes because in this theoretical world apparently I hold the balance of votes, Earth would be second in population only to Asto, is that correct?"

"It is." Oh, he knew this.

"And I understand that some sections in the society on Asto have a fascination with Earth."

"It's mostly about collecting ugly plastic figurines." That had turned into a bit of a fad recently. Some of the high-profile people in the Inner Circle had whole cupboards full of them.

"Most people there have some disposable income."

I did my best to restrain a chuckle. "You want to sell things to them?"

"Yes, but more than that. We can develop mutual industries and tailored products. We can provide ties to Earth economies and jobs and income streams."

"Yes, you could do that. Although Asto is still a restricted world, but that will probably change soon. These are benefits that will open up with membership." I could see the potential of all kinds of "interesting" situations develop around commercial deals, but that was outside my control.

He lowered his voice even further. "I hope you understand that we—the Cartel—control a serious business empire; I would say we directly and indirectly control more than half of all volume of sales conducted in the world. I own Sandowne Pharmaceuticals which holds sixty percent of the pharmaceutical market, and people in my circle of contacts own literally every type of company in the world. From mining to manufacturing to education. Building developments, clothing, communication, you name it."

And governments. "I understand that." I wondered where this was going and whether the fact that he appeared to have changed tack meant that he decided to give this a go or he was trying to lure me into a trap. I guessed both, if he could.

He continued, "We care little about politics as long as those politics stay out of the realm of trade. We like to do business."

Except that business and politics could not be seen separately.

"I would look very favourably upon being able to contact a person who will help us establish business relationships with Asto."

"You'd first have to delve into how their society works. Commerce is much more decentralised and generally is conducted within clans." A lot of deals involved paying back favours, and Coldi didn't tend to be very materialistic. Most lived in houses owned by their clan or the circle. They provided for their associations by way of payment. Like Nicha, Sheydu and Veyada, Reida or Deyu. I didn't pay them, but covered all their expenses. Not even Ezhya lived in anywhere near as opulent a dwelling as the house owned by Minke Kluysters. Coldi did not own houses although they sometimes bought the right to live in them.

On second thoughts I wasn't sure that business collaboration between Earth and Asto would take off anywhere beyond a few curiosities. Too much risk, too many differences.

But he continued, "I would be interested in talking to Asto directly. That's one of the things I want the office for." He had obviously been informed that one could not go to Asto.

"*Gamra* advises people to use one of their officers to make contacts. I can definitely help with that, once Earth has accepted membership. Maybe even if it doesn't. Deals can be made through the Trader Guild—"

He shook his head. "I don't want any middlemen. I want to talk to them directly. You don't understand. We control more than half the business flow on Earth."

"You did tell me."

"Yes, but I don't think you fully comprehend what this means. We control most of the business conducted on Earth. We would be interested—very interested—in collaboration with Coldi business partners."

"And I'm trying to make you understand that their society is very different, and that it would be prudent to get *gamra* contacts involved before bad situations develop." Such as writs and murder squads.

"No. I don't want them involved. I want to cut out the middlemen and speak to the people who make the decisions."

"But I'm telling you that their—"

"I want to speak with Ezhya Palayi. You have contacts with him."

What?

"This is my demand for promoting the yes vote: I want you to organise a meeting between me and Ezhya Palayi."

I stared at him, torn between bursting out laughing or asking him if he was joking, but his type of men rarely joked. He meant what he said.

I said, "Well, that's not easy."

"I didn't say it had to be. Easy goals are boring. You want me to say a good word for the yes vote? Get me the meeting. I don't really care whichever way the vote goes, but there you go. I will support it. If you can get me that meeting." He rose from his seat, went over to his desk and pulled out a piece of paper. He came back to the table, pushed the tea cups aside and put the paper down. "I'll put it in writing, scan and copy it, and you may quote me and remind me of my obligation."

He took a pen from his pocket—an old-fashioned one—and started writing in an even, loopy handwriting. Neither of us said anything while he scribbled. The sound of women's laughter drifted in from somewhere outside, followed by a large splash and another squeal of laughter.

"My daughters are having some friends over," Minke said, while writing. I imagined teenage girls pushing each other into a sun-drenched pool.

It was surreal.

This was a family home with a normal family life, and here we were, discussing the fate of the world.

He finished writing, blew the ink dry and handed the paper to me.

It said,

Hereby I, Minke Devier Kluysters, declare that I will lend support to the election campaign supported by Cory Wilson, delegate for gamra, *in return for the opportunity to meet with the Chief Coordinator of Asto, Ezhya Palayi.*

The paper bore the logo of Sandowne Pharmaceuticals, and it was signed with a loopy signature.

"I'm sorry for not adding your middle name."

"I don't have a middle name." I did—it was Morgan, after a grandfather I had never met—but that was none of his business.

"May I?" He took the paper from me and ran it over his reader. "I will send you a copy, too."

He gave it back to me, and I had no idea what to do with this utterly bizarre declaration. I put it on the couch next to me. I mean —why did he even say this and make a record of it? Wouldn't it be something liable to come back to bite him later? I had no intention whatsoever of honouring this request.

He got up from the couch. "Drink?"

He pulled two glasses out of a cupboard in the bottom of one of the bookshelves.

I hated drinking alcohol when facing important people. Far too often, I'd felt like I had lost control over the situation while sipping some kind of liquor. Probably a coincidence, but after having had president Sirkonen killed while sharing a drink, and having myself knocked out while drinking with Asha Domiri, I loathed to touch any alcohol while I was supposed to keep my wits. Yet I could barely refuse.

I took the glass from him. The waft of alcohol drifted past me.

"Oh, look," he said. "There are the elephants."

They were, too, a group of several adults and a couple of smaller ones, pulling at tree branches.

"They come to drink from the water trough." Minke went on to explain that this part of the reserve was a sanctuary, where hunting parties never came. "The females are smart. They come here because they know they're safe."

The rest of the visit took place in a more amicable manner. We spoke about little things, fishing and sailing. I cringed when he offered to show me his trophy room. I had half-expected it to be full of stuffed animals, but he meant horse-riding trophies. There were a lot of photos of a younger man, with dark hair, jumping over barriers, mostly while riding a jet-black horse.

"I always liked pushing the limits," he said. "I was a runty little boy, always sick. My uncle—who looked after me because my father died in the war—said I'd never amount to anything. A doctor suggested horse riding, because it strengthens muscles."

He set his glass down and opened a little cabinet. He took out the medal inside and handed it to me. "This is the biggest 'fuck you', addressed to him, that I have delivered in my life."

A gold medal, in show jumping, from the 2084 Olympics in Rome, the first time this event had been held after 30 years of war, one year after I was born.

The gold disk was heavy and meticulously polished.

I nodded and gave it back to him. He put it back in the cabinet.

This was not a man like any other I had ever faced. I had no doubt that he worked hard for all he had achieved. He was smart and brazen, and there was a spark in him that I recognised.

But above all, he was very dangerous.

What was even worse: I quite liked him.

10

———————

W HEN IT WAS TIME TO GO, I had not yet made a
decision about how seriously to take Minke Kluysters'
request.

We said our polite goodbyes in the marble hallway and the
driver picked me up from the house's entrance. I took in the
opulence of the hall and rooms I could see. It would be the only
time I'd ever be allowed near this man or his personal residence.

He shook my hand on the porch. "I'm looking forward to
working closer together. I think you're a man of high integrity."

"Well, I hope that you can match that."

He laughed. "Don't worry. I will."

And then I got into the waiting car. The driver shut the door
and slipped behind the wheel and we went back over the road that
crossed the green lawns of the golf course and the carefully mani-
cured gardens and ponds.

Well, that was one of the more surreal experiences of my life.

Now I would have to decide what to do with this strange letter
that I held in my pocket. My mind was going around in circles. All
my professional life, I had believed in the power of Nations of Earth
and the processes and international laws they had instated. But they
had become increasingly ineffectual because of men like Minke
Kluysters. Was this because businesses had taken control aggres-
sively, or because Nations of Earth had left a void? Without a doubt,

it was the last. The extent of damage and population upheaval after the wars was far too great for Nations of Earth to deal with. And right now, Nations of Earth was hampered by a political impasse it had helped create.

Why ever had Margarethe decided to call the election? Why had she thought the yes vote could win? Because the Pretoria Cartel controlled a lot of the communication and they could block whole countries on the day of the referendum, and change the outcome with the press of a button. And Minke Kluysters was willing to use that in my favour if I arranged a meeting between him and Ezhya Palayi?

Part of me wanted to see Ezhya tear into that aristocrat with his refined manners.

Part of me wanted to protect Minke from Ezhya's inevitable roasting.

Part of me wanted to run this past Margarethe, but she had not even replied to any of my previous messages. I didn't even know if she could or thought it safe to do so.

And another part wanted to just ignore the whole thing. Nothing good could come from a meeting between Ezhya and Minke Kluysters.

And yet, something worried me about the thought, too. What if they got on really well? After all, Nations of Earth had given Ezhya the run-around for more than twenty years.

Damn, I could see how the *no* vote would deliver just what Minke wanted: no cumbersome negotiations, no rules. Under Ezhya Palayi, Asto was not likely to break from *gamra,* at least I didn't think so. But Ezhya was not a young man, and he was at the end of his game. It was not a question whether he would be replaced. The question was when and by whom?

Damn, this was going into an entirely different direction from what I had expected.

The letter burned in my pocket.

Thayu and Veyada sat in the exact spot I had left them: next to each other on a wooden bench in the shade of the veranda of the security building. Their faces remained blank and emotionless, but I could see in their eyes that they were happy to see me.

I was happy to see them, too, and happy to see all of Minke's guards still alive.

The driver opened the doors, and the two of them came in, wordlessly. Thayu sat next to me. She met my eyes. I wanted to tell her about the strange meeting, but didn't want to talk in the presence of the driver, and our feeders didn't work, of course.

So we made some lame conversation, because every word we said in here would be recorded.

The driver dropped us off at the hunting lodge not much later.

It was midday; the sun was high in the sky, the light bright and pale, and the place looked deserted.

The place *was* deserted, we found out once we got inside. It was tidy, though, with only a few personal items, such as toiletries, left in the rooms.

"Any idea what they're doing?" I asked.

"An idea, yes, but I don't know for certain," Veyada said.

"They were going to fly the drones. I presume they planned to do that from here."

"Yes. They may have found something to check out."

"Or something found them?"

Veyada pointed to his emergency transmitter, which he carried inside his shirt, while mine was stuck to my thigh. "We would have heard." So there was nothing we could do except wait.

We went into the kitchen and made some tea. Klaus was also nowhere to be seen. I was guessing he'd be back to prepare dinner.

I opened the big doors in the living room because it was quite stuffy inside, and the cool breeze came in. We sat on the veranda drinking tea.

I told them about the curious meeting with Minke Kluysters.

"He asked you *what?*" Thayu said. "He wants to see Ezhya? Does he think he can just tell Ezhya to come?"

"Well, yeah, and he gave me this." I pulled out the letter.

While Veyada took it and unfolded it, I remembered how I had once sent a message to Ezhya and he *had* come. The similarities between myself and Minke Kluysters unnerved me. He was not *supposed* to be someone sympathetic. He *wasn't* sympathetic. He might not personally be aware of shady things going on in businesses owned by the Cartel, but he would have heard. He might even have said, "Just get it done, I don't care how."

But damn, I had expected . . . I wasn't sure. People with a lot of power were never of the over-the-top bogeyman kind. They were too smart for that. This was Robert Davidson's downfall, and why the Cartel had dropped him as quickly as they had.

Real people in power were not evil, and not good. They just had a lot of power, and they could only maintain that power for as long as they could optimise the situation for themselves while not falling foul of public opinion. Some people said Ezhya was evil. He certainly had a lot of power, and yes, he used it to silence certain people. Yet, he was my friend, because what he stood for overwhelmingly coincided with what I thought was best.

Minke Kluysters was the opposite. But where was the line between good and bad?

No. Why was I even thinking this? The man was ultimately responsible for the way his employees were treated. Those protesters had not been outside the courtroom for nothing. Sandowne Pharmaceuticals was unlikely to be clean. For one, manipulation with humans was most likely to be done by a medical company.

Veyada squinted at the page trying to make out handwritten Isla. Thayu looked over his shoulder, pointing at the words, and speaking softly.

"He's got a lot of courage," Veyada said.

And I had learned that, as a strange streak of evolution, Coldi leaders had an unhealthy fascination with individuals who were not in any of their associations who displayed courage.

I said, "Certainly, Ezhya would not seriously consider seeing him?"

"I think he would."

I'd feared that reply.

If I arranged the meeting and Minke kept his word, would it be worth risking claims of vote manipulation?

But manipulating votes was exactly what the Cartel was doing already by buying government debts and determining which projects were supported. Could the Cartel influence that much of the vote, since many weren't even registered? That was the big question.

"You think I should ask Ezhya?" I looked from Veyada to Thayu and back.

The sense of horror I'd felt when Minke first asked about seeing Ezhya returned. A Coldi person would take this as a serious offer, and I knew it.

They had no "government" other than Ezhya, and he could speak to whomever he liked. There was no protocol for who dealt with what except that Ezhya would deal with all of it, at least briefly, before passing jobs on to subordinates. That was why he had three feeders, to keep up with everything.

He would absolutely want to see Minke Kluysters if I could make the case sound interesting enough.

Question was: should I do that?

"Did he say what he wanted to talk about?" Thayu asked.

"I'm not sure. The meeting was more about what *wasn't* said than what was. Business, he said. He wants to sell things to Asto. This is a very strange group of people with far too much money to consider us mortals."

"Like the Vonayi clan," Veyada said.

I met his eyes. Vonayi clan represented old money on Asto. For many years, they were assured of providing the Chief Coordinator, before that honour went to the Palayi clan. Why exactly this had happened, or why the Chief Coordinators tended to be Palayi, I didn't understand, but it had to have something to do with entrenched loyalties.

The head of Ezhya's former guard association and the mother of his two daughters, Natanu, was Vonayi. I had a strong suspicion that this had something to do with why Veyada and Sheydu were no longer with Ezhya, but neither of them would talk about this.

"But Vonayi still have loyalty networks," I said.

"Vonayi loyalties often go through Azimi and Lingui clans, not Palayi and Domiri."

"Has that division always existed?"

"For a long time."

"Maybe then this Pretoria Cartel is like people from the Vonayi clan: distant from the day-to-day running of public life. They hand-pick who they get involved with, and ignore those that don't suit their needs. Nations of Earth, on the other hand, is forced to deal with everyone, rich or poor, friendly or hostile. That requires a certain degree of openness."

They both agreed. This was something Coldi could understand.

Then Veyada said, "But what do you think the Cartel are actually up to? He didn't tell you that, did he?"

"He said they were not interested in politics, and I told him I didn't believe that. He wants this office in Barresh, and I told him that he can have it when Earth joins *gamra* but if the referendum doesn't pass, he won't have it and I can't help him. And then he started talking about wanting to see Ezhya in return for helping with the elections."

Thayu snorted. "*Can* he help?"

I met her eyes. "Well, that's the question, isn't it?" I had told them about the projection Amarru had shown me of the areas of the world where the Exchange didn't have communication control and where I assumed the Cartel had their devices set up. What other influence did they have? I truly didn't know. I didn't *think* they could just tell people how to vote. I would like to think people were smarter than that and Nations of Earth had their voting system set up with greater security than that.

"I am very hesitant to let him anywhere near Ezhya. I suspect Ezhya will be curious. Minke Kluysters is an interesting man. He's pleasant, civilised, he seems to take you into his confidence." That trophy room was something different indeed. I could also still hear the laughter of teenage girls playing in the pool. "He seems genuine, and presents himself as far more vulnerable than he probably is."

But Veyada and Thayu didn't get that. Coldi leaders never showed vulnerability. It was not a sign of trust and was not appreciated or advisable.

I sighed and spread my hands. "Maybe he'd hoped to have an inroad into *gamra* but, whatever he wants, I can't give it."

"The only risk is that if you don't give what he wants, he'll be getting it somewhere else," Veyada said.

A dark look passed between us. I thought I knew what he meant.

"Do you really think the Cartel could be in contact with the Aghyrian ship?"

Veyada shrugged. "No evidence, but it wouldn't surprise me."

From having seen that off-world link that Amarru had shown me in the projection, it wouldn't surprise me either.

Thayu got up and walked to the hall. I guessed she could hear the others returning, but she came back a moment later.

I asked, "Are they coming?"

"No, it was just the breeze ruffling the trees. I'm wondering where they are."

My heart leapt. What had they been doing? "Tell me, what were they investigating?"

Veyada put his reader on the table. It displayed a map of a lot of nothingness with a couple of roads.

"One of Charlie's maps showed a place of interest not far from here at the edge of town. They had some information that they wanted to check out while you were gone. Jenny came with the bus and took them to a location outside the park, risking exposing herself. Someone must have held them up."

"What do you mean, *someone*? Not someone good, I presume?"

Veyada said nothing. Thayu said nothing.

My heart was hammering even louder. "What? Why didn't they tell us where they were going?"

"They did."

"They didn't tell me."

"We judged it safer for you not to know."

The sun sank towards the horizon, and I realised we'd have to stay here overnight. We tried to contact the park's office, but the little hub inside the hallway was dead. Thayu fiddled with it and took the box apart, but said she would need to rig up an antenna, and then it still might not work.

No one turned up, not even Klaus.

We improvised our own meal from the stuff in the fridge, but none of us were cooks, so it didn't taste very good.

We contemplated ways to get out of here.

We walked out in the dusk across the lawn to the thick metal gate in the tall fence that surrounded the property. Veyada wanted to know why this was necessary. Did the fence keep in the wallabies?

I explained the concept of lions. Both he and Thayu looked alarmed.

"Like a cat, but much bigger?" Thayu wanted to know.

"About this big." I held my hand waist high.

The gate was firmly shut, and we had no key.

"I should be able to get it open," Thayu said. "But is that desirable with these *lions*?"

"Not right now, while it's getting dark."

Because it was now getting seriously dark, we went back to the house, but it was also dark inside.

"How do you turn on the light?" Veyada asked.

Yesterday, it had come on by itself, like in most houses.

"I think there is a panel near the door," I said. I went to investigate, because both Veyada and Thayu had poor night vision. I found the panel, used my reader to light it, but none of the switches turned on any lights. Come to think of it, wasn't there meant to be a little light on the panel?

Ah. The power was off.

I went to check out the battery, which was under the house, in a concrete structure accessible via a little path past the side of the house, around the back and then underneath the main floor. The room functioned as pillar to support the main floor of the house.

It was really dark here, and I couldn't see much beyond the glow from my light. Animals scurried and snorted in the dark. Antelope or zebra maybe, or dogs. Were there snakes in this place?

I found the door and spent some time trying all the keys to open it.

The shed was even darker, with long and confusing shadows cast by spare furniture and garden utensils. The battery hung against the wall, and its lights were off, too. A lead dangled along the wall. I plugged it into the bottom of the battery. A screen flashed on, and said *Warning: power too low*.

Great. Someone had unplugged the panels this morning and the battery had not charged.

I left the shed again, and when I walked past the side of the house, an animal the size of a cat jumped out of the bushes and ran, screeching, across the lawn. It jumped into a tree and climbed up.

I stood there panting, trying to calm my racing heart.

Shit. A monkey.

Thayu and Veyada had come to the front of the house.

"Are you all right?" Thayu asked.

I had to explain what a monkey was. Could the animals see in the dark, they wondered.

We went back into the house, where we found a little oil light which I placed on the table in the living room. While we sat there discussing how we were going to get out, the Moon came out, silvering the forest outside. It was pretty in an eerie monochromatic kind of way. Ceren had two moons, but they were very small and moved through the sky at a great rate.

We had to wait until morning, and had to see if we could find a vehicle or some other way to get out of here.

It was too dangerous for us all to sleep at the same time, in case someone decided to pay us a visit at night, or if they needed help.

Veyada would sit at the door first, and then Thayu and I would take the early morning shift.

Thayu and I got ready for bed. I was tired, but I still found it hard to sleep. I listened to every sound, every squeak, every rustle. Even if Veyada sat at the front, what did Veyada know about such things as monkeys? What would Veyada do if a lion showed up?

I fell asleep for a bit but again woke up when Thayu left the bed to go out the front.

I was thinking that I'd have an entirely sleepless night when suddenly Thayu was shaking my shoulder. "Time to sit watch."

11

I **GROANED AND SLID OUT** of bed, found my clothes in the dark, took the gun from Thayu and padded out to the front door. When he had taken watch, Veyada dragged a chair out to the veranda, and I sat there. The seat was cold and damp from the chill air.

The night was absolutely still. The moonlight shone on the dewdrops on the grass on either side of the driveway. From my position, I could just see the moonlight reflecting on the top bar of the fence and gate which poked over the grassy hill. The bush on the other side was absolutely quiet. The resident wallabies sat in the far corner, grazing.

I was sure the fence had "accidentally" been closed because Mr Kluysters wanted me out of the picture for a bit longer. It was the way sophisticated people conducted kidnappings, because they could always claim that technical or personnel issues were at fault. They would eventually come to rescue us, but it wouldn't be soon.

Gradually the sky became lighter. A group of antelope grazed near the fence. I thought I saw a group of giraffes walking between the trees, on their way to the back of the lodge for their carrot.

Thayu and Veyada came not much later and we shared a breakfast of stale bread. There was some roast chicken in the fridge, but the fridge had been off for a day and I didn't want to eat it.

After breakfast, I first went to the shed to check the battery so that, if we needed to stay at night, we'd at least have light.

Veyada inspected the contents of the storage downstairs.

The storage was pretty useless, but in the tin shed that stood in the far corner of the fenced area we found a four-seater buggy. The tyres were flat and it had no battery, but Thayu removed one of the house's batteries from the shed, lugged it up to the parking circle and rigged it to the back seats. I used a squeaky foot pump to get air in the tyres. It was hot work, but at least the tyres seemed to have deflated from disuse, rather than from having punctures. Better toss the pump in the back, just in case.

Veyada found a few solar panels in the shed, which we hoisted to the roof of the buggy's frame and connected before pushing the buggy to the top of the grassy hill in full sunlight.

Phew.

It was now midmorning and we went inside the house for a break and a much-needed drink of cool water.

Veyada displayed the map of the area on his reader. We were about thirty kilometres from the park boundary where the main road ran past the perimeter fence. The main gate was further to the south, but I doubted that we could get out that way. There was a second service gate closer to us. The path to this gate went past a maintenance shed that maybe we could use to stay overnight if needed.

Then I remembered. "Klaus told me that there are trucks in that shed."

Veyada's face lit up. "Trucks are good."

Yes, they were. Trucks had a greater range than the buggy, they were safer, and they could be used to ram a hole through a fence after we'd emptied a couple of charges on it.

"Let's go that way, then."

A squeal came from outside.

"What was that?" Thayu looked alarmed. There were no people here.

All three of us got up and ran to the door—to find the buggy covered in squabbling monkeys. I ran onto the grass. "Shoo! Shoo!"

Most of them took off straight away, but the last two only jumped down from the seats and ambled off when I had almost reached the buggy. I had no idea what I would have done had they not done so. Monkeys had fearsome teeth.

Veyada and Thayu caught up. Thayu had drawn her gun and put it back in the bracket. I very much doubted that she would have shot, unless one of the monkeys had attacked me. Easy as the Coldi were about shooting people, they were as hesitant about killing animals as they were about eating them.

We walked around the vehicle, inspecting it for any damage, but there was none.

"We need to protect ourselves better," I said.

They agreed.

We found some wire fencing mesh in the shed, which we strung around the sides of the canopy frame. I suspected it wouldn't do much good if a lion decided it didn't like us, so we'd just have to hope there would be no lions.

I went for a test drive in the buggy along the driveway to the gate and back. It was surprisingly fast for such a primitive vehicle.

Meanwhile, Veyada and Thayu had used the house's solar panels to charge all our weapons.

We carried all our luggage to the veranda and judged that we could probably fit all of it in the buggy, including the useable supplies out of the pantry and the shed.

The buggy contained an old radio that Veyada had opened, dusted, and charged. He said it was a simple thing. It did nothing right now, but maybe we'd come into range of some transmission station. I trusted Veyada had received training in all the ways Earth technology could be used to suit Coldi needs, maybe even to ask for help from the Exchange. But not here. The Exchange couldn't reach us in this area. What about something in orbit? That was a thought that filled me with discomfort, but wasn't unrealistic. People were likely to be watching us from up there. Although to be honest I was more comfortable with being watched by Asha Domiri, even if he did come with a huge Asto military ship, than by the Pretoria Cartel.

When we were all ready, all batteries charged, water bottles filled, the mesh tied down over the open sides of the buggy, we got in. Veyada and Thayu had decided that I should be the driver, since they were better trained in everything else.

We drove up to the gate and stopped. Earlier in the day, Thayu had studied how to force the mechanism to open, and, knowing that forcing it open was likely to attract attention, had not done anything about it, because it needed to be done quickly and then we needed to get out quickly.

She pushed aside the mesh and jumped out of the buggy.

The gate's operating mechanism was located in a box that stood near the entrance. It had a sensor that would detect the presence of a device. She had also explained that it was likely to lock when damaged, so she dismantled the cabinet, took off the front panel and fiddled with the wires inside.

Veyada and I waited. A group of small monkeys had taken interest in us. They had jumped from the trees onto the top of the gate and were watching Thayu, no doubt deciding if her tool kit contained anything edible.

When the gate jumped into motion, pushing them all sideways, they ran off, shrieking.

Thayu had not noticed them and gave a shriek as well.

She came into the buggy looking shaken. "What were they doing?"

"They were just curious." I was sure monkeys could be a lot more annoying than they had been so far, but I left it. After all, I was now travelling in a wildly unsuitable vehicle through a stretch of wilderness that contained lots of "interesting" wildlife, with two people who were afraid of lap dogs.

Awesome.

I steered the buggy through the gate as soon as the opening was big enough. It was essential now to make as much headway as possible before the park rangers were warned that we had opened the gate.

At first, the road went through scrub. The sight of impenetrable thorn thickets made me nervous, because who knew what hid within. But then I figured that whatever was comfortable in the scrub was not going to be very big, so probably nothing we needed to worry about.

After a while, the terrain became more open, with larger trees and areas of grass. I spotted another group of monkeys under a tree, and we upset a herd of antelope drinking at a waterhole. Where there was water, animals gathered. I looked around, but saw nothing that alarmed me. The buggy was going well and even Veyada and Thayu seemed to relax when they realised that all these animals were afraid of *us*, not the other way around.

When we came to a larger open grassy field, I *thought* I saw a lion, but it was far off, lazing in the shade of a tree. It was a bit after midday and the light was bright.

So far, the only problems had been the dust and the heavily corrugated road surface, both of which were present in spades.

After a while, we turned off the main road to the track that went to the shed. The surface was much rougher here, and we had to go slower. On second thoughts, I wasn't so certain that coming this way was such a good idea. The wheels of the buggy were not very big and it was quite low above the ground. Veyada and Thayu even had to get out a few times to make the vehicle lighter. It was also getting later, and I feared we might not reach the shed until dark, and that would be a bad time to be out here unprotected.

We came over a rise, and I could see the maintenance shed surrounded by a fence. What was more, I could see the trucks underneath the overhang of a roof.

But first we had to cross a gully.

The path was pretty rough here, reduced to a set of wheel tracks. It zigzagged down the grassy hill we were at the top of, towards the gully, and then veered right to a spot where a concrete causeway crossed the gully, which contained a couple of waterholes. Undulating land continued on the other side of the gully. The hills were grassy, except for some straggly trees that cast lengthening shadows over the land.

Veyada sucked in a breath.

He was looking at the other side of the gully.

A lone tree stood by the side of the road. The grass had been trampled in the shade, and a couple of fairly large animals lay there, looking out over the grassland. Their ears twitched and they turned their heads in our direction.

Lions. Six of them.

Well, drat.

I stopped the buggy.

"What are they?" Thayu asked.

"Those are lions."

She and Veyada gave me alarmed looks.

"What are we going to do about them?" Thayu asked.

"Good question. Maybe we can scare them off."

I had expected either her or Veyada to offer to shoot at them, but they did not. So we waited a bit to see what the group would do.

"You didn't offer to shoot them," I said.

Both Veyada and Thayu gave me sharp looks.

"You don't shoot anything unless it's for self-defence," Thayu said. "That's the first thing they teach you at the academy."

Veyada agreed. "Anyone caught doing otherwise gets a quick ticket to the Outer Circle."

People called Coldi society lacking compassion, and every now and then, it surprised me with strong rules like this. If one was allowed to carry a weapon on Asto, military training was mandatory. And the Asto military held the badge for being the most non-confrontational while also being the most terrifying.

Shooting lions was not an appropriate thing.

Not even to scare them? I asked, but they said they had no idea what the lions would do. They might want to retaliate. I didn't think that lions were that vindictive, but I didn't know enough about lions.

We waited.

The lions looked at us.

We looked at the lions.

It was kind of boring.

The male yawned, showing a pink tongue and huge teeth.

"You're right. They are like a cat," Veyada said, using the Isla word. He'd spent evenings studying my father's cat. "Only bigger."

"That's what they are: big cats."

Veyada didn't like cats and how they always wanted to sit on him, with his higher than normal body temperature. I could see the thoughts working behind his eyes, that having a lion sit on him would not be a good idea, given the size of those teeth.

After a while, Thayu said, "They're just going to sleep here."

"Looks like it."

"How about we go that way?" Veyada pointed at a second track, probably made by vehicles during the times that the main track was too wet and the causeway was under water. The track was partially overgrown.

"It doesn't look very well-maintained. We might hit something."

"Then we just get out and—"

"No. You do *not* get out when there are lions."

Thayu said, "If that is so, then this mesh isn't much protection either."

"Nope."

Horrified looks.

I didn't think they'd realised until then. Thayu touched the gun in her arm bracket. Veyada nodded.

"Not unless there is trouble," I said.

More nods. They understood.

We had to keep going, because the sunlight was already turning golden. There was no point choosing any of the alternative tracks, because we had to cross at the causeway. We would just have to see what we'd do when we got to the other side.

I slowly drove the buggy down towards the causeway. The track ran along the bank for a short distance avoiding a marshy area. Thayu and Veyada kept close watch on the surroundings and especially the spot where the lions were. The grass was quite long in places, the track overgrown.

Veyada said, "Look. They're getting up."

I stopped the buggy. They were, too, you could see the backs of the lions as they slowly walked through the grass.

Thayu asked, "Coming this way?"

"No, I think they're going the other way."

"Good."

I steered the buggy further along the path.

We were perhaps fifty metres from the causeway, and perhaps a hundred metres away from the shed on the far side. We'd still have to figure out how to get into the enclosure, but that seemed a minor problem.

Thayu made a small noise.

I was traversing a particularly bumpy part of the track and had to keep a close eye on the terrain, but the strangled tone in her voice made me look. She sounded terrified. Thayu did not often sound terrified.

I looked back.

On the ridge we had crossed stood an elephant.

And it was some *elephant*.

He was huge, with tusks that would not have looked out of place on a mammoth, and huge flapping ears. He leaned forward as if he was going to come running down the hill any moment.

And then, while I was not looking at the road, the bottom of the buggy went *crunch* into the dirt and we stopped so abruptly that I almost fell off my seat.

Oh, fuck.

Veyada got up. "I'll lift it up."

I wanted to say, *no,* but we had to keep moving. If we were stuck here, we'd be sitting ducks. Hopefully the elephant was more interested in the lions.

Veyada slipped from the side. He lifted the buggy up and shoved a stick under the wheels. I pressed the accelerator and we moved forward again.

The elephant was coming towards us, down the hill, pushing aside the grass.

I called, "Quick, get in."

Hopefully we could—

No such luck.

Thayu yelled.

The elephant ran forward with alarming speed, ears flapping, trunk held high. It stomped over bushes. It trumpeted.

Veyada pushed the buggy and yelled, "Go, go, go!"

He yanked his gun from its bracket. Fired.

But it wasn't his big gun—it needed time to recharge—and the charge merely glanced off the animal's head. If anything, it made the elephant angrier.

Veyada jumped off the track, down into the marshy part of the gully. The elephant took off after him. I flat-footed the buggy. It jerked and jumped over too-rough terrain. We were either going to get struck or bogged or we'd hit something and damage the vehicle.

But we needed to move fast so that we could pick Veyada up on the other side of the causeway, where his shortcut would rejoin the track.

Veyada ran, charging through the grass, jumping over bushes. He reached the bottom of the gully, tripped and fell face first in a puddle. He scrambled to his feet and tore up the far side of the gully.

The elephant splashed into the water.

Thayu yelled, "Faster, faster!" I didn't know if she meant us or Veyada. The buggy didn't go any faster.

Veyada reached the top of the hill, the elephant just behind him, trumpeting, flapping its ears.

I knew Coldi could run much faster than us, but I didn't think I'd ever seen any of them run as fast as Veyada did. He took off across the grassy field in the direction of the shed. He jumped over bushes, he cut a path through the waist-high grass. The elephant followed. Sticks and clumps of grass flew in its wake.

Veyada was almost at the shed, but the shed's grounds were surrounded by a similar fence to the one that had surrounded the lodge.

I was afraid what would happen once he got there, but Veyada simply vaulted the fence, tumbling over the top.

The elephant pulled up, flapping its ears, trumpeting.

Veyada ran into the safety of the shed.

The elephant watched him for a while, snorting and pacing along the fence. But eventually it calmed down and walked off.

Phew.

Thayu's face was pale. I think she understood how little protection we had in the buggy.

I judged it safe to continue to the shed and steered the buggy carefully across the field. I hoped that one of those trucks in the shed was going to be useful for us, although to be honest I wasn't sure how much protection even a truck would be against an angry elephant of that size.

Veyada came out. He had a scratch on his face and a dark trail of Coldi blood ran down his left arm. The rest of his face bore splatters of mud, and drying mud flaked off his clothes and shoes.

He looked, in one word, ragged. There was no need to ask him how he felt. Lousy.

He opened the gate from the inside and we made pretty damn sure it was shut properly.

Safe.

12

———————

W**E WERE ALL SHAKEN** after that episode.

We sat in the shelter of the shed, drinking water, saying nothing, realising how close we'd come to being wiped out by an angry elephant.

Veyada's tumble over the fence had left him with some bleeding scratches that needed attending. He was also visibly exhausted. He closed his eyes and leaned against the shed's wall while I retrieved the first aid kit from the buggy and found disinfectant and bandages.

I had to be careful not to get Coldi blood into any open wounds. The part of the Coldi DNA that was artificially added to the base of Aghyrian DNA tended to create all kinds of trouble with DNA that didn't have this addition. That was why I'd had to have my sperm treated—in order to make sure that the places where it replicated and latched on were already occupied by molecules that were not easily dislodged. Or so Lilona had explained it to me.

In any case, I'd seen the infections and tissue death and other horrible things that could result when coming into contact with Coldi blood. I used gloves, while Thayu walked around the shed.

The cut in Veyada's arm turned out to be quite deep. Looking at it made me feel sick. I used surgical glue from the first aid box, knowing that it would probably need to be looked at in Athens.

He'd likely picked up a raft of local bacteria from that barbed wire fence.

After having taken care of his arm, I pulled out a fresh medical wipe for his face.

He said, "You know, at the military academy, they put you all in a dorm and then when everyone is asleep, they call the alarm. You have to be out and ready, with all your stuff, before the inspection comes. Anything they find that identifies you will lose you marks. They line you up outside, give you points and then send you back to sleep. Sometimes they make you run for your life." He watched as I bandaged his wrist. "That was obviously a long time ago."

"You don't need that here."

"Don't I?" He gestured with his uninjured hand. "This tells me I do. We've become soft and complacent about our training. We should set ourselves some training programs."

And the *we've failed in our job* thread continued.

I scrunched the tissue into a ball and wiped his cheek clean. Fortunately this wound was just a scratch. His skin was very muddy, though, and I worked my way from the scratch to his nose and forehead, where a bruise was developing.

I could tell him that I thought it was fine and that they did their jobs perfectly well, but I knew he would never listen, and also there was a grain of truth in what he said. We did find ourselves in dangerous situations quite a bit, and they had received the training, but training was worth little if you didn't maintain and update it.

And here we were in the middle of the African wilderness, sharing this very Coldi moment of closeness. Touching was important. We'd been so busy I had kind of ignored it. I had also never shared anything special with Veyada.

When we were home, I should book a private pool for just the two of us at one of the many bathhouses. I should show him that I appreciated him.

I finished with his face, then loosened his hair, raked the sticks and grass out of it with my fingers and retied it.

The scent of his Coldi sweat—earthy and reminiscent of the smell of rain on hot stone—brought back memories of times past. Meeting Nicha for the first time, sharing a bed with him in that freezing cold hotel in Russia.

I bent over and touched his forehead with my nose. His skin was warm and damp. He grabbed my left hand with his uninjured right hand and squeezed briefly before letting go.

Thayu had come back, but sat down at a distance, her back to the wall. She nodded to me.

I said, "All right. We'll organise some regular skills update sessions, whatever is necessary."

Thayu now joined us. "Did you hear that, Veyada? He actually *agreed* with you."

She told us that her walk around the building had not revealed any sign of recent activity in the shed. There were two doors, but they were locked and might be armed, so we would have to be careful. Power inside the shed was turned on. The garage held two trucks, and both were locked.

We had a few things to do before we could worry about the contents of the shed and any way to get inside or into the trucks.

After we had taken the solar panels off the buggy and leaned them against the wall of the shed to catch the last rays of sunlight, we ate a quick bite. The sky was turning orange and soon it would be dark. A group of elephants wandered past. These were smaller animals with a number of babies. One of them couldn't have been more than waist height. It kept tripping over its own feet.

Both Veyada and Thayu watched them with extremely wary expressions.

"This is a group with females and babies," I said. "I don't think that one is more than a day old."

Veyada gave a sniff. He did not want to talk about elephants.

We went to check on the battery, to find that it had not charged more than twenty percent. Thayu suggested there would be batteries in the shed that we could use. With a bit of luck, we could find a key to the trucks.

By the light of my reader's screen, Thayu wrenched open the door into the shed. It led into a fairly narrow corridor, with the walls made from corrugated metal sheets, with a few doors on either side.

This was one hell of a strange farm shed. I had expected a big open space with farm equipment like rolls of fencing wire, tools, graders, tractors and things like that. It looked more like a field office. We tested all the doors, but the rooms on the other side were dark, and they contained shelves of what looked like agricultural chemicals. The last room had a small office space, but it contained nothing of interest. I presumed that the work was done electronically, and the person who had worked here had not left any computers behind, nor was there a communications hub.

"This is strange," Thayu said, while we walked back to the door. "I thought that the building was much bigger judging from the outside."

She was right, as we found out not much later when we walked around the building and found a large rolling door to allow vehicles into the other half of the building. Judging by the view through the dusty window, this was the farm shed I had expected. The large door looked heavy and cumbersome to open, but next to it was a normal door.

Veyada decided that it was worth some of his precious gun charge to use it as a laser-cutter and cut through the lock. Thayu used a screwdriver to wrench it open.

On the concrete floors stood several tractors and a grader and various implements used for digging or making fences. A bench along the side held a variety of tools.

The back wall contained a door which led into another passage with doors on the left. The air smelled stale in here, the only light came from a little window at the very end of the passage. The polished concrete floor felt clean under my feet.

Thayu led the way with the glow from her reader.

In the first room, which had a single, blinded-out window, we found shelves with stacks of drums and bottles containing chemicals. I took some pictures because I had no idea what this stuff was used for.

The next room, without windows, was a store of medicines, all packed in little boxes, which displayed the logo of Sandowne Pharmaceuticals, the company owned by Minke Kluysters.

I was no expert on chemical or medical components, so the long names on the labels meant nothing to me, but this store of chemicals in the middle of nowhere was starting to worry me. There were too many of them to be farm chemicals. No one used this many chemicals in country like this. This was more like a storage facility.

Or rather, a place to hide these chemicals away from where people could easily find them.

Klaus had told me about this shed. He'd said there were trucks, and that was true, but it had sounded as if he'd *wanted* us to come here. He had also said that there were other useful things here, which meant that we'd go looking for them—and find something else?

The next room, also windowless, was a dressing room, with benches around the sides and hooks for hanging clothes. One wall was taken up by cupboards which contained thin overalls that could be hazard suits or medical scrubs.

The next room contained chairs, all empty, like a waiting room.

Then the next room was full of computers and communication equipment. This room had a window, but because it was now almost dark, little light came in.

Lights blinked and screens idled in sleep mode, but all of it was operational.

"Wow," Thayu said.

She went into the room and brought a screen to life with a single touch of her hand.

She read, and frowned. "This looks like a communication hub."

I agreed. What for? Who used it?

Thayu set the reader on the desk and dropped to her knees in front of the desk. She often did this, pushing the desk chair aside, and I never understood why she didn't just sit in the chair. Veyada placed his reader on the desk and flicked through a couple of menus to connect it to the network.

Thayu spent some time copying as much as she could onto her and Veyada's devices. I watched, leaning against the doorframe as they worked, their faces lit from underneath by the light from Thayu's reader.

After a while she said, "There are records of off-world contacts here, but we'll have to determine where they come from at the Exchange."

Then Veyada said, "Look at this."

He stepped away so that I could have a look.

The screen displayed a schematic map of a building that I recognised to be the shed, with its two compartments. It showed the rooms and the power points and status of those points: whether they were live and idle or in use. It showed the status of the building's battery and a projection of how long the charge would last at the current rate of use.

I frowned. "It's just an energy monitoring system."

"Yes, but look." He pointed to the side of the image, where there was a second map, smaller than the other. Clearly marked on one side of that map was a set of stairs. "This building has a top floor?"

I looked at the ceiling. If there was a top floor, it wasn't here. I could see the underside of the metal roof. I didn't remember that the farm shed had a low ceiling either.

"There is a level below us," Thayu said.

Crap, yes, that had to be it.

We went back and searched every room in the building, first on the warehouse side and then on the farm shed side.

Then Veyada discovered a floor plate in one of the storerooms off the big shed. We had to wheel a cabinet aside to see it fully.

"Open it," Thayu said.

But how?

There was no handle. Thayu found a crow bar, which she inserted between the plate and the surrounding concrete. She heaved and pushed. The plate moved a bit, so Veyada helped her. But they only succeeded in bending the crowbar.

I looked around the room to find a better metal bar, and discovered a cabinet on the wall next to the door. I opened the door, finding a panel with buttons inside. I wondered . . . I pressed one button. Nothing happened, then another one and nothing happened, but the third one turned on a mechanism that hummed.

"Whoa!" Veyada and Thayu jumped back.

Slowly, with a low hum, the cover rose out of the ground. Now it became obvious why Thayu and Veyada would never have been able to open it: it consisted of a thick slab of concrete.

Inside the rectangular hole that opened up, a stairwell led into the darkness.

The door was now fully open and the mechanism stopped humming.

Thayu put her finger to her lips. She preceded us into the hole, holding her scanner. Veyada produced a small light.

The stairs went at least two floors into the earth, coming out into a short passage, where the walls and the floor consisted of plain concrete. The air smelled of chemicals and was stuffy and breathless, with an unpleasant tang that I couldn't identify.

At the end we came to a closed door. Thayu tried the handle, but it wouldn't open.

Both she and Veyada dropped to their knees, studying the lock.

Sweat trickled down my back. I wished they'd hurry up with trying to open this door. I was sure that when we opened the trap door and went into the tunnel, some sort of alarm would have gone off, and we would probably meet some angry people with guns soon.

The door clicked open. Thayu pushed it, shone the light inside and sucked in a breath.

I asked, "What?"

She pushed the door further. A light came on automatically, revealing a room that was very, very different from the storage rooms upstairs. The air was clean and cool here, with a tang of disinfectant.

According to the floor plan we'd seen, this was a long, narrow room, divided into several compartments. Along the walls stood tables and benches with equipment, shelves with glass bottles and packets of medical supplies: needles, tubes, bandages, foil-packed things.

We walked through the central aisle, our footfalls muffled in the stifling silence. The floor was clean and the tables were spotless, the medical supplies neatly stored on the shelves. The floor consisted of scrubbed tiles. At regular intervals, there were bays with a power hub hanging from the ceiling and a drain in the middle. It looked like a table would be wheeled in here, messy work done on it, and the mess hosed through the drain.

I was beginning to have a very bad feeling about this. In fact, the chemical smell was starting to make me feel nauseous.

Thayu had pulled out her gun. It was not just a weapon, but also scanned for body heat and electronic activity that transmitted out of this room. She found nothing alarming.

Yet the place was clean and tidy and looked like people came here every day. In fact, it felt like someone could come out of the shadows any moment.

We passed under an archway into another segment of the room. We waited while lights flickered on through motion sensors.

This looked like a hospital room, partitioned into sections with cubicle walls. Each cubicle held a bed, surrounded by medical equipment.

Thayu took in a sharp breath, raising her hand to her mouth.

"Look," she whispered.

There were people in the beds. Most of them were barely recognisable as such, with their heads bandaged, their bodies encased in a shell of resin, with tubes sprouting from the casing to various machines that surrounded each bed. I counted sixteen of these beds.

"What are they all doing here?" she asked.

I went to the computer next to the closest bed. The screen displayed a table with live metrics: heart rate, blood pressure, and a whole lot of figures that represented I had no idea what.

I didn't dare touch the screen, but it must have sensed my presence, because it changed to display text that looked like a treatment log. Apparently, the person in question, identified only by a number, had come in a few weeks ago and had been declared clinically dead two days later, after which a raft of treatments had started. At the bottom it said, *Transfer to hospital* with a date in two days' time.

I went to the next bed. That person had been here for a shorter amount of time, and was due to be transported next week.

The person in the bed after that was encased in a cabinet that contained hazy air. The top was made of glass, and you could see the person's face, eyes closed, not breathing.

The other beds in the room were also like this. Some of the patients had surgical cuts in their skin—mostly in the stomach—and others didn't.

"Look," Veyada said.

He stood at the far wall of this room, which was taken up by an installation that looked like an aquarium shop. Well, minus the fish and with the addition of equipment with blinking lights.

The space in the tanks was taken up with fluid, softly glowing with red light. Inside each tank floated irregular, ragged hunks of flesh, all of them with wires and tubes attached.

"Wetware," I said. "Artificial body parts designed to be implanted into people with illnesses."

He waved his scanner in front of the glass. Lines on the screen squiggled. He nodded. The chunks of tissue contained an electronic device that would perform a particular function, and that had been coated with bio-mesh that would grow and attach itself to the surrounding tissue as if it were the real thing. Hearts could be programmed to grow arteries, and kidneys and stomachs and sections of intestines to develop the attachments that allowed surgeons to implant them in a living body.

Each of the tanks had a label with its contents affixed to the glass, mostly numbers, but underneath, someone had scribbled *livers*, *kidneys* and *hearts*.

A wave of nausea and dizziness forced me to look away. I leaned on a nearby table, breathing deeply.

I thought of the report I'd received from the Exchange on Jemiro. He had been revived in this way.

Thayu had been taking pictures and recording any information about the people.

"You know that they all died two days after coming here?"

Veyada and I met each other's eyes. I could see in his expression that he thought the same thing I did: what's the chance that they were killed especially for this purpose, while they were led to believe that they would be cured of whatever ailed them, real or made up?

"This is disgusting," Veyada said. His voice reflected how I felt. That scent of disinfectant suddenly became suffocating. "What is the point of this?"

"To show the world that they can do this?" And make everyone afraid of those terrible *aliens,* never mind that the aliens who gave them this technology and the ones wanting to stop the import of this knowledge were two radically different groups.

One reason that was always quoted why people had never bothered with artificial humans was that the universe had plenty of humans who came for free, and that, bluntly spoken, a random human life held much less value than some of the tech it could produce. One could argue that without humans, there would be no tech, but the battle became about *which* humans with valuable skills were worth keeping.

Another line of thinking concerned the creation of thinking automatons who would have common sense but no capacity to critically evaluate orders. The Tamerians were in this class.

If you made a superhuman, by definition you lost control over that person. If the person remained happily under your control, it was not a superhuman.

Thayu handed me her reader. "I should also show you this. I found this in a list of people to be treated."

In the middle of the screen was the name *Jacko Awaba*.

"Charlie's brother?" Charlie, in the wheelchair whom we had met in front of the court building in The Hague and who had told us of his brother and his illness, and how his brother had disappeared.

13

THAYU AND I stared at each other.

"Here is our proof," I said. "They take in people who are ill and have no money, promise them a cure and medicine, and turn them into Tamerians."

"And that happens in Barresh as well."

"We need to record all this for evidence." And I needed to get in touch with Lenka Trnkova, who had done the initial investigation of people without ID. I could get her to join up her data about faceless assassins who had murdered heads of state with information about people who had come through here, and I could talk to the police in New Zealand about the men who had been killed in their attack on us.

While I ran around taking pictures, Veyada and Thayu took data dumps of as many pieces of equipment as possible in the room.

When I finished, I searched through the computer system, finding a database with names, their origin, and a list of programs that the people were in.

"Come on, let's go," Thayu said.

I agreed with that. We'd been here far longer than we intended. It was revealing and important, but we still didn't know whether we could use any of the trucks, and someone would certainly turn up to check on their project soon. And we were still in a wildlife park surrounded by angry elephants.

Thayu tucked her scanner inside her armour. I took my reader off the connection cushion, stuffed it inside my shirt and zipped up my jacket. It would be too hot, but it was not to be helped.

We made our way out of the lab, through the connecting room into the underground passage, where it was still stuffy and breathless.

We were about to go up the stairs to the concrete plate trapdoor, when a sharp thunk rang through the building.

We stopped. Thayu, who was in front of me, took her gun out of the arm bracket. Veyada stood so close behind me that I could hear his breath.

We listened, but the only sound that reached this room was the muffled call of some bird and crickets outside.

Blood roared in my ears.

Thayu continued, slowly, step by step, into the upstairs room. I followed her and Veyada came up behind me. Would we close the trapdoor to hide the fact that someone had been here? They probably knew about it already, even if Thayu had not been able to locate any bugs. Closing it would make a noise. Thayu went to the door and into the hallway. I was the last to leave the room, and pressed the panel as we went out. The door's mechanism started humming.

Now I could hear footsteps. A door clanged open. A man spoke in a language I didn't recognise.

Veyada pulled me into another room—the one with the hazard suits. Two or three men tromped past in the hallway, heavy boots on the tiled floor.

They went into the room with the trap door.

As one, Thayu and Veyada shot into the corridor, half-dragging me with them.

We ran through the big hall with the grader and tractors. Out through the side door.

A truck waited outside the shed. The faint glow of the dashboard lit the face of a man in ranger uniform. Not Klaus. I wondered where he was and whether he knew what was going on.

Thayu ran to the vehicle, yanked open the door and dragged the poor driver out by his shirt, pointing her gun at his face with her other hand.

He was quite young, blue-eyed and blond-haired, wearing a game park uniform. His eyes were wide. He raised his hands.

Thayu hissed into his face. "Take us to the town."

He stammered, "I don't . . . I don't . . ."

I said, "She wants you to take us into town."

He cast a quick glance at Thayu's body. Probably hadn't realised that she was female.

"Get in the truck. Take us there." I would like to say nothing would happen to him, but we might need the truck, and I doubted his bosses would be happy if we took off with it, or even if he provided us with an escape.

Thayu motioned with the gun, while her expression remained hard and without emotion.

To be honest, she frightened me a bit like this.

The young man clambered into the truck. Thayu grabbed the reader from the passenger seat and turned it off, and pulled the portable hub off the dashboard and turned that off as well.

Veyada had run to the buggy and grabbed a few things we might need. Armour, bags which probably contained electronics. I was glad to see that he had also brought my small travel pack and Thayu's backpack.

It was a tight fit with four of us in the cabin.

Thayu sat next to the driver, with her gun still pointed at him. "Go."

I had never heard her say a single word in Isla. I knew that she had a basic understanding of it and I should not be surprised that she could speak a few words.

Her dark voice and clipped accent made the command all the more pertinent.

The driver nodded, sweat shining on his face. He reversed the truck, turned around and drove up to the gate. It moved aside at our approach.

I watched the driver from between the seats. The truck was fitted with a GPS device that also displayed a map of the area.

"I want you to take us to where the rest of our team is."

"But sir, I don't know—"

"No nonsense. Take us there."

"They're not in the park, sir."

"Then take us out of the park to wherever they are. Out the service gate."

"The road is much worse than the main road, sir. I don't know if the truck can make it."

"Take us there anyway."

"But sir . . ."

Thayu flicked the gun.

He nodded, lips pressed together.

I suspected that he was trying to channel us through the main gate where I assumed the surveillance and security were better. We'd come here in a buggy, and this truck was much further off the ground. It was winter and this was their dry season. There were not likely to be any boggy areas. And why have a service gate if service trucks were unable to use it?

I hoped I was making the right decision. If not, it would be the end of the line for us. We had no connection to Amarru, no help, no way of reaching anyone, not even the rest of my team, whom I doubted would have left voluntarily; and Klaus and Jenny . . . might be asleep and unaware of our situation.

We got from the driver that the others had been taken to a motel in town, because "Mr Kluysters doesn't like people snooping around." No, they hadn't been mistreated and yes, we would have been taken there tomorrow anyway and "Can that woman please stop pointing the gun at me?"

He was quite young, had been working at the park for six months, but came from Johannesburg. A lot of young men worked here for a year or so to get experience.

He was not being paid.

"Are you going to vote?" I asked him.

He glanced sideways, his expression bewildered. "Vote?"

"In the referendum?"

"Oh. If Mr Kluysters likes us to vote."

"If? That's not up to him, is it?"

He said nothing. It clearly *was* up to Minke Kluysters whether he allowed his staff to go into town to vote.

"Ask him. Because you should. Mr Kluysters has nothing to do with whether or not you vote. It's your decision. What you vote is your decision, too."

"I like Mr Kluysters and his advice. He gives us jobs. There are none in town. No job means no girlfriend, because the girls don't like losers, and my parents got sick of me hanging around the house."

"So you like the way he does business?"

"That's not my business, sir."

"Isn't it?"

Another sideways look. "No, it isn't."

"That his company takes in poor and ill people and makes them disappear is not your business?"

"We don't talk about that, sir."

"Maybe you should, because you're young, and I don't think you're a bad man. You wouldn't like anything like that to happen to your family, right?"

He pressed his lips together and stared at the road. He said no more.

The truck rumbled along the road. The surface was rough, bumpy, with ridges and corrugations, dust pans and dried-up bog holes.

Next to me, Veyada peered into the darkness, where the sky had acquired a faint blue glow.

Once, the truck had to slow down for a group of giraffes crossing the road, but we saw no other animals.

Then the perimeter fence loomed up in the glow of the headlights.

It was now definitely starting to get light, with a band of light blue along the eastern horizon.

The map on the truck's dashboard showed that the gate was not too far away, and I spotted it when we crested a hill.

The road looped into the scrub for a little bit, and as we came out, in full view of the gate, it opened, with a truck approaching from the outside.

"Who are they?" I asked Thayu in Coldi.

She gestured *I don't know*.

A service vehicle, emblazoned with a park logo.

Thayu gestured with the gun. "Keep going. If you give us away, you're dead."

I had to translate that for him.

He nodded nervously.

Veyada and I ducked out of view.

The other vehicle stopped as our truck went through the gate that was only wide enough for one vehicle.

The driver raised his hand in greeting to the other driver.

We passed the other vehicle. I held my breath. A few more seconds and we'd be free of this prison, a few more seconds—

The truck stopped.

Veyada and I gave each other a sharp look.

Someone called outside. The driver opened the window. A man spoke to him, but his dialect was hard to understand. But over the sound of his voice came another very distinct sound: the *thwup-thwup-thwup* of the blades of a gyrocopter.

Shit.

Our driver said, "I don't know, man. I got a job in town."

The other man asked something, I couldn't hear what. The sound from the gyrocopter was getting louder.

The driver replied, "Oh man, it's got nothing to do with me."

And then the door on Veyada's side of the vehicle opened.

And Veyada's gun discharged with a blinding flash.

The driver screamed, opened the door and dropped out of the vehicle. Thayu discharged her gun as well. I thought she missed, but the flash blinded me. Veyada pulled me out of the truck and handed me our bags.

"Run."

I stared at him. "Where to?" The view from my position in the back of the truck showed a regional road in the middle of nowhere; there was no traffic and no sign of habitation.

"Run."

I shouldered the bags and ran.

The park gate had closed. The second truck was on fire and a man lay face down on the ground. The gyrocopter had come much closer. Searchlights lit the ground underneath it, and the clouds of dust it threw up.

I had no idea what purpose it served, but I ran away from it, because I trusted Veyada with my life, because I trusted that they had plan.

Thayu caught up with me, and then Veyada.

The gyrocopter circled us and then came towards us from the other direction.

"Run," Veyada said.

A rush of air, a moment of silence, and then:

Boom!

I almost tripped.

The landscape that surrounded us bloomed with orange light. One of the trucks behind us had exploded.

The gyrocopter flew so low that the downward blast of air made it impossible to keep running.

Someone yelled over the whoosh of air, "Come!"

Reida. Thank the heavens.

I could see him and Sheydu inside the open cargo door. The gyrocopter landed on the road in front of us, blowing up dust and leaves. I ran, holding onto the bags. I handed them to Reida and scrambled into the open back door, hauled up by Sheydu. Nicha was also there, as well as Deyu and Devlin.

The gyrocopter took off again.

I lay on the dusty floor, panting, glad for my team, glad to be alive, glad to be out of the clutches of the Cartel.

When I had caught my breath, and the chill breeze blasting through the open back door was getting a bit much, I made my way to the front of the cabin, where most of my team were gathered on the seats. The pilot of the gyrocopter was a man I had never seen before, and the only other people on board were the members of my team.

"What happened?" I asked Nicha.

"When you were gone, Jenny came with the bus. She said she was under orders to take us to a place in town. I said we weren't leaving without you, but she said you'd come later. She was quite insistent and told us this was the usual process and that we'd be safe and you'd come later. But then you didn't come, and there was no one for us to contact. Neither Jenny nor Klaus responded to our messages, if they even got them. We contacted the park, but they said to wait. We were through with waiting, so we 'borrowed' this vehicle."

"Klaus is all right?" I asked Sheydu.

"I think he had to keep his head down to avoid being discovered. He's worth a lot to Amarru."

I'd feared as much. That also fitted with my impression that he didn't want us here. He had not been joking that he thought I was an upstart. I was interfering with his mission. Risking it.

Well, that was sobering.

Were we still on the same side?

I thought we were, although I could see how the Zhori on Earth were like the Ezmi on Hedron, and had no love for answering to the established Coldi hierarchy, the Palayis, Azimis and Domiris who were still very much linked to Asto. The Zhori ancestors had fled from a brutal Chief Coordinator, many of them in the period immediately following the establishment of the first Coldi outpost in Athens in 1962, and these families were never likely to return to Asto, or even acknowledge Asto's rule.

Amarru trod a much more careful line. She wanted more independence, but she was also a much more recent immigrant from a time where Coldi settling on Earth did so of their own volition and were happy to maintain contact with Asto.

Klaus was stuck between those two worlds.

But Earth joining *gamra* was not about that at all. *Gamra* was not about Asto.

Klaus would see that, wouldn't he?

Another question: did he work for Amarru because he believed in the benefit of *gamra* or did he work for her because he wanted to make her see his point of view?

That was a disturbing thought.

Everyone in this game had their own goals and reasons for taking part. And we'd just have to steer this huge monster, this giant, bumbling *machine* in the right direction.

The pilot took us into town to the airport, where a couple of police officers waited for us with a van. Apparently, the gyrocopter that the team had "borrowed" belonged to a local transport business, the owner of which had been slightly unimpressed that they had taken off with it.

The officers informed me that they were obliged to arrest us, but when I talked to the senior officer, he was clearly unhappy that we had fled a run-in with the Pretoria Cartel. It seemed that some part of their integrity got lost in between "these people stole a gyro-copter" and "these people were here by invitation of the Pretoria Cartel". I guessed the police force was very much afraid of this proverbial elephant that inhabited this area.

I also guessed that they were few and backup was a long way away. The police were likely understaffed and underfunded, even with the help of private security firms.

The station looked like a regular residential house. The garden was paved over for the vehicles. A few steps led up to the veranda and the hallway had been turned into a reception area. A single officer sat behind a desk, greeting the others as we came in.

They showed us a room at the back of the house.

It was fairly large and had a door with multiple locks and bars on the windows. It contained a couple of beds and couches which could be turned into beds. There was a shower further down the hall.

We dumped our bags on the dusty lino floor and set about making sure that everyone could sleep.

The officers brought us breakfast and coffee and told us that we had to be out of there by tonight. In return, I asked them for access to their communication channels.

14

WHILE MEMBERS OF my team were traipsing back and forth to the shower, a wave of sudden fatigue took hold of me. I simply could not keep my eyes open any longer. I lay down on one of the couch beds and dozed.

In a corner of the room, Reida was doing the same.

Thayu and Evi had annexed a computer, and, after consulting with the police officers, managed to get onto someone from the Exchange register who could help us get out of here. Apparently. I didn't hear everything or understand all the code. I kept drifting in and out of sleep.

I felt terrible that I was resting and Thayu was still working, but I was so incredibly tired.

When I woke up, Thayu showed me the data analysis she had done on the material we had copied from the lab.

She had established that those people we had seen in the lab had all been listed as missing by their families. Nicha had obtained a missing persons list from the police, although he said they'd been reluctant to share it.

She added, "Probably because they're scared of upsetting the Cartel. They've probably known that this happens for many years and have been unable to do anything about it, because of a lack of people or funds."

"I'd say so," Nicha said. "Even the storeroom in that lodge we were in had nicer floors and neater walls than this excuse of an office."

I looked over the list of missing persons. Presuming they had integrity—and maybe it was naive but I'd like to believe people who signed up for the police had integrity—it would have been incredibly frustrating for the police officers here to see what was happening and to be unable to do anything about it.

Most of the missing people were listed as having left their families because they had been promised a cure for their conditions. Some had come from the cities, others from smaller towns. All were Africans, from black, white and Indian heritage. All came from poor backgrounds.

According to the data that Thayu had compiled, they were first given medication to clear up the short term effects of their conditions and when the body was as healthy as it was going to get, they were "put to sleep". When the body was technically dead, they were operated on to insert the implants we had seen floating in the tanks to replace their diseased organs. The thought of the chunks of flesh floating in the tanks still made me feel sick.

Sometimes they even replaced sections of the patient's brain, by inserting biochips through a tiny hole in the skull, which took a few weeks to permanently fuse with the brain. The X-rays of these people showed the lead from the implant going to a point in the side of the head in the recipient's hair.

I remembered seeing that in the X-rays from Jemiro.

This was not technology limited to Earth. It was done right under our noses in Barresh.

I asked, "Did you find out where they get all these medical information supplies?"

The medical profession on Earth used implants for certain limited conditions, but I'd never seen anything as extensive as this. This was not Earth-based technology.

"The supplies don't come through the Exchange," Thayu said. "These chips are produced in factories owned by Sandowne Pharmaceuticals. There were boxes on the shelf in that lab with the address."

She showed me a picture of a shelf in the lab full of medical supplies, and zoomed in on a small part of the picture. In light blue print on a white box was written an address in Kenya.

I remembered the solar gliders we had found in use in Ethiopia when we went there. They were an Indrahui design but produced in Sudan.

Nicha said, "The companies buy the knowledge and blueprints, but they make everything here."

I asked, "Who sends them this material?"

"This is where it gets interesting," Thayu said. "When we were back in the shed, I did notice that there were some communications coming in from off-world, but they're not coming from the Exchange."

We both looked at her. Apparently, this was news to Nicha as well.

"Then where does it come from?" Nicha asked.

"There is a satellite in geo-stationary orbit. Maybe there is more than one, but this particular one seems to be dedicated to the Cartel and this region of the world."

"You need to give Amarru the coordinates."

"Yes." That was a very definite yes from Thayu.

"But I guess we don't have Exchange connectivity here?"

"Nope." What a surprise. "But maybe the information packets that they received contain enough information so that we can work out where the communication comes from. We may be able to find out."

"Someone will be here to take us to Cape Town later," Nicha said. "They have Exchange connectivity."

"Good," I said. "I will need as much of this information as possible for presenting to the Nations of Earth assembly. If Amarru can find out who the satellite communicates with even better."

I had my suspicions, of course, but it would be nice to see the hard evidence.

Some time after lunch, Devlin came to me with the message that there had been a change of plan and our pickup would not be here until the next morning.

I went to the front of the building to tell the lone police officer on duty at the desk, who was clearly not happy with this.

"I'm sorry, but we're dependent on the schedule of others." We were in a remote area, and most of the people on the register were in the south of the country, with the exception of Klaus and Jenny, but Amarru clearly wanted them to stay undercover.

"We cannot be seen to be partial," the officer said.

Sure. That was just a way of saying he was scared of the Cartel.

I looked at the virtually empty street through the barred windows, and wondered how many of the people passing by were spies from the Cartel hovering around and making threats.

"It seems to me that everyone in this town is afraid," I said.

He didn't respond. He looked quite young, although I tended to think that black Africans held their age much better than white people.

"Are there any employers in the town other than the game park?"

He shrugged. "There are the shops, but those people own everything. You can't get away from them."

"And you don't like it that we have some evidence they won't like?"

He was not inclined to say more. The fear of the Cartel was drummed into him. I could understand this, because his life was here and he needed to keep himself and his family safe.

"Just do me a favour and vote."

He laughed. "You think we have a free choice? You think voting is private? That they won't find out what we voted? They can see, because our identification is right there. They will just not send my vote across, because they own the network."

"What would make you feel safe enough to vote?"

He shrugged. "Even if I went to Cape Town and voted there, they'd find out. They own the network, so they will find out. There is no way to question the operation of the Cartel and be safe."

———

The police officers took us to the only hotel in town after a plain lunch of soggy sandwiches. Being out of their limited protection meant that we needed to provide our own, and also we lost whatever little connectivity Devlin had been able to restore. I hoped our contact wouldn't need to change the details of the pickup at the last moment.

Our three adjacent rooms looked out over a courtyard with overgrown garden beds and spaces for vehicles that looked to have been empty for a long time.

Business clearly wasn't booming.

Evi, Telaris, Reida and Deyu took turns standing outside, but if the Cartel watched us—and I had no doubt that they did—they kept quiet.

I sat on a little hard chair on the veranda while others inside our room continued to examine the data Thayu and Veyada had collected in the cellar lab.

The night was restless, with people traipsing in and out of the room, and others still hunched over their screens. The glow was annoying and the level of noise just high enough to keep me awake.

I also hadn't had a regular night's sleep since we left New Zealand, and my body was probably still on New Zealand time.

So I listened to the soft sounds with my face turned to the wall, pretending to be asleep, and wondering if I should help them, but knowing that they'd need to explain stuff to me, and we'd wake up even the people who were able to sleep.

Very early in the morning, Devlin shook my shoulder to announce, "We have located the coordinates of the origin of their information."

I sat up, rubbing my face.

Devlin continued, "The satellite in orbit is owned by some communication company that's probably owned by someone in the Cartel. We don't have enough connectivity to check that. But the incoming communication has the galactic coordinates embedded. It comes from Tamer."

Here was the evidence.

Damn it. Whoever had started this business in Tamer had been building this network for a long time. We had even accepted Tamerians as normal in Barresh.

In truth, Tamerians were people without the ability to think for themselves, who did mindlessly what a ruler ordered.

Who were the people behind Tamerians? I didn't *think* they

were directly related to the ancient Aghyrian ship. The Aghyrians had come across to me as being obsessed with perfection. They didn't like the Coldi because they thought them imperfect even if the Coldi were Aghyrian creations. Tamerians had turned out to be much less perfect than Coldi.

Tamer was governed under a sub-council at *gamra* because it had no native humans and none that had been there long enough to qualify as such. I should write to that sub-council and ask what was going on. They would probably laugh at me.

Did they know who was behind this? Did everyone know about this except us?

Here was another issue why Earth needed to join: without *gamra*, there was little the authorities could do to stop the people at Tamer experimenting on Earth. The idea of mindless zombies would frighten anyone.

The key points of my presentation were slowly working their way up in my mind.

We ate a breakfast of stale bread and some sort of spread that smelled funny and that most of us didn't want to touch.

Our contact picked us up around mid-morning, a surly Coldi man with a minibus that had seen better days. The fact that he was on the register meant that we could trust him, but I didn't feel terribly confident.

We spent most of the morning bumping along a badly maintained road through uninviting scrub country. We passed several guard posts, where surly militia guards slowed us down and talked to the driver but let us through. I had heard that the Cartel had long campaigned for "their" country in the northern half of South Africa to become a separate state, and it seemed a separate state already, if not in name.

The driver could only take us as far as Pretoria. That suited us fine because we disliked being dependent on others.

We booked the high-speed train to Cape Town and hung around for a few uneasy hours in the cafeteria in the station until the train left. People were watching us. Even I noticed the same people walk past several times, pretending to be looking at their readers, but probably taking pictures of us and sending them goodness knew where. In all the time we sat there, I did not spot a single Coldi person.

It was evening when the train left, and boarding time couldn't come soon enough. I was also glad that we'd hired cabins, because we could sleep, away from the prying eyes of whoever was watching us.

We ordered meals to be brought to our cabins. Both the service and the food were terrible, but we were safe in our little bubble.

We appointed guards—two at a time on each side of the narrow corridor—and tried to sleep as the train sliced through the night, speeding away from the unsafe zone.

———

I woke up very early, as pale blue light came in through the cabin's tiny window, to Nicha and Thayu talking. They were sitting hunched over a reader on the bottom bunk opposite me.

I raised myself on one elbow. "What's going on? Where are we?"

"Almost there," Nicha said. And indeed the train appeared to have slowed down. "We just regained some news coverage from non-local channels."

The news channels other than those approved by the Cartel.

I pulled out my reader and read while lying on my top bunk and holding it above my head.

I came into a world I barely recognised. I was used to the sensationalist headlines from Flash Newspoint, but even the normally staid World Newspoint had gone into a frenzy.

Headlines screamed:

Kazakhstan conflict instigated by off-Earth interests.

This covered the Zhori clan's mafia and the way they had controlled much of the rebel factions. After what I'd seen from Klaus and Jenny, I didn't think Zhori could still be classified as "off-Earth".

Another headline said:

We will be overrun.

The author went on to describe how people from *gamra* would be flooding to Earth and that they would "take our homes and jobs" just like they had done in Athens. Never mind that in Athens, many Coldi often did jobs no one else wanted to do.

I felt disturbed to see Fiona Davidson's face in some of the articles, being interviewed and fanning up this kind of paranoia.

Either these people didn't want or couldn't understand the concept of the non-confrontational Coldi society.

There were reports from people in the street shouting for the "No" vote. Riots, attacks on businesses owned by Coldi.

I searched, but couldn't find much campaigning for the Yes vote.

What was going on? Where were Margarethe's people? Where was Dharma?

A sense of horror came over me.

I needed to contact them urgently, but we were still in transit and I couldn't do much from the back of a taxi.

Evi had reserved accommodation in a hotel close to the airport from which we had a flight booked to Rotterdam at some ridiculous time the next morning. That was a measure of how remote Mr Kluysters' house was: it took us longer to get from his game park to Cape Town than it would take us to get to Rotterdam.

I wondered when Eirani, Karana and Ayshada were going to meet up with us. At the airport, probably. I wished I knew where they were—just a simple message that they were safe and all was still right with the world.

At the motel, Sheydu told us to wait outside while she, Evi and Telaris checked our three rooms.

They established that there were no bugs, but my team remained tense.

We were not in safe territory, Thayu said when I asked. That was security speak for unsecured areas, where a higher level of alertness was needed.

I let them do their thing and tried to find any of the positive news stories that Dharma had planned to broadcast about *gamra,* but it was like they, and Dharma himself, had vanished off the face of the planet.

What was going on?

I sent a message to Margarethe when Devlin said it was safe to do so.

We are coming. Have explosive evidence. Need to present it before the assembly.

She did not reply before we went to bed.

The motel was close to the airport, and it was noisy. We shut all doors and windows before we went to sleep. I was afraid of worrying through another sleepless night, but I was so tired that I didn't even wake up when Thayu came into bed.

There was a short note from Margarethe the next morning. It simply told me to see her when we got to Rotterdam. I guessed she was very busy, but I didn't particularly like it. The only contact I'd had with her during this visit was when she came to me with the bus when we were at the court.

Was there another problem?

I had no doubt that the Cartel would already have complained about our escape from the park to Nations of Earth, even if they had no leg to stand on. We had evidence that they'd tried to detain us in the lodge, even if the people who had shut the gate on us were just lowly employees.

The members of the Cartel had clout in this area, they knew how to complain and let the bureaucracy take the greatest possible amount of time to consider the case. They knew how to stall important discussions. They had the money to hire the best lawyers to get things their way.

But even if Devlin said there was supposed to be Exchange coverage, I couldn't reach Dharma, I couldn't connect with the Exchange. I couldn't even contact my father. I debated asking Devlin how he'd gotten onto Amarru, but wasn't sure I wanted to know the answer.

And Thayu, Veyada, Sheydu, Deyu and Devlin were frantically working in the other room, too busy to come to breakfast that I shared in one of the other rooms with Evi, Telaris, Reida and Nicha, all of them with guns next to them on the table.

Sheydu came into our room. There was a change of plan. Amarru was sending someone to pick us up.

I was surprised that Amarru would bring an Exchange craft here under the noses of the Cartel. I began to think something significant had happened, but we weren't going to find out until we were in Athens.

"This is not a secure area. People are spying on us," Sheydu said. "They will be following us. The register will lose one secured spot that we can't use anymore for a while."

"We have our tickets to Rotterdam, why not use them?"

Sheydu shook her head. "It wouldn't be safe. Not for us. Not for the other people on board."

15

———

I STARED AT HER. Was she really saying that the Cartel wanted to prevent us going back to Nations of Earth so badly that they'd take down a commercial flight?

But it had happened before, and would happen again, and while the cause of an accident could be determined, the culprits were not always easy to find, especially not in an area where communication was compromised at best.

Right. Shut up, Delegate.

It was essential that we make it to the assembly. I was starting to wonder if I'd be allowed to speak, and when I did, whether I could sway enough people to make a difference. If the Cartel controlled so much of the communication, then I could say what I wanted, but no one would hear it.

The most pressing problem appeared to be, not people's opinions, but getting those opinions to the news channels. And if the Cartel controlled communication in so much of the world, who was to say they wouldn't meddle in the voting process itself? In fact, I was pretty certain that they would.

So this exercise in trying to convince people was futile if we couldn't reach the people we needed to reach and make sure that people's votes counted.

Getting to Amarru's pickup spot involved another trip in a bus that arrived as the light was turning golden.

The driver was someone else from the register, a Coldi man quite advanced in age. He had the same weathered skin that I had seen in Jenny, atypical for Coldi. He wore no earrings, but had many tattoos on his arms and disappearing under his shirt, on his neck and the back of his shaven head.

I suspected that he, too, was Zhori.

He had introduced himself as "Jack". One thing I noticed was that these Coldi used local names and didn't use the last name Chen. He even spoke Coldi with a halting accent.

"Don't speak it much," he said by way of apology when I asked him about it.

"Yet you work for the register?"

"Seems the right thing to do." He shrugged. "Some don't like it, but many of us still have families . . . over there." He glanced at the sky. "We want to visit them occasionally. Or rather, we don't want to be denied the possibility to visit them, maybe one day when it becomes cheaper. We also don't want our families to be denied the chance to visit us."

In a way, "Jack" was more from Earth than I was.

Funny how these things became messed up.

I sat on the steps next to him and watched the scenery slide past. It was pretty here, and not terribly dissimilar to where my father lived. The road wound its way along the coast, with views over bays from headlands, passing through little sleepy surfing towns consisting of little more than a single street.

Coming through one such town, we passed a police station. Through the glass doors at the front I could see a bored officer sitting at the reception desk.

I had an idea. I could take the list of missing people back to Rotterdam with me and let authorities deal with it. I could also . . .

I said, "Can you stop here for a minute?"

Jack did, pulling into a parking spot in front of a restaurant. Business had closed, and the owner was stacking chairs.

I jumped from the bus clutching my reader, and ran along the footpath back to the police station.

Inside, I crossed to the counter and put my reader on top.

The officer gave me a strange look. "Can I help you, sir?"

"I don't know if you can help me, but you can definitely help a lot of other people. I have with me a list of people who have gone missing from all parts of this country and some adjacent countries. I also have a list with where these people are right now. I have given it to the local police, but they are too afraid to do anything. I'm about to leave the country, but I'd like to give this information to someone local so that there may be a chance that some of these people on this missing persons list will survive."

I showed him the lists on my reader.

He ran his finger along the line of missing people. "We've been looking for that one, and that one, and we'd given up on that one." He met my eyes. "Are you sure that you know where they are?"

"Any who can still be saved, who are still alive, can be found at the locations in the second document. I'm sending these to you now. I trust you will check them out, and if you happen to be intimidated by the size of the opponent, you will ask for assistance, and more assistance. Call your colleagues. Call the relatives of these people. Get them out."

He nodded, stunned into silence.

"Good luck. The hope of many families rests on you."

Then I left and sprinted to the waiting bus. Once I was inside, the door closed and we continued on. I returned to my seat, where Thayu was dozing and didn't appear to have noticed my little trip outside.

Some time after the sky had darkened to black, the bus turned off the road onto a dirt track, towards the ocean.

We stopped at a parking lot on top of a cliff. I suspected that during the day it would have a nice view, but now all we saw was darkness.

The cessation of movement from the bus woke everyone up. We lighted on the dusty ground, yawning in the crisp air.

The lookout was so quiet that we could hear the rumble of waves on the rocks at the bottom of the headland. Except for the glow of light coming from the bus at our back, it was pitch dark. The Milky Way stretched above us.

"There," Sheydu said, and pointed.

I could see the craft coming this time, only because I was looking over Thayu's shoulder and it showed up on her scanner. It only became visible to my eyes once it had landed on the patch of grass in front of us.

It was a smaller model Asto-built craft and, when the door opened, the glow of light from within showed the Exchange logo on the side.

We carried our bags from the bus to the craft.

The pilot was a woman I had not seen before, but she was Coldi from the Lingui clan—according to her earrings—and Lingui were often pilots. She was a typical middle-class Coldi from Asto: neat, tidy, pale-skinned and confident. Our driver seemed a little uncomfortable in her presence.

I thanked him and then we climbed on board.

The craft was a lot smaller than the ones we had previously used, not in the least because some people were already on seats.

As Nicha stepped in before me, a little voice squealed. Nicha ran up and scooped up his son in his arms. Ayshada's way of showing affection was to hammer people in the face, and for once, Nicha did not tell him to stop it. Eirani and Karana were also there.

It was a tight fit with all of us and our luggage, and not a seat remained free.

While the craft took off, stories were exchanged. Apparently Eirani and Karana had stayed at someone's beach house where the scenery was amazing, even if Karana thought—and Eirani did not contradict her—that the owners were rude.

Eirani was also not surprised to hear that our adventures involved rather more dangerous moments. She and Deyu—who had only half-heard the story—were curious about the concept of an elephant and the fact that such a clumsy-looking creature—that didn't even have any toes—could run so fast.

It was comforting to see that mutual curiosity had not died. If worse came to worst, I'd be happy to cut ties with Earth and live in Barresh. Well, not happy, because of my father, and my mind wandered off thinking about ways to convince him to come to live in Barresh with me.

As the craft flew through the night, one by one members of my team fell quiet and went to sleep.

As was typical, I was more awake than I'd been during the bus ride, and I spent some time checking the news.

World Newspoint was full of negative propaganda against *gamra*. Apparently, there was favouritism in the hiring of Coldi versus non-Coldi people in businesses owned by Coldi. This supported the "they're taking our jobs" argument.

I could find nothing about the Yes vote.

The referendum was now less than two weeks away and things were not looking good for Margarethe.

I tried to contact Dharma, but he still gave no reply.

Eventually, I fell asleep, and woke up when Thayu shook my shoulder. I was surprised that we were still flying with no sign of an imminent landing.

Thayu held her reader under my nose. "The Exchange analysed the data I sent from the lab."

She showed me the results from the files that we'd sent them from the police station.

Coldi were masters in making reports. Their pattern-detection was second to none. In addition, they loved making things pretty and organising them according to their natural flow. This was why they hand-wrote legal writs. It had to be pretty.

Even medical reports and this one was a work of art.

First there was a diagram showing where supplies came from: most of it was sourced from within Africa, but twenty-nine percent came from Asian countries and two percent from off-Earth. Not much, but it was important material, some chemical components and electronics.

It contained a table of the origin of the victims. As I had suspected, they were all from African countries where the Cartel held power, tabulated by the amount of debt that Cartel companies had bought from the governments. Little Cartel involvement in a country meant that few people went missing there. Big government debt bought meant that the list of people from there was long.

It showed a diagram with all the bits that went into a body before it was revived.

A diagram detailed what happened to the victims after their treatment was completed. First, they went to a rehabilitation clinic where they were thoroughly checked for bodily functions and brain activity. Then they went to a few weeks of schooling. After that, each person received an assignment, usually with a group, and then they carried out the assignment, which often involved killing people (thirty-two percent), helping militias with the setup of technology (twenty-four percent), or providing services that were needed (twenty-one percent). Those services would be identified first, and the brain implant would contain that knowledge.

I realised with a shock that Jemiro had been one of that group, likely having received the knowledge about Pengali only a day before we required it.

It was disturbing.

"We should show this to Lilona," I said.

"Yes." Her voice sounded angry and full of conviction.

———

We landed in Athens when it was just starting to go light.

Here was another night with only a little sleep, and that, interrupted. Travelling and working through the night was coming to be a habit.

Amarru had sent one of her guards to pick me up and so, while the team went for breakfast in the canteen on the top floor, I went with him, hoping that there would be some food in her office.

I'll save you some, Thayu said. We'd put our feeders back on and she was again picking up on my thoughts, now we were in the range of the Exchange.

The guard led me through the corridors to the lift. There was a good level of activity in the building already.

I felt like asking the guard what had happened in our absence, but he was one of the faceless, nameless Indrahui men that Amarru tended to favour and would probably not reply with anything useful. I was very happy that my own relationship with Evi and Telaris had moved on from that.

Amarru stood in front of the window in her office that looked out over the hazy city in the morning. The sky was cloudless, light blue with a pale pink tinge. It promised to be a hot day.

"There you are," Amarru said, while keeping her back to the door.

I went to stand next to her. "What are you looking at? Anything happening out there?"

She looked at me. Most Coldi were a bit shorter than me and she was no exception. In the time since I'd last seen her, she had dyed the tips of her shag-pile carpet hair purple. More like someone from Earth, less like a Coldi leader. Her voice was dark. "You mean, other than that a few people with a lot of money are buying off-world tech to scuttle the referendum?"

I was going to say things couldn't be as bad as that, but I could see from her face that it was.

She jerked her head. "Come."

No breakfast, then.

I wanted to remind her—damn, I was hungry—but clearly, saving the world had a higher priority than eating.

I followed her into the room next door where I had been once before, a few weeks ago, when she had shown me the parts of the Earth where the Exchange was losing coverage and control. Back then, it had been quiet in the room. Now, it was full of people, seated at rows of tables with readers and other equipment. Many of them looked up when we came in.

"What's going on here?"

"This is where the referendum will be won—or lost."

"But no one has started voting."

"No, but the enemies of freedom are attempting to black out as much of the world as possible. No one will know, but the information will have passed through their system and they will have altered it."

"What do you mean—altered?"

"Look at this." She went to one of the desks and touched the corner of a reader. After thumbing through a couple of menus, she brought two pieces of text in Isla on the screen. Both were letters, from a German government official to another about the election.

One of them said that he supported the yes vote, the other did not contain this paragraph, but ended with a bland sign-off instead.

"This was intercepted by our spies, and we've since found a lot more. We noticed this pattern when you brought it to our attentions with your communication from New Zealand."

"*My* communication?"

"Yes. Did you really write this?"

She flicked to another screen, with a letter that I'd written to

Lenka Trnkova. I recognised the text, but in the second-last paragraph, it said not to worry about the referendum, that we were going home to Barresh and that everything was arranged.

I did a double take. "I definitely did not write that."

She shook her head. "It seems they're using some form of artificial intelligence to pick out which parts of your message to change, because this is what you wrote."

She showed another letter, which said instead that I'd be in contact once we came back from New Zealand and that she needed to contact our mutual friend—meaning Dharma—to see if she could help him.

It rattled me. I'd written this from the kitchen table in my father's house, before we discovered the block. "So, their system read my letter, took out the bit it didn't like and replaced it with something else that not only changed the meaning of my letter, but still sounded like it came from me?"

She nodded, her lips pressed together. "This has been going on over the past few months, especially in the areas of the world where we are finding it hard to get communication."

Which, as I remembered, included Rotterdam. "Can your systems even do anything as sophisticated as that?"

"They can, but manipulation of communication is illegal if that's what you're suggesting that we do."

"Well . . ." I snorted. "Sometimes you need to fight fire with fire." I remembered a few occasions where I had very much done so. Letting my father-in-law loose on a rogue settlement in Ethiopia from orbit came to mind.

"Not that simple. We're bound by a number of strict laws from *gamra*."

"Certainly they would understand?"

"Manipulation of information is forbidden. It's one of the five core laws. It is why Exchange communication is open, because everyone can check. We have been put on warning status several times already. They don't like us and don't understand why we don't join." *They* being *gamra* and *us* being Earth, or at least the Coldi on Earth. I wasn't sure where I belonged in all this.

I said, "Threatening you isn't going to be very productive. You make attempts to uphold *gamra* law."

"I know, you don't need to tell me, but that's the way *gamra* works."

Which sadly, was true, and none more so than under the leadership of Marin Federza. He loved his rules.

"So if you can't manipulate information, what are you doing in here?" I glanced around the room. All the people had gone back to work on their screens. They were talking on earpieces and dragging lines across their screens so that they joined the big, earth-spanning network.

"In this room, we're trying to strengthen our network and weaken theirs, but it is a constant battle."

"How exactly does that work?"

"We have our ways." She always said that, and I had enough of it. Time had come to get to the truth, and I needed to know it now.

I took a deep breath. "This is not something I can defend in the assembly. So tell me, Amarru, because I really need to know this. When I speak to the assembly, I don't like being surprised with any nasty comments I can't answer because I know nothing of the subject. There are rumours that ever since the advent of computer chips in household equipment built on Earth, the Exchange has inserted its own routines into these chips during their design so that they can be called up to perform tasks for you. Is that true?"

"That is the network you see in operation here." Not really answering my question with an unequivocal *yes*. She *knew* that this was a difficult point.

My heart was hammering. I'd always suspected this and had never been brave enough to push for an answer.

I glanced at the people working at the desks. There had to be at least fifty, and the room looked like a control centre of a major operation, with faces lit from below with a blue glow.

"So . . . you're saying yes?"

"I don't think it is what you think it is, a vast machine that we can just plug in a question and get the answers."

"Then what is it?" To me, it was starting to sound like just that. The network that was projected in the middle of the hub room looked like that.

Amarru blew out a breath through her nose. "I'd hoped to avoid this conversation in this manner."

"Well, me, too, so that makes two of us."

"There is a lot of history associated with this and you have to see it within the historical framework. The first Coldi here were refugees and they were scared."

"Yes, but that was a long time ago." The first Coldi who came here, over a hundred and fifty years ago, were Zhori. They were refugees from the harsh rule of Edyana Vonayi. But there was no excuse for keeping their secret network hidden all that time.

"I still don't know that you understand. Those first years when the refugees moved into Athens and started their community were all about hiding and setting up warning systems. A couple of Zhori who had been rich merchants before they fled figured out a way to embed tracking modules into electronic equipment. At the time, a lot of it was being manufactured in Japan. With a bit of disguise, we can pass ourselves off as Japanese, and some people went to work in the factories and helped design electronics that were shipped all over the world. The aim was to build a security trigger network that would warn them when any ships from Asto came close. Of course that became obsolete when Edyana was killed and Mizha took over. But the network proved useful for other things."

"Such as listening in on communication?"

"That was a by-product, when people started to use satellite and wireless communication a lot."

"But you still listened."

"If you'd been handed the information, wouldn't you have used it? The Coldi on Earth were still being persecuted by a good number of people both on Earth and off. If you have a resource like that, you don't just give it up while you're ahead."

"Maybe not, but . . . damn it, Amarru, how am I going to defend this? People will find out and then you'll have the scandal of the century and turn public opinion against you. The yes vote will never win."

"I'm not sure you understand what we're doing here." Her voice held a serious tone that chilled me.

"I think you're manipulating communication and spying where, in the minds of the native people of Earth, you have no business spying."

Her expression hardened. "This system here is the only reason why there wasn't a complete collapse of worldwide communication a few months ago. You have seen how the Pretoria Cartel can selectively block out messages or change the content of them. They've been doing this wherever Dharma visits. They're capturing the names of the newly registered voters and sending them their propaganda. It's only once we've freed up those accounts that we can send the information Nations of Earth sends these people."

I must have been tired, because I'd known bits of this information before, but this was when the full implication hit me.

Amarru must have seen in my face that I understood. "Yes. If we don't use our system, no matter how little Nations of Earth will like it when they find out that we can do this, we will lose the referendum."

Was it even worth winning if there was going to be a huge blow-up about the existence of a spy network that could look into people's houses and their work places, their vehicles? "If we lose, it will be a blow, but we'll ramp up to try again as soon as we can." Although that might be years.

She shook her head. "If that happens, Earth will most likely lose the Exchange as well, because *gamra* will recall us."

Another shock. "Seriously, after all those years the Exchange has been here? Wouldn't they keep you on provisional status like Indrahui?"

"They wouldn't. The *gamra* assembly will judge that there is no point in staying in a world that has decided it's not interested in joining. That was always part of the deal to legalise the Exchange in the first place: that they would join eventually."

That was something that shook me. "You would leave? Really?"

"We'd have no option. I know the Exchange used to operate illegally in the beginning, but those times are over."

"But that will just drive people to whatever the Cartel wants as alternative. Heck, that Aghyrian ship is probably cooking up something and handing out the bits of data to various groups of people who are angry for them to create havoc. Like whoever is at Tamer."

"Yup."

"Oh, fuck."

"So this is why we've been pulling out all our tricks."

"Maybe, but it's going to backfire when it becomes widely known."

She let a tense silence lapse. Damn it, I hated the idea of confronting Amarru, but she would *have* to come clean about this spy network, sooner rather than later. I wasn't sure that exposing it was up to me. It would not make me any friends in Athens, that was for sure. But they had to understand that this could not go on.

I wasn't sure where I stood with Amarru anymore. Did she work for Asto or for the Zhori clan? Who was her superior? Had she gone rogue, looking for an association to align with?

I pushed uncomfortable thoughts of an alignment of loyalties away. Those situations never went without dead bodies, and we could do without those.

Change of subject. "And are you making any progress?"

She sighed, tension visibly falling from her. "We're trying hard. We're especially trying hard to stay within *gamra*'s own rules, but we've been losing ground every day. New voters that Dharma is recruiting aren't registered. Communication is disrupted, documents are changed, messages erased. Most of the time we can't even reach Dharma."

"How much does Margarethe know about this?"

"Probably not as much as she should."

"Have you spoken to her?"

"Yes, but the security around her is nervous and I'm not sure how much I can trust it."

I saw the ominous look on her face: they were also losing control over Rotterdam.

"Are these people infiltrating the Nations of Earth administration?"

She laughed, not in a happy way. "They were always in Nations of Earth in the first place. Maybe they weren't affiliated with the Pretoria Cartel; maybe they're still not affiliated with them. But they're fine with what the Cartel is doing or don't see the potential harm. The Cartel's aims and theirs are enough aligned that they are happy to support them, and they can't see the dangers. This referendum cannot be won without any major upheaval."

And creating that upheaval, clearly, was up to me.

Me and my big mouth.

Me, who didn't go to school with the old guard, never played their games, never went to their dinner parties and didn't speak their language.

In normal cases, I would rely on *gamra* and their technology and communication, but we couldn't. Or I wouldn't. I'd be damned if I used the spy network to win the election.

"Well." I blew out a breath. "I've been asked to make a presentation to the assembly and will present the data on Tamerians to the full assembly. It should create some stir and change some minds." I hoped.

But that was all I could think of at that point. And chances were that it wouldn't be enough.

16

I MET UP WITH the rest of my association after I left Amarru's office.

While I ate the noodle salad Thayu had saved for me, I informed them of the things Amarru had told me. The expressions were dark around the table.

I wasn't sure they cared about Earth joining *gamra* in the same way I did, but they did care about losing entities from *gamra* and they cared about Earth because I did. They also understood how the Pretoria Cartel's blocking activities could reflect badly on *gamra* and the Exchange. And they knew of the danger posed by the Tamerian activities which might or might not be related to the Aghyrian ship.

"So what should we do?" Nicha asked me.

"In the short term, I can only stick to the plan: I will go the assembly and give that talk on what we discovered. We should keep our eyes open for information and people that we may be able to use. Trust no communication."

No communication meant especially no feeders because that communication was not encrypted. Feeders had a very short range, but they tapped into more extensive networks. I had already taken mine off, and I didn't mind. I was not a great fan of feeders.

"You said: in the short term. Is there a long term?" Sheydu asked.

"No. We have two weeks. I want everyone to think about what else we could do. It has to be quick, it has to be legal and, no, it can't involve the Asto military."

"I was afraid you'd say that," Sheydu said. "I hear that you didn't always have these objections in the past."

Funny she should remind me of that. "It was a different time and a different situation. I would have strongly resisted that action had the target been the property of local people, as is the case now. The Cartel is manipulating communication, but I can't see how we can prove that to enough people for it to have the desired effect in the short time we have. I'm not even sure that if we can prove it, most people will understand the seriousness of the matter. They will only see that because of Amarru's system, we are equally guilty. Trying to blame the Cartel of manipulating communication will never stand up in our defence. Mostly, I'm not interested in proving what the Cartel did wrong. That will be something for the lawyers. I'm interested in an action that will stop or circumvent their communication blocks so that the election can be held fairly."

Sheydu said, "We can ask Asha—"

"No. There will be no military action."

"—Not even to take out that satellite?"

A satellite. A clean shot, in deep space.

That was a tempting thought. Nobody on Earth would notice except the Cartel, and they couldn't complain publicly, because the satellite in question was not supposed to exist.

But I was sure that the people who operated that satellite would know about the *gamra* laws and would be the first to run to *gamra* to protest. They might win, too.

I needed some other brilliant idea about how to break the block that did not involve shooting anything out of orbit.

But my mind was empty. I knew one thing: the solution was unlikely to come from any Coldi technology, because it was too intertwined with Earth technology and was already corrupted. Bringing attention to that would open up a can of worms of unprecedented magnitude and the discussion might not go in our favour.

I wanted to go to Rotterdam on the train, but Amarru said that there were security issues with ground transport. She could guarantee a flight in the afternoon. She also knew this because of the network and because of the register. She had suggested safe flights to me since I started in the job, so I couldn't even claim ignorance.

So we had the best part of a day to kill. I could, of course, talk to advisors and more advisors, and answer messages with the same text over and over, but there would be enough time for that later. I needed ideas and I needed them now.

Veyada said he needed to do some work. The strange way that he said it and Sheydu's suspicious glance made me wonder whether he was going to meet up with Mereeni instead. I let him be. Veyada had been a bit insecure lately and I was sure we'd hear of any changes in arrangements when he was ready.

Nicha wanted to sleep. Ayshada was already out cold on his lap. Eirani and Karana had expressed interest in a tour of the building. I told Devlin that he could go with them. Evi and Telaris wanted to sleep as well. There would be enough work at strange hours for them in the coming days.

Having heard of elephants—although not from Veyada himself because he remained sore about the subject—Deyu wanted to see them, so she and Reida were going to the zoo. Sheydu would go with them.

"Let's go for a walk," I said to Thayu. "Just the two of us. I need some space to think." And a change of scenery to come up with an idea.

We went to the ground floor foyer of the building, where I hired a taxi driven by a local young man. I asked him to take us the harbour front at Piraeus.

By now, it was almost lunchtime.

The day was sunny and quite hot, but that bothered only me.

The quayside was full of restaurants and stalls where people sat in the shade of olive trees or under umbrellas. Food from a wide variety of nationalities was being served. Over the many years, Athens had been a little enclave where the effects of conflicts in the world had been felt, but conflict itself had never penetrated. As a consequence, the city was a melting pot of refugees: from Turkey and further to the east, all the way to Pakistan; from central and eastern Africa; from parts of Europe that were now underwater; and most recently from Egypt.

We walked hand in hand along the quay where yachts, cruise ships and fishing boats lay moored. A lone fisherman was checking his nets.

As we walked by the restaurants, shops and the various street businesses, I wondered how they were going to be affected by the referendum. I wondered how they would vote. There was no sign of politics anywhere. It looked like this little enclave was one of the slow places on Earth: a forgotten pocket of resistance in a world where technology had not penetrated. Did they even know of the fight raging over their heads? In the same city even?

Did they know that if the referendum was defeated, their existence might be threatened, since the strictly patrolled border of the enclave would open and everyone could come in as they pleased? Did they know that all the Coldi people who were sitting at restaurants, walking along the street, people who worked for them or gave them jobs, would disappear? They would go underground elsewhere or return to Asto, or, if that was not an option, they would go elsewhere altogether.

We came to an authentic Greek place that served strong coffee, where we had been on occasion. The owner, a woman with an infectious laugh, bushy hair and a large bosom and hips, used to know me and Nicha, and even further back, when I came here with Inaru. Damn, I had not thought of her for so long.

Thayu and I sat down at one of the little tables outside.

"You're very quiet," Thayu said.

I blew out a breath. "I wanted to go somewhere I could think about something that we can do that might have a remote chance of being successful."

"I take it that your talk with Amarru did not go well this morning?"

"The referendum is headed for a disaster. The Cartel controls communication, we can't contact Dharma, large parts of the world won't be able to vote, and there is no time to prove that the Cartel is doing this and convince the court—who are all Cartel stooges anyway—that anything is wrong. I really don't want to authorise your father to shoot that satellite out of orbit, and I doubt it would solve the problem anyway. We desperately need an idea that will turn the situation around. I'd hoped to get some thinking space away from the Exchange, but all that happens is that I remember that I've been to this or that restaurant before, with whom and what they said. It's all just thoughts about the past."

"Then maybe that is where you need to find the solution."

I met her eyes. Thayu was a reserved type of person and did not normally offer deep thoughts. It struck me that this was a strange remark from her. "What do you mean?"

"I don't know. It's just something I thought."

Thayu never, ever, "just" thought something. She was likely to be considering, mulling over something that she might tell me later, hopefully in time for me to do something about it.

The owner came to bring our coffee. She gave me a sideways look, and then looked again. "Have I seen you before?"

"You remember me?"

"You do look familiar."

"I used to come here a lot more often. I think your name is Ania?"

"Yes, it is. How long ago was this?"

"Oh, years." I always got confused. Years in Barresh were much longer than Earth years. I was fine with remembering months, but could never remember which year things had happened. It was . . . 2121, right?

"Oh," she said, squinting at me. "Maybe I was wrong."

"I had much shorter hair then."

"I remember that there were not as many Exchange people back then, and some of the restaurants used to serve them in separate areas. We didn't want to do that, but the city council said that we must, and we had to keep track of everything they ate and how much they spent."

"Whatever was that for?" I had neither noticed nor known about such a thing.

"They wanted to make sure that Exchange people didn't get money they shouldn't have. I know we were all very suspicious. I mean—look at this place now." She spread her hands.

About half the tables around us were occupied, two of them by groups of Coldi. The two groups amounted to more people than all other patrons combined. At the restaurant next door sat another three groups of people who were Coldi.

"If they weren't here, we would have no business," Ania said. "Many people here would have no customers, because no one else in the world cared about us when we had it tough." She nodded to Thayu. "Enjoy your coffee."

"What was that about?" Thayu asked when Ania walked back to the kitchen.

"Those are the type of people we need to appeal to. We need to make sure that all these people vote."

"You should ask her if she's registered."

True.

I sipped from my coffee, watching Ania stack cups on the counter. Then I put my cup down and went up to her.

Her eyebrows rose. "Is there a problem? Can I help you with anything else?"

"No, but if you will forgive me the question, Ania . . . have you registered to vote?"

She frowned. It was probably the question she had least expected.

"Well . . . that's for . . . you know, educated people. White class."

"It's not. It's for everyone."

Her frown deepened.

"Has no one asked you to register?"

"No." She shook her head.

"You said you'd be out of business without the Exchange."

"Oh yes, that's for sure."

"There is a real chance, if the referendum is defeated, that the Exchange will have to leave."

Her eyes widened. "I didn't think it was as serious as that."

"It is. Could you register and tell all the people in the street and your family and friends to do the same?"

"Oh. I wouldn't even know where to begin. I don't have one of those fancy readers."

"Use mine."

I went back to the table to get it and then guided her through the process. I had assumed it was simple, but it was not for her, but eventually we got through. And then I wondered that since she didn't have a reader, how was she going to see the documents that would now be put into the account? I explained the two sides, and then told her that since she didn't have a reader, she would need to find a voting station.

I had to look it up, but it turned out that any mail delivery centre took votes, but only on the day of the referendum and the day before.

"I know where it is. My brother used to be a postman. I will do it."

Yes, but how many people would not bother? Had it always been this difficult to register? Had it always been primarily for White citizens?

I spoke to Thayu about this on the way back to the Exchange. "It looks like it's been set up this way to make it difficult for people to vote. I wonder what Dharma has been doing. Literally collecting people's contacts one by one?" I knew he had a whole army of people ready, but still.

"But you were just saying that he had communication problems?"

Yes, he did, and this way, the Cartel were trying to stifle a process that was already hard enough.

Seriously, had Margarethe thought we'd *win* this election?

———

So we went back to the Exchange building without a plan.

We weren't going to use the Exchange to travel to Rotterdam, of course, but we needed to collect our things and the rest of the team in order go to the airport. Our flight was in the late afternoon.

We found everyone up and in the process of packing. Thayu and I checked our bags, but there was little to be done, because everything was already packed.

We took the taxi to the airport. The cheerless guards and airport security let us through their respective checkpoints without a hitch.

It was a normal commercial flight and the trip was uneventful.

My team studied the news; Sheydu spoke to Deyu and Reida in a low voice. I had noticed her doing a lot of teaching since the three of them had been travelling together. To be honest, I felt like Sheydu—who worked under Thayu—was poaching the pair for herself, and Nicha seemed to be fine with that, but it did mean he would soon need a new pair of *zhayma*s to make up for their loss. And my team would expand yet again, a common problem of someone whose standing in Coldi society was growing. I wasn't sure how much I wanted it to keep growing, because there was only so much I could keep up with.

On top of that, I really needed to solve my financial issues. More team members would mean more money spent. Eventually the expense was going to be worth it, but when we got home, I needed to put some thought into how we could sell some of our skills, or into which type of business I could invest in order to stop the bleed of money from my accounts. It was not that I didn't think I could do it, but that finance bored the crap out of me. While I could outsource accounting, I had to make the decisions myself.

I spent most of the flight reading and preparing my speech. I had written some of it at my father's house, but had forgotten most of what I wanted to say in South Africa, and as it turned out, some major things needed to be changed. Also, a report came in from the New Zealand police about the autopsy done on the four men who had attacked us in the bay. All four were Tamerians, as I had expected.

I also kept an eye on the South African news.

First an item came up about a police raid in the north of the country.

The next report said, *Number of missing people discovered in warehouse raid,* and this was further expanded to, *Over 100 missing person cases solved.*

Other news services in the world also took up the story. It seemed there was a special database for photos of news events, because not all of them used the same photos. Most showed the outside of the warehouse and office building where the people were found, but one or two showed the more gruesome pictures of ill and emaciated people in beds, waiting for the "treatment" that was going to save them.

Then I came across an article with a photograph of a familiar face: it was Charlie Awaba in his wheelchair next to a hospital bed that contained another man who was little more than a bag of bones, his emaciated hand holding Charlie's.

The caption stated, *"He's my brother," Charlie Awaba said. "He will come home with me. He may not have long to live, but he will live it with his family."*

My eyes briefly misted over. The skeleton-like figure reminded me of my mother. I remembered spending a lot of time in the hospital back then. Those days would always be part of my life.

I collected the photos I wanted to use for my presentation, a combination of news stories and my own. I used part of the report from Jemiro and the report from the New Zealand police. I'd use Lenka Trnkova's findings about the nameless, faceless assassins. I'd show pictures of the boxes of medicines we'd found in the warehouse in the game park.

Thayu sat next to me, staring into the distance, but I didn't miss how she was reading on my screen. At one point, she said, "You should also talk about the attack on Marin Federza's apartment by Tamerians. It will show them that it's a problem not just this world faces."

Yes, I had almost forgotten about that attack. "That's a good point. I will mention it. These people are the enemy of us all, Earth and *gamra* alike, and we cannot fight them if we don't fight together."

In Rotterdam, we had booked in the normal hotel. I hadn't been there for a while, but the staff still knew me.

We got the top-level suite, which consisted of three bedrooms and a sitting room. In times past, when I first came here, I would stay in the cheapest room they had available, and now we got the most expensive one. This trip never ceased to remind me of the fact that I had become a fairly important player, and that it was probably in my power and ability to do something outrageous that would upset the Cartel's hold on communication, if I could just think of what it would be. Something that would not pander to any of the Cartel's demands, including arranging that meeting, because I could not see that leading anywhere good.

Devlin started setting up the communication hub in the hallway. He appeared to have taken on the role as the team's hardware specialist. Telaris helped him, while Evi arranged our luggage. Eirani and Karana took a bedroom with Nicha, Ayshada and Deyu.

Ayshada was filthy and hungry and needed to go to bed.

I checked in briefly with Devlin. A fair number of messages had arrived for me, all of them from Nations of Earth. I thought of Amarru's words about losing contact with Rotterdam.

It was true. I used to be able to speak with Amarru from here, and found it hard to get through these days. Amarru either chose to remain silent except for emergencies, or she could not get through either.

I was filled with a sense of foreboding. This really had been going on for quite a while and we hadn't noticed or thought it serious.

My speech was not until tomorrow morning; and, after a quick dinner that the hotel staff brought up from the kitchens, I kept working. I would speak to the full assembly, my second-ever time of doing so. I felt restless.

I asked Eirani to get my uniform ready, but she had already done so. It was warm enough to wear the thin *gamra* shirt and I would be going in full blue dress. Eirani would need to do my hair tomorrow morning.

As usual when getting ready for a big event, I slept poorly. I kept going over all the things I intended to say, knowing that I had rarely given a more important speech in my entire career.

17

———————

I **GOT UP REALLY EARLY.** Thayu was still asleep when I tiptoed out of the room to the hall, only to find Devlin and Telaris already up. They were at the communication hub, looking at something on a screen.

"Anything going on?" I asked, feeling a sense of dread coming over me.

"The news is that there is unrest in South Africa," Devlin said.

"In Cape Town?"

"No. Pretoria."

I went to look over his shoulder. His reader's screen displayed pictures of angry mobs of people outside the head office of Sandowne Pharmaceuticals.

The article said,

No one has yet heard from Sandowne's reclusive owner, Minke Kluysters, who is said to have personally assured many of the contributors that the experiment was all above the table.

Wait. "What is this about? Contributors?"

"Yes, this crowd is not the usual crowd of rabble," Telaris said. He, too, so rarely voiced a remotely political opinion that it was worth noting when he did. "You see, these people are all well-off and neatly dressed."

They were, too.

I kept reading.

Apparently there was some dispute over investment loans made to Sandowne that the investors wanted to know about, after the missing people were found.

"We were assured that everything they did was legal and there was no improper experimentation on humans," one man was recorded as saying. "That was clearly a lie. This company has been involved in foul experimentation, and has deceived us. I don't want to be involved in this project anymore. I want my money back, paid with interest, plus all the payments we've been due."

Nicha also came out of his room and had a look at the news, balancing Ayshada on his arm.

"How likely would it be that these people have a fair bit of influence?"

He was right. Ultimately it would take people from all walks of life to make a difference. After assuming we'd lost the White vote already, this was an encouraging sign, even if only a very small one.

We still hadn't heard from Dharma, and we faced having to go to the election without the benefit of the work he had done.

The others got up, too, and breakfast arrived on a trolley. The hotel did quite a decent Coldi-style breakfast, with spicy mushrooms and roast prawns on skewers. There was a large pile of pancakes for those who were so inclined, and a big, hot, steaming jug of coffee, rich and black.

While I ate, I looked through my speech and Eirani did my hair.

I had requested to speak to Margarethe, but did not hold any hope that the request would be granted, and there was predictably no reply. I would have to use one of our personal channels, although I was not sure that they still worked or were secure. All our correspondence had been handled by her staff.

Thayu went into our bedroom and came back fully dressed in *gamra* security uniform, with armour and guns. The loops on her belt held her weapon. Sheydu and Nicha were already walking around in very similar gear. Veyada changed into his white gown and Reida and Deyu wore simple black with armour and one weapon each. They looked proud. As usual, Evi and Telaris completed our group. They were the most heavily armed of all. Evi's weapon was so large that he needed to sling it across his back. I wondered if that was necessary, but who was I to ask?

A minibus came to pick us up from the hotel. Driving through the city, I didn't notice anything unusual indicating the lack of communication. We usually had some Exchange coverage here. If anything, security seemed more lax, or maybe this was just because my most vivid memories of this place were from the aftermath of the attack on President Sirkonen.

A steady stream of people were filing into the marble-pillared building of the assembly. Some were delegates, but most were journalists or administrative staff.

The bus dropped us off at the main entrance. We attracted quite a bit of interest while walking up the stairs to the building.

The foyer was filled with a buzz of voices, and people congregated around a table where coffee was being served.

I had to meet someone for a brief about the equipment and rules of the assembly floor. This employee was a stern woman who told me that she'd meet me at the entrance of the hall in twenty minutes.

In that time, I was able to grab some coffee. While I stood in the queue, waiting for the staff member to serve the woman in front of me, I spotted a very familiar figure walking across the hall: a slender, dark-haired woman whose infectious smile used to warm my heart. She wore a dark business suit, a comm pack clipped to the back of her waist band and was talking to someone via an earpiece attached to her left ear.

Eva.

She saw me, too. Her eyes widened. She stopped and turned off the earpiece, and came towards me.

I cursed myself. While I had often wondered how she was, and I'd been toying with the idea of contacting her and asking, now, mere minutes before I'd have to give the speech of my life, was not the time for discussions about what a jerk I had been to leave her.

"Cory."

I'd forgotten how small she was, how slender and delicate. I was disturbed to see flecks of grey hair at her temples.

"You look . . ." She spread her hands and let them sink again.

I filled in the rest of the sentence. *Like an alien? Like one of them?*

I asked, "How are you?"

"I'm good, thanks."

"What are you doing here?"

"Doing my job. I work as political consultant."

"So you did finish your degree." I felt as awkward as hell, and yes, that was a stupid thing to say.

"Did you ever think I wouldn't?"

"Of course I didn't think that." Yes, I had. I had often wondered if Eva only did her degree because I wanted it, or because she wanted to stay in the diplomatic circuit. She had never struck me as an ambitious person.

She bridged the uneasy silence. "So, what are you doing with yourself now? You're all . . . dressed up nicely."

"I'll be addressing the assembly today."

Her eyes widened. "You will? The agenda says 'Executive representative of *gamra*'. Is that you?"

"I certainly didn't come up with that title, but I guess that's me. I work as security and diplomatic consultant for Ezhya Palayi detached to *gamra*."

She smiled, awkwardly. "That's a bit of a mouthful."

I glanced over my shoulder, where my team was waiting for me. I really should go into the hall and prepare.

"Look, can I buy you something after the session? Can we have lunch or something?"

She glanced aside. "Yes, maybe. I think that should be fine."

"Meet you here, then?"

"Yes, yes, sure."

"I'll see you then."

She reattached her earpiece, and scurried off, apologising to someone on the other end.

I grabbed my coffee and joined Thayu and Nicha, who had seen and heard everything.

"She looks nervous," Thayu said. She knew who Eva was, and, being Coldi, had no problem with my talking to her.

"Yeah," Nicha said. "But she was always a bit like that. Really keen to please everyone."

That was also true.

I couldn't see Eva in the crowd anymore.

We progressed through the crowd to the hall entrance. A line of security guards was checking the passes of the first eager beavers to get into the hall.

I had been prepared for the increased security. Thayu and Veyada took off their weapons so they could come with me. The others would stay outside the hall. This was expected and planned. Still, Sheydu especially thought it extremely rude to separate a high-ranking person from his security.

Both Thayu and Veyada had to subject themselves to a weapons scan and I was a bit surprised that the guards didn't find any on Thayu, disappointed even. I still didn't think that it meant she had none, but we weren't using feeders so she couldn't laugh at me for thinking that.

The stern female employee met me on the other side, where she stood talking to a young male employee who carried a crate of router boxes, microphones and earpieces.

We walked through the hall, where it was still relatively quiet, and were met by a woman who showed me through the process I was meant to follow. She introduced me to the staff who were going to deal with the projection of my photos. The sight of my reader raised some eyebrows, but one man said there would be no problem. He asked me to turn it on and then fiddled with some of his equipment. The large screen in the hall flickered and came up with my login menu.

"Thank goodness," the woman said. "Someone knows what they're doing."

He grinned and then gave me a sincere look. "Good luck, Mr Wilson. Everyone is keen to hear you."

His nametag said *Roban Wisher.* He was clearly someone familiar with and sympathetic to *gamra.* Maybe he had grown up in a mixed household like me. Maybe he had a Coldi partner. Little things like this gave me hope.

With all this set up, I was directed to a fenced-off area at the front of the delegates' seating. A man brought a jug of water and cups. Thayu was looking around the vast hall, squinting at the ceiling, probably wondering where bugs or weapons could be hidden. There had once been an attack on this hall. I'd been nine and living in the compound with my father. The attackers had been anti-*gamra* terrorists. Even my father's wedding to Erith, the next year, had been interrupted by a heckler.

These days, the enemies of *gamra* had much more sophisticated methods. They were in this hall, even if they weren't here physically. They listened to what we said, and if they didn't like it, they made sure that no one else would hear it. The world was so terribly dependent on electronic communication, and there was no fallback for when that communication didn't work.

At least at *gamra* they had the Trader network, and they had been given greater autonomous powers since the Exchange went out a few years ago and it took them weeks to re-establish contact.

Over shorter distances, the Trader couriers were the last resort and safest delivery method. Even Margarethe had used them. A Trader Guild courier delivered a hand-written calligraphed message on a pretty piece of paper. Very old-fashioned. Very safe.

People now started to file into the hall, both from the back doors and the front, where I had come in.

Each continent had their own seat allocations. The number of delegates varied according to population and contribution to special Nations of Earth committees. This was a plenary session, and all those delegates were allowed to attend. This hall was going to be jam-packed.

I was wondering if they were truly interested, or if I was merely a curiosity and should have come with a betanka drum and some players.

My muscles were tense. I had to force my leg to stop jiggling, and then wanted to bite my thumbnail, which was worse than jiggling, so I jiggled my leg anyway. Thayu put her warm hand on my knee.

The hall was full and guards shut the doors. People sat down and lights dimmed.

Doors opened on the other side of the hall, and Margarethe came out, accompanied by two men, neither of whom I'd seen before. That was strange. I thought her personal secretary was much older than either of these two men. They looked more like bodyguards, to be honest.

She sat down. The men sat on either side of her, and both

looked around the audience. I was probably right to think *body-guards,* but where was her secretary?

She opened the meeting. I was surprised to hear that they had called the session early especially for me. Margarethe said that the assembly should hear my information and that they would be getting a copy of my speech.

Then she gestured me forward.

I had spoken to the full *gamra* assembly a few times. Less often than one would think. It was a similarly huge hall, at times filled with a partially hostile crowd.

I was always tense when coming up to speak, but never had I felt ill with nerves. So much hung in the balance, and part of me suspected that my speech came too late to change any of it.

I put down my reader on the dais, and stared at it, afraid that my mind was going to blank out on me.

I took a deep breath, and another. Touch the corner to bring the projection to life. One thing at a time.

By this time, the applause had died down.

I glanced at Thayu; she nodded. Veyada nodded, too.

And so I began my recount of all the things that we had discovered, not just in New Zealand or South Africa, but in the past few years in Barresh. I spoke of the Tamerians who had attacked Marin Federza's apartment in Barresh. I spoke of the communication block around the court, and how we had captured a Tamerian-type person in The Hague on a trip to the beach. I showed them what we had found on the man's reader, the contacts, the pictures of the shed in the Cartel's game park in South Africa that turned out to be the origin of some of the Earth-produced Tamerians. I asked the chairman if it was all right to show some of the disturbing images. She said it was, and a blanket of silence fell over the assembly while I showed the—rather graphic—images of how these people were revived, including the image of the organs floating in the tanks.

At this point, a man in the audience objected. "Is it really necessary to show this?"

Several people agreed with him and a murmur spread through the hall. The sophisticated, cultured diplomats didn't like these graphic photos? Good.

The chairman nodded to me.

"I think it's more than necessary to show these images, because without them, you will not be able to comprehend the full extent of the disgusting atrocities committed. These people were poor and ill —too poor and ill to raise money for treatment, and too poor and ill to raise their voice in protest. It is time that the truth is told about what has been going on in Africa and other countries around the world."

I told them that we'd had a Tamerian in our team without realising it. I showed them the report on Jemiro, that he was artificial, essentially a resurrected corpse—some people showed real discomfort about this—and then I told them that Tamerians were not a population group. They were a tool used by people who needed people to blindly carry out orders. I showed them the picture of the carnage in the pristine bay in New Zealand and details from the report on the autopsy of those men.

"The Tamerian reconstructed—zombie, if you like—agents are disposable. They have no identities and no voice. Most of them can't communicate. They kill themselves in preference to being arrested. Or they simply disappear. We have seen it in Barresh, and Earth has seen this many times over. No one was ever blamed for the killing of the Nations of Earth's Court prosecutor Conrad Martens. Similarly, there are many political murders, especially in Africa, where no convictions were ever made. If perpetrators were caught, they were people without ID, without names, untraceable even through countless police searches. Tamerians are from off-world, but this variety are people from Earth. They are produced from the many brothers, fathers and sons who go missing both in African countries and other poor regions of the world. Why poor regions? Because the makers know that poor people won't protest, and if they do, no one will listen. This has been happening all over *gamra* as well. The 'translator' we hired came from a fallen family who were not in a position to register their complaint. The people who are involved with Tamerians operate by stealth, by staying under the radar."

Some murmuring broke out. I waited for it to calm down.

"Who are these people who commandeered Tamerians? On Earth, they are the Pretoria Cartel, a powerful business lobby group which adheres strictly to the free market principles of Lucas

Wright. In a nutshell, they want no rules. No rules means no laws. It means free trade of everything including weapons. It means Kazakhstan. It means Ethiopia. It means lawlessness. It means that if any of you, in any of your countries, suffer an act of violence through people from off-world, you have no means to bring them to justice. It means *gamra* won't be keen to offer help in solving the problem. Moreover, it means no voice for the poor countries whose debts the Cartel have bought. It means exploitation of workers, indenture or slavery. Because of all these things, and many more, I strongly urge you to advise your constituents to vote for joining *gamra* and do so urgently. The Pretoria Cartel is working to stop fair elections. The sooner you notify people in charge of the elections, the better."

With that, I'd finished the speech. In the murmur that broke out in the hall, the speaker asked for calm.

I was not happy with how that had gone. Not because I'd screwed up things, but most of the audience seemed distant and passive, as if they didn't care or had already made up their mind.

The speaker asked for questions from the audience.

Someone called out, and there was some commotion as spotlights shifted and another microphone came on.

A man yelled, "I have a question."

The accented male voice was disturbingly familiar, and there in the spotlight sat Piotr Zbrowsky, Eva's father. Eva sat at the table with him. Right, that was how she came to work here, and also why she was so nervous. I should have thought of that earlier. Eva had always been terrified of her father.

He took the headpiece that an employee handed him. "You speak as if there are two options. Yes means we join this deplorable organisation of yours, no means we are therefore evil and must run with the Pretoria Cartel. You have not mentioned the other 'no' option: that we tell all these people from other worlds to pack up and leave. We have enough problems of our own to indulge in trying to solve theirs. We are not interested and your people can stay away as far as we're concerned."

"It is impossible to turn back the clock. Those people are here and this has become their home. We're talking about second and third generation immigrants."

"Deport them!" someone yelled.

A couple of protesting voices drowned him out.

The speaker called for calm and gestured to me in order to continue.

"You can stick your head in the sand and pretend none of this is happening, but Nations of Earth has been doing that for the past thirty years and it hasn't worked out so well. Thirty years ago, Ezhya Palayi came to this very assembly and spoke to you about accepting his people and making steps forward to join *gamra*, and in thirty years, nothing has been done about that invitation. Meanwhile, numerous conflicts and situations could have been prevented or greatly reduced by membership. The issue is coming to a head, because there is now a group trying to move into the vacuum. It is not a benevolent group. It is not a group that works in any interest other than their own. It's not a group that Nations of Earth exerts any control over, or even knows exactly who they are. They are blocking communication, even in this very hall, and by blocking it they are trying to rig the referendum. They don't want us to join, and they don't bank on us having the knowledge and resources to survive on our own, so they're courting with unknown entities in deep space."

"We survived by ourselves for thousands of years."

An applause went up, from what I could see mostly the European section of the hall. Yes, those were all the old-school diplomats, all those people I'd met at dinner parties with Eva's family. None of them were ever going to change their mind, because they hadn't done so in the past thirty years.

The referendum was not about those people. It was about all the people who weren't in this hall, the ones Dharma was trying to sign up to vote.

"We may have survived for that time, but I have shown you why those times are never coming back."

"Let the people speak," Piotr Zbrowsky said.

Again, applause.

"I'll be happy to let the people speak when they can speak fairly and their votes are not interfered with."

"I'll grant you that. It has to be fair."

"Yet even as we speak, people are manipulating the vote."

"The Exchange with their spying devices."

Ouch, Amarru. "I can prove to you that these people are manipulating communication, that these same people are speaking to others on a non-*gamra* world. If only we could get a fair process, if only we could be certain that no one is interfering with the voting data, then I'd be happy. *This* is what they're doing." I gestured at the screen that showed the last of my images, that of the organs floating in the tanks. "If you want this stopped, if you want any of the similar schemes stopped, then you need to inform your people to vote yes. Because if you don't, these people will take control of our governments." I brought up the last image, the one showing the line of off-world communication going from South Africa into space. "There are people at the end of this line. They're on a world called Tamer, which is not a *gamra* member. We don't know who they are, but they have been supplying the Pretoria Cartel with the knowledge to make these artificially adapted people. Without *gamra*, Earth will be open for these people to move in and take control."

18

———————

I **HAD HOPED FOR** a thunderous roar of voices after my speech ended. *Gamra* meetings were often like that: people who agreed or disagreed would go into shouting matches.

But today, people merely applauded—they didn't even do so with particular enthusiasm—and left their seats to go for lunch.

I had expected people to come up to me to ask questions, or dispute me or thank me. A few people glanced in my direction, but they didn't come to me or say anything.

Would no one even congratulate me, no matter how perfunctory, on the speech? It was all very strange.

"Let's go," I said to Thayu, who stood watching the people stream out the door.

As I was putting my reader away, Margarethe came past, flanked by her guards. She met my eyes. I greeted her, but she just nodded and kept walking.

Well, that was even stranger. Wasn't she even going to stop and chat?

Thayu frowned at me as well.

We walked across the floor and met the rest of the team at the door.

Tables had been set up for refreshments in the foyer, and catering staff in neat uniforms were handing out little parcels with packed pita bread and salad to the attendants.

Several people nodded and greeted me, but none came to tell me that they enjoyed my speech. I guessed the subject matter wasn't the type of thing that could be described as enjoyable in anyone's language, as some of the images had been pretty horrific. But no one offered me any support either. It was like they wanted to distance themselves from me, as if they were reluctant to be seen with me, supportive of a cause that might land them in trouble with the establishment on whose approval they relied for their jobs.

The Cartel and their money really had their claws into the establishment.

I had probably risked myself and wasted my time by talking to them. But at least my standpoint was now official, and people could watch my speech at any time—as long as the Cartel didn't block their communication.

Damn, I was running out of ideas and this referendum would end in utter disaster if we couldn't break through the Cartel's block.

I had asked to see Eva for lunch, but I couldn't see her anywhere in the hall.

I spotted Piotr Zbrowsky in a group of dour, similarly dressed people, men all. I recognised the type of dress worn by the people who used to come to Eva's house: straight-laced, serious-faced men who brought wives in frilly dresses and smoked pipes and spent altogether too much time dwelling on a time a few hundred years before their birth. Eva was not with him, and I didn't really want to go up to him and ask. After his attack on me, I wasn't even sure that I should see Eva, but deep down I still felt terrible for the way we'd split up, and the way I'd left her hanging on while I'd known for a long time that a marriage between us would never work, but I just failed to admit it to myself.

Maybe I'd be better off writing that letter to her that I'd started and abandoned so many times. It was not as if I didn't have any other things to do right now. I should make an effort to see Margarethe to ask her what was going on.

"Cory."

I turned around and there was Eva, behind me.

"Oh. I couldn't see you. I was just going to ask your father where you were."

"Oh. He wouldn't have known anyway. Where do you want to go?" Again, she seemed nervous.

"I thought we'd just get some food from the buffet and sit somewhere." People were queuing up to be served there. Through the open doors at the side of the foyer I caught a glimpse of people sitting in a leafy courtyard.

"I know this nice cafe across the road."

"All right. But don't you have to be back for the continuation of the session?"

"They won't miss me if I slip in a bit late."

That was not how I had experienced the assembly sessions, but I was happy to roll with it. She seemed keener for us to talk than I was. A feeling that I should urgently *do* something about the election kept gnawing at me, but until I knew *what,* I couldn't give in to it.

We left the building, Eva with her skirt and heels. Thayu walked behind us with Nicha and Sheydu, and Telaris and Reida in front and the rest of the heavily armed assembly to the sides and behind us.

Our team got some strange looks.

The cafe in question was on the ground floor of the building of the International Relations department. I didn't remember if it had always been here.

It had paved seating outside and the two walls facing the street were entirely made from glass.

About half the tables were occupied.

"It's not very busy today," Eva said. "Probably everyone is having lunch in the assembly building?"

Thayu gave me a look like she wasn't sure where I wanted her to sit, but I decided we were all one group, so we pushed a couple of tables together and I introduced every one of my team to Eva.

She bowed her head to everyone, especially Veyada and Sheydu when I mentioned that they had been part of Ezhya's guard. Bowing was how people at Nations of Earth were taught to greet *gamra* people.

We studied the menu on the table display screen.

I told Eva, "I have a no-restrictions ordering card, get what you like."

Her eyes widened. "You *have* done well for yourself."

When we were at the court, my team had developed a liking for flaky pastry, sweet or savoury, so we ordered a couple of big plates of that and chatted while we waited. Nicha remarked that it was a pity Ayshada wasn't here, and I had to explain who Ayshada was.

"Nicha has a *son?*"

"Time moves on. I heard you're married."

"Yeah." And some of the spark left her eyes as she said that.

Not happily, I presumed. "What does your husband do?"

"He works for Nations of Earth, because . . ." she smiled awkwardly. "Who around here doesn't?"

"But?"

"But what?"

"It felt like there was a 'but' in there somewhere."

She looked down at her cup. "Do you know they don't want me to talk to you?"

"So it's not like you didn't know it was me on the agenda."

"I figured. I asked my father if I could help in the meeting, because I normally work in the office, not in the assembly hall."

"Does your husband work there, too?"

"No." She looked at her hands. "He's . . ." She let out a breath. "He's a spy. I'm here because of what he's doing, to warn you."

This was such a major departure from the demure Eva I knew, that it astonished me. Was this really Eva, going behind the back of her father and husband?

"So what is really going on at Nations of Earth? What's going on with Margarethe?"

She hesitated. "That thing you said, about infiltration by the Pretoria Cartel of the assembly, every word of it is true. The older members of the assembly don't understand what is happening. They simply think that their conservative views are winning. They don't like *gamra*. They're scared of 'aliens taking our jobs and money'. They don't see that the true enemy of the world is not the group of people who made their homes here on Earth many years ago, but the interlinked businesses that have hollowed out government autonomy from within, and whose aims are at direct cross-purposes with that of a free society."

I stared at her, kind of stupidly, I assumed.

Was this really Eva? Timid, demure Eva. "How long have you been seeing things this way?"

"I met someone by chance. In the library." Her cheeks coloured.

Romantically-met, I guessed.

"I understand you know her. She's a professor in International Studies. Brilliant mind."

Another blast from the past. Could it really be? "Alma Savage?"

She nodded and looked down.

All right. I saw the "husband" issue. I hadn't met Alma since my days at school on Midway Space Station, but I had spotted her name occasionally, mostly as a quoted expert.

"The academic world is behind you," Eva said.

"How good is their penetration in parts of the world controlled by the Pretoria Cartel? They do have their own network, don't they?" An idea started to form in my mind. We could not hope to defeat the communication blocks put up by the Cartel, but we could try to circumvent them.

"There are universities in those countries, but their funding would be dependent on the Cartel."

"True. But we need to circumvent the Cartel's blocks. We need to ensure fair elections. I believe that when most people who want to vote can vote and most of their votes are counted fairly, we have a chance of winning. The problem is that the Cartel filters and outright controls communication. We don't have the time to prove that they're doing this. We have to reach the people in some other way."

"You have really powerful friends, don't you?"

"I guess."

"Why don't you ask them to take out the network."

"Sabotage the election? That will go down well."

She shook her head. "When there is no connection available to hold the election electronically, it must be done on paper."

I stared at her.

She spread her hands. "The law says so. Believe me, I've studied it."

"And we're going to print and distribute billions of voting cards in seven days?"

"No, just in the places where the network is broken. That's still a big job, but then people who do vote get to vote fairly, and technicians and lawyers can bicker later over how the network was corrupted."

Damn it, this sounded crazy, but we *could* try to do it. Except we would not need to bring down the Cartel's communication. All we needed to do was quote the copious evidence that there was some sort of block in place and, therefore, the trustworthiness of the reports on the election results was in doubt. Therefore we had to run the vote in the old-fashioned way.

"How would the votes be counted?"

"In the normal way, by election officials in each country. They always get a small number of paper votes because people live in remote areas or can't access the network for other reasons. They will get a shock with the amount of work they'll get, but they are obliged to count the votes."

"Damn it, Eva. I've been looking for a solution to this problem for weeks, and you just . . . give it to me. What can I do to thank you?"

She looked up at me with the familiar dark blue eyes. "Succeed. I don't want to live in a world where these people control us—"

She gasped. Her eyes widened.

A dry voice behind us said, "What a surprise to see you here."

The voice was sharply accented and more familiar than I wanted to admit.

Piotr Zbrowsky had come into the cafe. He normally resembled a scarecrow, with the dark suit he wore, and the long-haired eyebrows fashioned into horns.

He said something in a sharp voice to Eva, and she jumped up from the table so quickly that her knee hit the table leg. Coffee slushed in the cups.

I got up, too, turned around to face him. "I invited Eva for lunch. I'm sorry if I wasn't supposed to do that." I let the words *she's an adult and can meet whomever she pleases* hang unsaid between us.

Since the last time I'd been close to him, he had become greyer and grown more hair out of his ears and nostrils.

He snorted. "Look at you, strutting around in your pretty clothes, playing with the hearts of honest girls, cheating on them under their noses. You dare to invite my daughter to lunch after all this? My daughter is an honest woman, with a husband who doesn't cheat on her. Eva needs to be back in our office. *We* have work to do. *I* suggest that she belongs with her husband and would do well not to speak to traitors."

"Traitors? Do you even know what that word means in this context? Do you know who the real traitors are? Hint: it's not us and it's not you. It's the people who are pulling the strings of the court and the assembly, who have bought government debts. They want full control of the assembly. They want Earth to become isolated so that they can do whatever they want."

"How dare you talk to me like this, young man? You know nothing about the assembly or indeed about anything to do with Earth. You lived with your father in one of their stations. You have no idea of hardship and what we had to do to survive during the years of war. I was there when Nations of Earth was founded. I watched the signing of the agreement. Nations of Earth is *ours* and no one will get any say in what we decide. I watched you come into my house and talk like you know it all and you haven't changed a bit. Look at you and your fancy suit. Look at you with your 'independent analysis', studying us as if we're mice in a little cage. I wanted to believe so badly that you could see the truth and understand, but you understand nothing. You never deserved my daughter and you are not taking her away from us now. Go away with all your filthy chans. They will never rule over this world."

"Why can't you understand that no one is interested in ruling the world? That we're on the same side?"

He laughed. "On the same side? Never."

He grabbed Eva's arms and frogmarched her out of the cafe. I could see them go through the glass front of the cafe, across the outdoor seating area, across the street.

A man waited for her on the steps of the assembly building, standing with his arms crossed over his chest. He wore a suit and white shirt with the Nations of Earth assembly tag attached to his jacket. His hair was blond and longer up top than down the sides. To my surprise, I knew him.

It was Jarek Malicki, Robert Davidson's lawyer.

When Eva and her father reached him, he spoke a couple of

sharp words to her. Eva replied as I would expect Eva to do: by lowering her head, and letting her shoulders sink.

He did not touch her, but walked next to her on their way back into the assembly building. She seemed small and dainty compared to him.

Well, that was . . . *interesting.*

I met Thayu's gold-flecked eyes.

She asked, "Her husband?" Using the Isla word.

"Apparently." Although what sort of marriage that would be worried me. He was brazen and bold. Voicing outright opinions tended to make Eva shrink into the shadows.

"So that whole thing with being captured on the boat was a game? Why? For the reason that you might trust him and tell him about your plans?"

"Apparently. He failed because I didn't trust him. I immediately disliked his face, and my gut instinct has rarely been wrong in that respect." Except, perhaps, for Marin Federza, who had made an admirable Chief Delegate of *gamra* even if I still disliked him.

I didn't think Jarek had seen me in the cafe, but he would know Eva had met up with me. I hoped she wouldn't get into trouble. He didn't seem a very compromising guy. In fact, Eva looked positively terrified of him.

I felt bad about it. Eva could have lived with me in Barresh, but I also didn't know whether, if I'd stayed with her, I'd have been able to pull her from the sucking mud of demands placed on her by her family and her background.

I was happy that I was no longer involved. I would have been much happier had she been happy, too.

We gathered everyone in a big group and left the cafe in the direction of the bus stop to go back to our hotel. I was sure that we could get one of the many Nations of Earth vans to give us a lift, because that was how we had arrived here, but I didn't want to be under anyone's control anymore. There was much work to be done, and we needed to go back to Athens to make use of whatever reach Amarru still had.

We got onto the bus at the terminal just outside the entrance of the compound. It was a driverless vehicle that trundled over the dedicated lanes at a slow but steady speed.

We arrived back at the hotel with no problems, because the bus stopped not far from the hotel and no one followed us.

While we were out, Eirani and Karana had been to the park with Ayshada and had busied themselves making tea and securing cakes.

The members of my team were young and muscular, or both, and hadn't thought much of the portion sizes at the cafe. The cakes vanished in no time.

While we ate and drank, Eirani informed me that they had also managed to watch my speech online.

"You did well," she said. "We can all be proud of you."

That met with approval from the others. I guessed not being heckled, as was common in the *gamra* assembly despite the amount of protocol that forbade it, was a distinct sign of success.

If only things were that simple.

While we were drinking tea, I explained to my team what Eva had said. "The law guarantees that if electronic voting is not an option, voting in person on paper is an acceptable alternative. The law also guarantees that in each district in each country, there should be designated officials for processing of paper votes. They are probably going to get a nasty surprise with the amount of work we're going to send their way, but those provisions are already in place, and we are going to use them. The trouble comes with the fact that we now have seven days to distribute as many voter cards as possible to affected regions."

"We should use the Coldi register," Nicha said. "There are sure to be people on it who own printing plants in various regions. We can send them the designs and they can produce the cards, and we can use other people on the register to distribute the cards, because there are plenty of people on the register who own forms of transport—"

"*Legal* forms of transport," I insisted. "We can't do *anything* illegal. We can't use Amarru's secret network, not even to block communication. We can't use people with illegal craft or illegal weapons."

"Of course."

Sheydu said, "We need to leave this area, where communication is compromised. Because otherwise, they will know what we're doing before we've even started."

I agreed. I told Devlin to contact Amarru with the news that now I'd completed my speech, I wanted to return to Athens.

I told my team to find as many useful people in the register as possible. I tried to reach Margarethe—and was fobbed off by a secretary—and Dharma, but the last time he had sent me anything was when we were still in New Zealand.

Devlin came to get me a little later.

Amarru had asked to speak with me.

I followed Devlin to the temporary hub he'd set up in his room and I took the earpiece he handed me.

"Amarru?"

"Yeah, I wanted to make sure that I could tell you this in person, because I don't have any safe trains or flights."

What? She always told me to go this way or that. "What's going on?"

"I'm sorry. We're extremely busy because a lot of people are coming back to Athens, and on top of that, we don't have as many safe openings. I'll let you know when something comes up."

She closed the connection. I turned away from the screen and faced the dark expressions of my team. For a while, no one said anything.

Then I said, "We're going. I don't care whether it's safe or not. We're going back to the Exchange. We need to be away from the control and spying by the Cartel."

19

———

WE HAD TO FIGURE OUT how to get back to
Athens safely and quickly.

I preferred the train and most of us were inclined
that way. But Sheydu, Evi and Telaris, with help from Thayu and
Devlin, could not establish a safe route.

Sheydu said that as soon as we purchased tickets, our travel time
and names would go onto a database that was searchable by police,
customs and other authorities. There was no guarantee that no one
we didn't want to know would see it. I knew better than to protest
that it was "just" Customs and police who had access to this data.
Many of those organisations were infiltrated by the Cartel.

Normally, when the Exchange needed to find a flight, Coldi
routines in the various database systems caused a slight delay in
synchronisation of data. That way we could book late, and our
names would not go on the passenger list until the very last
moment, which would not be updated for the public until the flight
had already left.

I had always wondered how Amarru could let me know that
certain flights were safe to use and others were not, and this
was how.

But that system was no longer safe and, what was more, just like
happened after the shooting of President Sirkonen, Coldi people

were flooding to the Exchange enclave to be safe in case the *no* vote won.

Nicha wondered if we could book train tickets under false names. In the past, the Exchange had created false identities that people without valid Earth ID could use, but they'd stopped doing this about ten years ago. The false IDs still existed, but no one knew how to access them.

Flying was a problem, catching the train was a problem . . .

Then Nicha said, "Why don't we hire a vehicle and drive ourselves?"

I said, "None of us has a licence for a vehicle that's big enough for all of us."

"Then we hire a bus from the register."

It made sense, but now we were back to the problem that in order to access the register and find out who owned a bus, we needed safe communication, and we didn't have that.

"Do you know anyone locally who could help us?" I asked Nicha.

But he didn't. He'd grown up in London, not Rotterdam.

I had once known most of the Coldi in Rotterdam, but that was so long ago that I doubted those people were still here. In any case, I no longer had their contact details.

Reida suggested we search for their names in existing databases, but Sheydu said that such searches were certain to be tracked.

Ayshada had gone for a nap, but now woke up and came to sit on the floor in the middle of the room where we held our war council.

Damn it, we faced having to do dangerous things with a child and two innocent domestic workers in our group.

"There is no option, we're going to have to use one of *their* vehicles," Telaris said.

I asked, "You mean Nations of Earth's?"

"Yes."

Sheydu shook her head. "They are tracked. I propose that we ask help from outside."

Meaning the Asto military. "No, we can't do that. Only in extreme emergencies, and preferably not even then. Once we do that, we've lost whatever chance we still have at winning."

Sheydu leaned back with her arms crossed over her chest. She didn't like it, but she also answered to Thayu, who gave her a warning glance.

There would be no Asto military. *Strictly* no Asto military. Well, except when the whole situation went to hell and we needed saving, maybe. Just *maybe*.

We were back to finding a bus. I couldn't drive a bus, so we needed a driver. We couldn't get a driver from the register because we couldn't contact them. We had no way to judge the safety of any random driver. On top of that, we had no way to pay the driver, because all our finances went through the Exchange.

Then I had a thought: maybe using a Nations of Earth bus could be a solution after all. "When we were at the court, Margarethe came to see me in a bus. If we could get *that* bus or one like it, we'd have no trouble getting through at least the first couple of checks."

Nicha thought it was a great idea.

Thayu was less keen.

The others thought it was worth a try.

Deyu said, "That vehicle is going to have a fully capable communication hub, isn't it?"

"Likely." Margarethe's bus did, at any rate.

"So we can start to work on all these things we need to do while we travel. We could even take all of the time between now and the election to roam the areas where we can safely communicate."

That was a very sharp suggestion.

The next question, of course, was how to get one of these buses.

Time was ticking and we needed to move quickly to retain the element of surprise.

Of course, Sheydu proposed that we go in and simply borrow a bus. We had satellite images that showed us, clearly, where the buses were.

But I would not allow that. "Believe me, even if we can escape the compound, we wouldn't get far. The police will block the roads, they'll be able to see exactly where we're going and once they stop us . . ." I spread my hands. "Nothing good can come from that."

Nicha and Thayu agreed.

"Well then," Sheydu said, crossing her hands over her chest. She was clearly fed up with not being allowed to do things her way. "Maybe we can use *subtle persuasion power* to convince someone to let us use a vehicle." She stared at her knees. I knew she would much rather shoot her way into the compound, hijack a bus and take off with it.

But my bluff and power to bullshit my way out of tight spots were going to have to do the heavy lifting. "Let us try just for the rest of today. If it doesn't work, we can break in and borrow a bus tonight." But I would kick myself if that ever came to pass, because my welcome at Nations of Earth was already wearing thin and I didn't know how much longer I'd be allowed to come here.

It was now late in the afternoon, and we went back to the complex to see what we could find out. It was our luck that the assembly session hadn't yet finished, and my name was still on the list of people to be allowed to enter the compound, and we could pass the gate without any questions.

The vehicle depot was located between a couple of buildings near the residential section of the compound. It was the first time I had been down the alley, which was closed off with a gate at the end. We had no pass to open it. Nicha lifted Thayu up so she could see over the top, and she reported that there was a shiny black bus parked in the courtyard on the other side.

"The same one Margarethe used?" I asked.

She didn't know this—not having seen the bus in question—so she lifted me up so I could see.

It was the same bus, unless Nations of Earth had more than one, which was always an option.

I couldn't see any people in the courtyard, but Nicha located a transport office in the building whose entrance was next to the alley. It probably had an exit into the courtyard.

We went to this office. It was only one fairly large room, where a couple of people sat at workstations, some talking into earpieces.

A young man came to the counter.

"My name is Cory Wilson, Delegate of *Gamra*. I was invited to make a speech to the assembly, but I'd like to borrow a bus for myself and my team to travel around for a few days to talk to people before we return home."

He frowned. "Did someone tell you to come here?"

"No, but this is a transport office, right?"

"We look after the vans that drive around the compound and the train station. We're not a taxi service."

"I understand, but you sent a bus to pick us up this morning. I would like to hire a bus like that."

"We don't have buses here."

"What about the one in the courtyard?"

He did a double take. "That's the president's personal vehicle; you can't hire it."

"Oh, I'm sorry. I didn't know that. But we are in a rather tight situation and there are quite a few of us. I was wondering if you could help us."

"You need to go to the transport office. They might have something."

He sent us to another part of the building.

It was surprisingly busy in the hallways, and people coming the other way gave me and my non-earthly companions strange looks.

The office was at the back of the building, and in walking there we came through a ground floor corridor where one side was glass. Through it, we could see the black bus—and there was someone with the vehicle: a woman in Nations of Earth uniform. She came down the steps, shut the door, and crossed the courtyard in the direction of an entrance a bit further down the corridor.

I sped up, so that I met her as soon as she came into the building.

"Excuse me."

She turned around. Her nametag said Maya.

"Can I help you?" Her eyes widened. I presumed that she recognised me.

"I'm looking for a bus that my team and I can use for a few days, and I was wondering if you could help us. We're happy to pay."

She opened her mouth, as if she were going to protest, and then shut it again. A frown came over her face.

"You're the president's driver, right? I'm sorry if we've got the wrong person but please tell us who we need to contact. We have an appointment to make, we have a young child with us, and all the flights and the trains are full."

She nodded. "I understand that there is a scramble of people trying to get into Athens ahead of the election."

I hadn't said we were going to Athens. I didn't contradict her.

"I'm sorry. I should have booked earlier, but I'd thought we would be staying longer."

I was totally winging it now, and she kept looking at me with a disturbing intensity. I explained to her that we wanted to visit a few places and that some of them weren't terribly accessible by train. I felt rather terrible that I couldn't tell her the truth about where we were going.

She kept walking until we ended up in some sort of locker room.

She stepped around us, and pushed the door of the room shut.

"If you're trying to get out of here, don't use the airport or the train. They'll find some dumb reason to hold you until after the election. None of your group's members are covered by citizenship laws."

"We know. That's why we're trying to get a bus."

"You're going to drive it to Athens." It was not a question. "You won't get there. All the stuff that you said in the assembly today . . . it's all true. Some people have known about this for a long time, but it's always been swept under the carpet. The old guard doesn't want to hear it, because if they acknowledge it, they also acknowledge that they've been bought out by the Pretoria Cartel. So they will resist the facts for as long as they can. I'm one of two drivers who work directly for the president. You wouldn't believe the amounts of money I've been offered for information about her, to let people share the bus with her, or even for me to casually leave material or mention things to her that will bring her into the Cartel fold."

"You? But surely Margarethe has a personal secretary?"

"She sacked him two days ago."

I remembered Margarethe coming into the meeting flanked by two men who looked like bodyguards. "And she hasn't found a replacement?"

"She *won't* accept any of the replacements suggested to her. The president's office staff are appointed by the Interior Department. She has the final say, but they bring up the candidates."

My heart jumped. This appeared to confirm the feeling I'd had since arriving here for the court session, that Margarethe had become isolated because she refused to dance to the Cartel's tune.

The election might have been her final attempt to use the vote to get rid of these people.

Maya opened a locker and took out a bag . She dug into it, retrieving a card and a pen. She scribbled something on the back and gave it to me.

"An access code?"

"There is someone on the end of that who would like to talk to you. Tell them I sent you, but don't mention it to anyone else, and don't use the code while you're still inside the compound."

"Will that person be able to get me transport?"

"I don't know, but I have heard your request."

"We're on a very tight schedule."

"I know. If you haven't heard anything by nine tonight, do whatever you want. Just give me some time."

She preceded us out of the locker room, chatting about the weather.

We parted ways in the corridor. Maya went in the direction of the transport office, and we made our way back to the exit. I was extremely curious about the contact she had given me. I didn't know if it was an office or personal contact and didn't want to risk missing this person, so I sent a message introducing myself and mentioning Maya as soon as we had left the compound.

My reader pinged not a minute later.

"Mr Wilson?" The voice was male. This gave me hope, because Margarethe tended to surround herself with male assistants, many of them significantly younger than herself. I knew this gave rise to stupid gossip, especially since she had no partner, but that just showed how vicious the Nations of Earth gossip circuit was.

"Yes. Maya gave me your contact details, but didn't say anything about the reason I should speak to you. I'm keen to arrange transport for myself and my team." I wasn't sure if it was a good idea to mention this, but if people were listening in, *transport arrangements* were less interesting than my asking *What the hell is going on in Margarethe's office?*

"I understand. I will meet you downstairs in a minute." He broke off the connection.

What the hell?

"Anything wrong?" Thayu asked.

I repeated what the man had said. "We're not even downstairs."

"We could go back there."

Yes, we could. "Maybe not all of us, so that we attract less attention."

I chose Thayu, Evi, Nicha, Reida and Deyu. Nicha because he spoke Isla, and Reida and Deyu because I wanted them to have the experience.

It was the middle of summer, and though the offices were closing and people were going home, it was still broad daylight.

I figured that "downstairs" was probably in the foyer of the building that held the president's office. It was next to the assembly building, and was the focus of a good handful of dreadful memories of the attack on President Sirkonen. Back then I'd been full of respect for the assembly. To be able to speak before a plenary session was a lofty goal. The president was someone I'd put on a pedestal.

How things had changed.

There were guards at the top of the stairs into the building, and I had no invitation that would let me in. I wasn't going to press for access, because that would draw too much attention to myself.

I had no idea what this man looked like, and I couldn't see anyone who was waiting. Surely we had taken much longer to walk back than he would have taken to walk down one flight of stairs.

Then Deyu said, "There." She gestured with her eyes.

A small side street ran in between the assembly building and the press building. No traffic was allowed into the street except for authorised vehicles which had to pass a gate when turning off the main street. Pedestrians, however, were free to walk through, underneath the covered footbridge that linked the two buildings and past the juice bar and coffee stands, where the owners were stacking away chairs for close of business. Underneath a tree stood a man looking at a device. As we stopped on the corner, he looked at us, pocketed his device and strolled in our direction.

When he reached us, he said, in a low voice, "Pretend you're tourists."

So I asked him if he knew somewhere good to buy dinner, and he replied that there were some good restaurants in the street on the southern end of the compound, and that he was going that way anyway so he'd walk with us.

So he did. We crossed the street, crossed the park and walked between the Archive building and the International Law building. I was familiar with the wide pedestrian-only avenue, because the school was behind the Archive building and the residential area behind that. We used to come here to roller skate, much to the annoyance of the guards.

It was not until we'd gone past the school that our silent companion spoke.

"I apologise for having to see you under these rather extreme conditions of secrecy. My name is Max Shaeffer, and I work in the president's office. Apart from that, I'm also fortunate enough to call myself a good friend of hers. Margarethe has wanted to speak to you ever since you left the court and especially since she called the referendum—"

"I've been sending her messages all that time."

"And she has received them."

"Then why hasn't she replied?" Why had she been so distant in recent months?

"We have to go back to the election that she nearly lost. A big part in the opposition's arsenal was always the network of Coldi intelligence that we all know exists, but that every politician has thrown in the too-hard basket for far too long by pretending it didn't exist."

Sure enough, there it was.

"Margarethe was extremely lucky that her major opponents all had issues that weighed down their chances of winning. Fiona Davidson never stood a chance as long as she was married to her obnoxious husband. Ricci Gutierrez was never able to mobilise enough of the centre-right voters, and she did have some crackpot ideas. Margarethe won because the opposition was too fragmented, not because she ran a strong campaign. But every single opposition party addressed that issue of the Coldi network. It got them a lot of votes. Whichever way the vote goes, it *has* to be addressed. We can't say 'Oh, this is just how Coldi society works,' because while it may be the way Coldi society works, and the way every Coldi person thinks is normal, we are *not* on Asto, this is *not* a Coldi society and people very much mind being spied on. So, that *has* to be addressed and the Exchange will *have* to cede control of this network."

I knew in my heart, as I'd known for a long time, that he was right. I said, "But I'm one of the few people who could provide a gateway to those types of discussions."

"Precisely. That's why the Pretoria Cartel doesn't want you to talk to her. It wants to foster the us-against-them mentality. It's an easy position to maintain within the assembly, where conservatives like Piotr Zbrowsky have the upper hand and are easy prey for the Cartel. They have manoeuvred their supporters so that any finger that the president extends towards the Exchange is seen as 'colluding with the aliens'. They whipped the anti-Coldi sentiment into a frenzy, at least in the circles of people who will bother to vote. These people actively *support* the communication blocks that I'm sure you've noticed operate in this area."

"So why then did she call the referendum early?"

"Because this is the only chance we have. There is an election coming up for a good part of the African continent. I'm sure I don't need to tell you what is likely to happen."

Holy crap. Every time I thought the situation couldn't get any worse, it did, by magnitudes.

"Is Minke Kluysters going to run for president?"

"Unlikely. He's too smart for that. Wait. I'll show you something you might find enlightening." He dug into his pocket and produced his reader. He flicked through a few menus and showed me a photo. In it, a blond woman in a red Victorian-style ballroom dress stood next to a man in riding gear. The younger versions of Margarethe Ollund and Minke Kluysters looked regal and stunning, in a way that only the very rich and privileged could.

"They were both students of economy trailblazer Lucas Wright, who was a professor at the University of Berlin where they were in the same year. She was smart and stunning. He was charismatic and an Olympic medallist."

"Hang on, were they a couple?"

"No one quite knows how serious it was, but one might be forgiven to think that all the Pretoria Cartel has done has the aim of sinking Margarethe's political career."

"Holy shit. Remind me to never piss off my exes that much."

He raised his eyebrows. "Did anyone say Piotr Zbrowsky?"

"Yeah."

He chuckled and glanced at Thayu, who—very proper—pretended not to understand anything. "Anyway, since calling the referendum, the Cartel has significantly stepped up its blocking of communication. And a permanent guard of newshounds is on the lookout for any step Margarethe takes towards 'appeasing the aliens'. This includes any visits to places owned or operated by Coldi. They're been going through her personal patronage and published a list of companies she uses in her *personal* life, that have Coldi connections. We're sure the Pretoria Cartel has sent these gutter press lowlifes, but everything we've tried to stop them is met with 'you're trying to hide how much you're in the aliens' pockets.' This is why she hasn't contacted you. This is why she hasn't been able to arrange a frank discussion with Amarru Palayi. Because every step she takes gets turned against her, and her words are twisted, and because we've effectively lost communication control of this area, there is not much she can do. And because the Cartel control most of the local employees of Nations of Earth, like the court, we have to be extremely careful whom we trust. We've been going through the files of all employees at the president's office and have sacked a lot of people. I'm sure you've heard about that."

"So what can you do?"

"We're going to mount a last-ditch offensive. We were going to do things differently, but since you were here, effectively stranded, we've come up with a new plan."

"I have a plan that, if acted upon quickly, may circumvent some of the communication blocks. But I need to leave this area as soon as possible."

"I understand. I think our plans will work together. Let's do it."

Exactly what we would do, he didn't say. To be fair, I didn't say anything about our plan. He told us to go back to the hotel and wait there.

We said very little on the way back, and there was little to say. Time was ticking, and whatever he might or might not be able to do was at the hands of people outside my team—something I didn't like.

At least Nicha would have understood the seriousness of the

situation. Both he and Thayu would know how much I feared that it was already too late to turn public opinion. I'd hoped that the speech and images from our discoveries would do that but, instead, this world I no longer recognised had become incapable of being shocked into action. The established elite no longer cared about the lives of less fortunate people. And I wasn't sure if I still wanted to be part of a world like that.

From *gamra*'s perspective, an election loss would be bad, too. They very rarely lost worlds. It was true that Indrahui seemed to be on permanent probation, but that was because *gamra* believed that it was better to keep them that way, and because various local authorities were genuinely trying to put an end to feuding and other practices that made the world ineligible. It was not that Indrahui rejected *gamra,* not at all; it was that they seemed incapable of organising themselves. Yet *gamra* forgave them, time and time again, by extending the probationary period.

Never had a world spoken against *gamra*, and I would bet that, if people at *gamra* were following the pre-referendum jostling, they would be thoroughly baffled.

We returned to the hotel, where Eirani and Karana had managed to procure dinner for us all. The table in the largest room, where Reida, Deyu, Evi, Telaris and Devlin had their beds, was full of food parcels which turned out to contain everything from Moroccan pita to noodles and pizza. They couldn't decide what to get, they told us, and so they'd gotten a bit of everything.

With so many young and fit Coldi, the pile vanished quickly.

I spent some time looking at the news, but it was utterly depressing, with no mention of my speech at all, and little mention of the South African protests. I turned off World Newspoint and instead doodled with circles as I often did when faced with a difficult problem.

Instead of a person or institution, I drew the referendum in the middle. But literally every other circle I drew, which represented a person or a group of people, had something to do with it or wanted to influence it, and the problem was not that people wanted to influence it, because that was the nature of elections, but that some people couldn't.

The page turned into a mess, and I wiped it before tossing my reader aside and staring morosely at the table.

Thayu sat down next to me, handing me a steaming mug of manazhu.

I took it from her, meeting her eyes in an exchange of mutual understanding. There was no need to speak about the desperate situation. She hated waiting as much as I did, and very soon we'd have to switch from referendum-campaigning mode to survival mode.

We drank.

While the others chatted about the food, I still considered things we might do, knowing that I wouldn't sleep well tonight, because if nothing had happened by tomorrow morning, I'd pull out all stops and ask for emergency assistance to get out of here, from Asha and his military units, if necessary.

We were about to retire to our rooms, when a message appeared on my reader.

Leaving now.

What?

"Who is this from?" I showed the reader to Thayu.

As I did so, another message came up, *Out the front*.

I pushed aside the curtain. A big black bus sat in the street in front of the hotel.

20

———————

I RAN INTO THE HALL and knocked on the doors of the other two rooms. "We're going, quick, the bus is outside."

None of the adults had gone to sleep yet, so the announcement was followed by a complete frenzy. Members of my team ran around, half-dressed, collecting items from the apartment. The final parts of the hub had to be dismantled and packed away, the weapons and armour donned, toiletries collected.

I didn't know that we had ever packed as fast as we did then. This included all our clothes and weapons and all the things for Ayshada because he was the only person to have been asleep.

He woke up cranky and let his displeasure be known.

Nicha had to do his utmost to keep him quiet.

But a short while later, we were all packed and crammed into the lift. Nicha had been down to check that the reception was empty, and it was.

"What about the room?" Thayu asked.

"I'll let them know that we've checked out a bit later." It wouldn't be the first time that I left unexpectedly.

We went out the front door into the darkness where the bus still waited. Dark, menacing, black.

Thayu was the first up the steps to check it out, and when she said it was fine, I climbed into the luxurious interior. It did look like the same bus that Margarethe had used last time.

Maya was there, behind the wheel. She smiled. Max Shaeffer sat in the seat behind her.

About halfway down waited another familiar person: Lenka Trnkova. I greeted her with a smile. She would be good to have with us.

And a row further down, someone even more familiar: Margarethe herself. She wore very non-presidential clothes: wide trousers and a loose shirt with floral patterns. Her hair was tied back in a simple ponytail.

I sank down opposite her, while my team climbed on board and stowed away luggage.

"What's going on?" I asked her.

"We're going on a field trip," she said, her tone belying a smile.

The last time I'd met her in this very bus, she'd been dressed much more officially, and she'd had an entourage, security and at least two vehicles to accompany her.

"Interesting field trip," I said, using Thayu's meaning of the word. *Interesting* might be the new way to spell *constitutional crisis*. "You know where we're going, right?" Just making sure she was on board with this.

"I believe I can guess." She met my eyes. "Everything is under control. Max has arranged most of it. I've told the vice-president to hold the ship for me. My security is following secretly. I've checked out every single one of them for trustworthiness. Officially, we're going campaigning."

Campaigning or escaping?

Meanwhile, my team had settled in the seats, the doors closed and we were off. *They* thought nothing of the fact that the president of Nations of Earth was with us. Ezhya would do stuff like this all the time. Come to think of it, the relationship between Margarethe and Ezhya was unclear to me. Neither of them had ever elaborated on the three weeks they had been forced to spend together at Kedras when the Exchange went down.

Maybe there was more strength and cunning to Margarethe's actions than appeared on the surface. People had painted her as being weak and having made crucial mistakes, but of course no one got to a position like hers without having a fighting spirit.

"You want tea?" Margarethe asked. She'd already turned to the machine next to her and pressed a button. A cup fell into the holder from above, a spout came out of the back of the cubicle and hissed boiling water into the cup. The tea bag floated to the surface. She picked up the cup and gave it to me, and made one for herself.

She called through the bus, "If anyone wants tea, feel free to get it."

There was an odd energy to her actions.

"Why?" I met her eyes over the steaming liquid.

"The Pretoria Cartel thinks they have everything stitched up. Most of the assembly is turned against me, and my communication is compromised. I've raised these issues with the guards and the Special Services Branch, but *they* are compromised, too. They've waged a fear campaign against *gamra,* but Minke Kluysters forgets one thing: in a referendum, the assembly doesn't vote. The people do."

"He doesn't forget. Many parts of the world are cut off and compromised, too."

"I know. That is where you come in. That is where Amarru can help. Let's have your plan. I give you the transport you wanted. Do your thing."

So I called everyone around me. Everyone except Maya, that was, because she was driving the bus through the darkness. They sat on the benches, the floor, the armrests. They leaned over the back-rests of seats and stood in the aisle.

I explained—for the benefit of Margarethe and her people—about the law that if electronic voting was compromised, voters could submit paper votes. I explained about the Coldi register and how we could—legally—recruit people to print and distribute these cards. It pained me that this was Eva's idea and that she was stuck with that authoritarian father and double-scheming bastard of a husband.

I said that we weren't going to tell anyone which way to vote; but that Dharma Yuwono had been hard at work recruiting people who did not normally vote. His message was that if they wanted to stop the de facto takeover of their countries by companies aligned with the Pretoria Cartel, and if they wanted better working condi-tions and wanted to fight organised crime, they were better off voting yes. I hoped that I had been able to support that message with the things I had discovered about the Pretoria Cartel, although in hindsight the Nations of Earth assembly had been the wrong venue to talk about it. But I could still fix the mistake. The speech had been recorded by many news services. I would use our own network to distribute the information to the places where it would have the most impact. People from the register would distribute the cards.

As I spoke, I noticed how first Max and then Lenka started smiling. And then Maya said from the front of the bus, "Let's go get them!" And the other people—two technicians and someone who'd been frantically writing since we entered the bus—all cheered.

For our benefit, Margarethe said that she had informed her office that she would do a last campaigning tour in the local area. In the past weeks, the chorus that it was unsafe for her to travel outside a mythical "safe zone" had become ever stronger.

"They were constantly talking about being unable to guarantee my safety. I took their advice in the beginning. After all, that's why I have security people—to look after security so that I don't have to. But I've had enough of their stalling and scheming. I checked out every single one of them. The people with dubious connections, the people who were protesting loudest at my wish to leave the area— for example, to speak to Amarru—those people, I sacked every single one of them. The people who are with us, observing us and keeping an eye on our safety, are a team I trust."

I wondered how big that team was. Not terribly big, I thought.

"Anyway, I'm sure that you are aware that this bus comes with excellent communication equipment. I believe you could use this."

We could, indeed, once we were back in Exchange coverage, which was not too far away.

Various members of my team moved over to the communication hub and the technicians went about explaining how everything worked.

Devlin touched a keyboard and was rewarded with a login screen. Lenka showed him how to log in.

There was no Exchange coverage yet, and probably wouldn't be until we left the city, but we prepared everything to send out the moment coverage returned: messages to Amarru and Dharma, messages to countless Coldi people asking for help, including Klaus and Jenny. We would have to look for additional contacts once the register became available, but those were the people we already knew about.

Until coverage was restored, there was little for me to do. I waited nervously as the bus continued its journey into the night.

Most of the time, I couldn't see anything out the window, but occasionally we passed a building or street light.

I told Margarethe about my meeting with Minke Kluysters, about his beautiful house and his stylish life.

"Oh yes, he will wow you with his manners and style and suck you in to think you're a friend of his. Then behind the scenes, he will have his minions do despicable things which you will find impossible to believe because he's such a nice charismatic man. I used to think that he didn't understand where the boundaries were, but since he never shows any of his unpleasantness in face-to-face meetings, I've concluded that he knows very well, but he truly doesn't care about the suffering of other people. He's in it only for himself. He climbs to the top over the dead bodies of the people's killed along the way. Take it from me: you do not want to trust him in any shape or form."

I was glad I hadn't, and as I remembered that I felt I liked the man, a chill went over my back. He had invited me to his house so that I could arrange a meeting with Ezhya. He'd presented the carrot of instructing his people on how to vote, because he truly didn't depend on the outcome of the election. His minions, like Robert Davidson, probably did, but he didn't. Everything he did was behind the scenes anyway. He had his ways to get what he wanted and didn't need the election. I feared we hadn't seen the last of him, but for now, I was going to ignore Minke Kluysters as much as I could.

Then the bus turned off the main road into a small town or a commerce hub deep in the suburbs. We were at the side of the road in front of a row of restaurants—all closed. It had started raining a bit, and a number of people coming out of a brightly lit entrance put up umbrellas as they crossed the street.

It was a station, and a train had just arrived.

Two women ran out of the entrance, sheltering themselves against the rain by pulling their jackets over their heads.

Maya opened the door to the bus.

Both women climbed, panting, into the bus.

The doors shut, and the bus started moving again.

The two women moved down the aisle to the group of seats where I sat. The first one pushed down the hood of her jacket.

It was Eva. One of her cheeks was red and a drop of blood ran from the corner of her mouth.

"What happened to you?"

As she sat down opposite me, I recognised the shape of a hand-print in the red mark on her cheek.

"He did that to you?"

She wiped her mouth, saw the blood. "Oh, sorry. I guess I look sufficiently like a vampire to scare everyone."

Her chuckle fell flat.

Then she met my eyes. "I've had enough. I'm leaving him. I tried to do the right thing, please my father, marry a nice Polish boy that he approves of. But he's a butcher. I should have listened to you long ago. As always, I'm late to the party, but here we are."

Then I looked at the second woman, who had also pushed down the hood of her jacket.

She was in early middle age, with a round, friendly intelligent face. Her curly hair was cropped short, greying at the temples.

"We meet again," she said.

"Alma." The last time I'd seen Alma Savage, she'd been thirteen. Tall, bushy-haired, a know-it-all, who had, nevertheless, stood by me and had become my friend at Midway Space station. "I never thought I'd see you again."

"Well, here we are, all on Team Cory Wilson."

Someone in the cabin called out, "Contact!" I thought it was Devlin, because he'd been monitoring the connections.

Thayu, Deyu, Reida, Nicha and Veyada sprang into action. They scrambled over seats to reach the communication stations.

All the messages we'd pre-written, requests for assistance from a huge range of people from the register, were all sent within a few minutes.

I recognised the familiar Exchange logo on their screens. Thank heavens they were still up. Thank heavens no disasters had happened while we had been out of contact.

As I had expected, Amarru contacted us soon after, baffled at the barrage of requests on the register.

"You almost brought it down," she said.

"I need all of it that you don't absolutely need for emergencies." I explained to her what we planned.

She listened, making a few suggestions along the way. Never once did she say that it was a silly idea or wouldn't work. She just contributed her—very practical—thoughts about certain aspects. It was probably the human in me expecting opposition to the idea.

Coldi went to work, no questions asked.

And work, they did.

Since we still didn't get a reply from Dharma, my entire team scoured the news in search of information that indicated where he was and what he was up to.

By the look of the image on Nicha's screen, Nations of Earth had released the voting portal.

It consisted of a map of countries and their voting regions, with a coloured dot in each. A lot of voting stations had already been taken offline—indicated by a red dot—with as reason *objectivity compromised*. Many of the stations in African countries suffered that fate, as well as a lot of Asian ones.

"That is our task," I said. "To make sure that as many as possible turn green again, or have enough cards to record votes."

That earned me some frowns from my team. Yes, I knew, the choice of colours was unfortunate, because most in my team could not see the difference between red and green.

"Is there a percentage point below which the referendum result will no longer be valid?" Eva asked.

Margarethe said, "There is, and it varies per country, but it's surprisingly low. Nations of Earth made a major mistake when they judged that voting should be voluntary. Decisions like this can be made by a very small percentage of people, as long as each country is represented."

And that was, presumably, why each country had some voting stations green. City ones, mostly, because none of the remote stations were good.

We might have lost Dharma until the place where he was came back onto the network, but Amarru was amazing.

Before the sky started to turn light, as the bus continued its long way south, she had arranged printing, using sixteen companies owned by people on the register. She had lined up a string of legal aircraft to deliver the cards; she had to get clearance from the local air traffic control to release several visiting ships from the Exchange. The local air traffic control was very happy to do this, because, without the Exchange, Athens would be nothing. The visitors were Traders, she said, who had a vested interest in being able to continue to come here. They would be met by referendum officials and local people from the register, many of them Zhori Coldi. Not all Zhori were happy to help, and I wasn't surprised to hear that. I was rather surprised that quite so many of them did want to help.

Klaus and Jenny were in Cape Town, from where they could communicate with us. Pretoria was in turmoil, they reported, with hordes of angry protesters roaming the streets. People had already tried twice to set fire to buildings belonging to Cartel companies. A police cordon stood in front of the glass façade of the head office of Sandowne Pharmaceuticals to stop people smashing their way in. Hundreds of stories of missing people were coming out, and people were demanding the truth about their relatives.

Had they heard my speech, I asked; and Klaus said that virtually no one in the country spoke of anything else.

It was encouraging to hear this, except all the voting stations in the region still showed red.

He *had* to make sure that people could vote, I told him, and he said that he had a group of people with Sudanese solar gliders ready and waiting for when the cards arrived. It was a step in the right direction, but there was so much still to do.

We stopped for breakfast at a roadside restaurant somewhere in southern Germany. Eva and Alma went inside and brought back a mountain of pastries and heavenly coffee, which we ate and drank inside the bus.

Maya said she was tired. She looked tired, too. She retired to a cabin in the back of the bus, from which a young man emerged by the name of Logan, and he continued driving. My eyes were scratchy, too, and my team looked equally tired.

We'd take the best part of three days to get to the Exchange enclave. There was much work still to be done, even when we got to Athens.

Were we being followed, I asked, and Veyada showed me the screen of his reader with lots of little yellow dots. We were the bigger dot in the middle; the others were people who were likely to be following us, because they had been going in the same direction and travelled at the same speed. None of them had attempted to make contact with us. Some would be Margarethe's security, although when pressured, she said she only knew of three vehicles following her.

"What about all the others?"

"There is likely to be lot of attention on us from journalists," Margarethe said. "I may have 'disappeared', but it won't be too hard to figure out where I've gone, and they only have to draw a straight line to figure out where we're going. Someone is going to try to stop us in between here and Athens, I'm sure of that. I don't know what grounds they'll use to close the road, but they will be there. We had best be prepared for people trying to prevent us from reaching our destination."

"Don't worry. We are prepared," Nicha said.

He was not normally a combative type, and far less likely to reach for arms than most of my team. To hear him talk like this disturbed me.

We continued on, with Logan as our driver. Daylight came and we were all tired.

There wasn't enough room in the bus for us all to lie down across a couple of seats, so we took turns sleeping.

I felt reasonably awake and volunteered to take the second shift. But as soon as I'd sat down in order to read the news, I could barely keep my eyes open. I fell asleep with my face leaning against the edge of the window, which made for an interesting impression in my cheek when I woke up.

I had woken up because we had stopped at a roadside rest place consisting only of a park with benches and children's play equipment and a charging station, which the bus used to top up the battery. Most of us stayed on board because we didn't want to be recognised. Besides, some people were asleep, including both Thayu and Nicha. Ayshada lay face down on a blanket at Nicha's feet. Eirani lay back in her seat, snoring softly.

Evi went to get coffee and a giant bag of biscuits which we consumed silently, at least those of us who were awake.

"You have a rest," Margarethe said to Logan. She got up, produced a beret from a cupboard, put on a vest—which I suspected to contain armour—and slid behind the wheel.

"All ready to go? Sit down, we're going to keep moving."

The bus started moving.

I sat down next to her on the steps. "When did you learn to drive these vehicles?"

"I worked in the mines on Taurus. I was a machine operator and would travel as a passenger in the large trucks. My father always told me that I should learn to drive one in case of an emergency, so I begged the guys and they did. They thought it was funny."

I remembered Margarethe as she used to come to our house on Taurus. She was quite young, and—a politician even back then—was much hated by the mine operators for driving through changes that made the mining work fairer to those going down in the trucks.

It should not have surprised me that she could drive a truck. Beneath the elfin appearance lay a tough personality. I looked up at her, with her hair stuffed under the beret and her vest zipped up.

"You're enjoying this, right?"

She did not take her eyes off the road. "Well, it's certainly different from sitting in an office being waited on by everyone all day."

"What do you hope to get out of this?"

"A victory. Fairness."

Fair enough. "What about you personally?"

She shrugged. "By the time any agreement comes into place, my term will be over. I can help with the transition once I've retired." She gave me a sharp look. "Yeah, we have to assume victory. The alternative would be too awful."

I considered asking what she would do in case of a defeat, but she was right; it was too awful. Because I would have to talk about ceding my citizenship and permanently moving to Barresh. And worry about my father's safety. "We have to win."

"Yes."

And then she didn't say anything for a while. I was about to get up and return to my seat when she said, "I need to have a frank discussion with Amarru."

"I can imagine. It's been a while since you spoke personally to her."

"Never."

"But I thought . . ." I remembered some sort of function where they had both been present.

"Never in my current position, as an official visit. I've spoken to her in snatches here and there, but have rarely addressed the important issues."

Which, I presumed, included that Coldi spy network.

"I have addressed the Exchange in my speeches often enough, while my security insisted that it wasn't safe to travel outside an 'approved' zone, and stalled on my initiative to invite Amarru to address the assembly. I didn't realise until much later that her lack of reply was not because she wasn't interested, but because the network lines were broken and obstructed. I only realised this when we were unable to contact Dharma and you."

"Certainly, you knew that there was a communication block in place at the court?"

"Oh yes, but that's fairly normal, so I trusted my advisors. I shouldn't have. I was busy with many unimportant things while forgetting the most important issues. I tried to contact you before you gave your speech."

"I never received anything."

"I know. This is how much control they have over our communication. That's when I knew that if I wanted to reach people who hadn't already turned away from my message, I needed to leave Rotterdam. I want to speak to Amarru before the public. I want to make a joint statement."

"You've left it to the last minute."

"I didn't want to give them the chance to reply."

"Would you have gone anyway if I hadn't come?"

"We were looking into a trip in the jet. I had asked several people to find reliable security."

"So why come on my hare-brained trip?"

"Because we hadn't yet found enough reliable people in the

Special Services, and I wanted at least two other craft to follow mine. I knew some units were compromised, but I didn't realise how strong the stranglehold of the Pretoria Cartel was. I sacked a lot of my personal security. The only additional people I could find were those you already know. They're on a list that Amarru's people can draw from if they're in trouble."

Well, it would have caused major upheaval if it came to light that the president had used the Coldi register.

"So, is this a constitutional crisis or simply a road trip?"

She didn't reply to that. I watched her face, showing no emotion, as she drove the bus.

After a long silence, she spoke. "A lot of mistakes were made over the years. By me, and by people before me, and by people who were in power when I hadn't even entered politics. Nations of Earth should never have stripped Coldi residents of their citizenship. It should never have allowed the native Zhori clan to become isolated and driven into the cesspool of the third world cities. Nations of Earth should never have allowed companies to take over the debt of countries. I should have realised that Minke Kluysters could not possibly be a different person from the student I knew at university. Also, the Exchange should have come clean about their spy network a long time ago."

I nodded. Yes, to all those things.

"It's time for talks."

I was really tired and excused myself to return to my seat. Thayu was awake and offered me both seats. She had some communication to attend to, and she joined Eva and Alma who were busy at work gathering news.

I lay down across the seats and was asleep in minutes.

———

I woke up quite abruptly through people talking in excited voices. I sat up, blinking. The light had turned golden, but the bus was still moving. At the back of the bus, there was some sort of consternation caused by something on Veyada's screen.

I got up and looked over Veyada's shoulder. Sheydu, Deyu and Telaris sat next to him.

Thayu was pointing at little dots on what appeared to be a satellite image. "There and there."

"What's this?" I asked, my tongue still feeling rubbery from sleep.

"A camp, by the side of the main road."

I could see the road, too, like a slice through a parched landscape.

"This was taken just now," Thayu said.

"What is the source?"

"Amarru."

"Who is in the camp?"

"That's what we're trying to find out. We've captured some electronic data from the vehicles. Amarru is looking at that."

Veyada zoomed in on the image. The level of detail on these images never ceased to amaze me. The Asto ships usually hung out somewhere in geostationary orbit, which was a heck of a lot further than most imaging satellites, but the quality of the images was stunning and would often even include live videos where you could see vehicles moving across the surface.

Veyada pointed. "These are personnel trucks. There is a building over here, which you can't see until someone goes into it, because the roof is under the ground. Each of these trucks can probably hold about twenty people. These trucks here contain supplies."

"Weapons?" Thayu asked.

"Probably, but also other things, I'm guessing."

"It does not look like they belong to Nations of Earth guards," I said. Those vehicles usually had identification on the roof precisely so they could be identified as peacekeeping forces from above.

"Nope." Veyada shook his head.

"So. They're gathering there to intercept us, I'm guessing."

There were grave nods from several people, including Sheydu, whose advice I'd value most on matters of security.

"Does Margarethe's secret security know about this?" In other words, *Are you in contact with them?*

"They might," Sheydu said. "We sent them these images."

"Is there a way we could all meet up and talk about this?"

There was such a way, Margarethe informed us, and she gave Eva a code.

When, about half an hour later, the bus turned off at another rest area, two vans waited for us.

Margarethe stopped the bus and opened the door. I stepped into the afternoon summer air.

The door of the closest van was open, and someone inside said, "Come in."

I did, followed by Thayu, Evi and Sheydu.

Inside, two men and a woman sat surrounded by a mass of electronic equipment. When we entered, there were seven of us in the vehicle, making it really crowded.

The woman was looking at the same satellite image that Veyada had shown me. "We got ID on this truck," she said. "It belongs to a local security company. They also own a hire company that owns these two vehicles here. This company is part of a worldwide business that's owned by Angelo Pardas."

And he was a Cartel stooge. "So they're Cartel militia of some sort?"

"Very likely."

Well, damn. "What are our options?"

Evi said, in the menacing tone that his voice took on when he spoke Isla, "Amarru has control of a few back-road gates into the area. We could use those."

"We could, but it wouldn't take much for these people to figure out that there are other gates." It felt strange speaking Isla to him.

The woman said, from behind her screen, "There are more vehicles coming into the area all the time. I don't know that simply sneaking in the back way is going to work."

No, it wouldn't. I turned to the men who were with her. "What sort of resources do you have on standby?"

"There are three other groups. They are armed with their own gear. We don't have any spares."

"What type of vehicles?"

"A bus, two vans."

"Can you get something that flies?"

"We'll have to look into that."

"Good, do that, with urgency. We'll wait here until you have something."

I gestured at my team. We left the van and went back into the bus. Deyu rushed at me, saying that Amarru wanted to speak to me. I sat at her workstation.

"There is a concerning development," she said. "We checked the ID on those vehicles and—"

"I know. They're allied with the Pretoria Cartel."

"There is also communication coming in from a satellite in orbit that coordinates their activity, and probably ours."

"They're trying to stop us."

"What do you want done about them?" Not *what should we do about them?* I guessed the Cartel wasn't trespassing on Exchange territory, being outside the enclave, and Amarru rightfully did not want to upset any people by authorising illegal activity, not this close to the referendum. But it was the first time that she asked me to make a decision. I couldn't tell if this was a shift in loyalty—it would have been if I had been Coldi.

"Well . . ." I took a deep breath and let it out again. "We have no time to mess around. They are not in the area in any formal capacity either. They're probably hired guns, or they might even be Tamerians. We can't negotiate or complain about their presence, because there is nowhere to complain." I took another deep breath. "All right. Give the satellite data to Asha. Tell him to take out the satellite. Then send backup and support to the border region. Don't tell me where they come from and how they get there. I don't want to know. I need some vehicles, people—"

"Weapons?"

"Where these people turn up, I assume there will be appropriate weapons. We need everything secretly and urgently."

Amarru said she would arrange this, and when I logged off, I found my team gathered around, and everyone else in the bus looking at us with wide eyes.

It was time to do something I had never done.

I reached out and touched the shoulders of each of the members of my team. Veyada and Sheydu stood in the subservient position, looking down with their arms by their sides. Thayu also looked down, but touched my arm affectionately while I put my hand on her shoulder. Nicha nodded gravely, his lips pressed together.

"We're going to win this," I said, once I'd given everyone attention. "We're going to reach the Exchange safely, and we're going to carry out all our plans. We'll show that no one messes with us. We'll defeat those who stand in our way and prove wrong those who tell lies and treat others cruelly. The truth will win. Honesty will win. We will win. *Iyamichu ata!*"

My voice had risen as I spoke, and when I finished, Thayu, Nicha, Veyada, Sheydu, Reida and Deyu all raised their fists and shouted as one, "*Iyamichu ata!*"

I met Eva's wide eyes over the backrest of a bench. She looked scared, as if she no longer knew me. The others, too, gave me alarmed looks, including Margarethe, who had stuck her head out the door of the cabin at the back of the bus, where she was getting ready to rest.

"It's all right," I said to them.

But as we shouldered our gear and clambered out of the bus, I knew it wasn't all right at all. If the no vote won, I would lose whatever tenuous connection I still had with Earth. I would become well and truly Domiri, and de facto Coldi. And the bond between me and my team meant I was pretty much Coldi already.

21

———

W E COLLECTED OUR GEAR.

Nicha, Devlin and Reida were going to stay with the bus, as were Karana and Eirani, both of whom looked positively terrified.

I took Reida aside, because his expression had turned morose.

"Anything the matter?"

"No." But he looked down and avoided my eyes. I knew that he had hoped to be included in our group, and didn't like the thought of babysitting the bus.

"Your task will be extremely important. I want you to defend the president, and our people, with your life. I want you to coordinate Devlin with Amarru and all the information the others are collecting."

He nodded, still not looking convinced.

"You have a talent with spying and security. Why do you think Nicha chose you with Deyu?"

He shrugged. If he'd been an Earth teenager, he might have said, *I have no idea. She is better at everything than I am*, but he was Coldi, and had a solid, inborn, understanding of his place in our group.

I continued, "She is the practical, brute force of your team. You are good at sneaking into things, whether that is by breaking locks, climbing balconies or using your charm. I was considering, now you've completed some of your training, sending you somewhere you could learn to develop those skills, because they are very valuable. I was thinking I could ask Asha if he could recommend you to the Academy." That was the Inner Circle Spy Academy, which Thayu, Nicha and several others on my team had attended.

Now Reida looked up. The morose look was gone. "Really? But . . . could I even go? I mean . . . with where I come from?"

"The Outer Circle. I admit the background isn't great, but there is a tendency these days to be much more open with their acceptance criteria. Especially if you come with recommendations. But only if you would like to go."

"Oh, I'd like that very much."

"Then I will see what I can do. You just do your job. The best things come to those who wait for the best opportunities." That was a Coldi proverb.

"Thania Lingui." That was the Chief Coordinator who had originated the proverb. The game of citing proverbs and then the other person naming their originator had gone out of fashion a bit, but Asto Coldi would still do it in formal settings.

I patted his arm. "Wait. The opportunity will come."

He went to work happily.

Not much later, we got news that a gyrocopter had been located and was on its way.

The bus, again with Maya at the wheel, stopped and I got out in the company of Thayu, Sheydu and Veyada, Deyu, Evi and Telaris.

We scaled a fence and walked through a paddock where the cows were all standing in the corner. Not until we'd passed a copse of trees could we see the reason for their behaviour: a gyrocopter had landed in the paddock. The back cargo door was open and the engines were blasting the surrounding grass flat on the ground.

We ran through the blast of air, clambered into the open door, dropped onto the hard benches and did up the safety harnesses. The gyrocopter took off while the door was still open, with cold evening air blasting through the cabin and the air vibrating with the noise from the rotating blades.

The noise only dampened somewhat when Sheydu slammed the door shut.

Phew.

The craft was of military origin, very basic inside, with hard seats and a dusty metal floor. There was no one else in this part of the craft. A narrow opening joined the cabin to the cockpit and, through it, I spotted the two pilots. One was definitely Coldi, but I couldn't be sure of the other. So, were they from the register?

Both Thayu and Sheydu had pulled out their readers, and communicated in short messages of plain text on a black screen.

I leaned in closer to see what Thayu was doing.

Her text was in Coldi and concerned coordinates—I thought, though I was pretty uninformed about military code—and a list with times and "phase 1", "phase 2" and "phase 3".

People were on their way, she said when I asked, but she was busy, so I didn't disturb her.

This might be the most stupid decision I'd made in my life, but I'd made it, and there was no going back. If there was going to be any fallout, we'd deal with it later.

The gyrocopter travelled through the night on our way to the checkpoint. Through a tiny window in the door, I could occasionally see pinpricks of light indicating towns.

After a while, Thayu put away her reader and leaned back in her seat. Without the bluish glow from the screen, the cabin went dark. Sheydu had already turned off hers, and the others were silent in the dark, asleep.

It was too noisy to speak more than a few words to each other, so I leaned into her warmth. She put her head on my shoulder and slept. It was none too warm in this bare-bones cabin, and I was glad of her warmth, but I couldn't sleep. I worried about Margarethe and the others on the ground, in the dark, on the long road to Athens.

———

It was still dark when the gyrocopter landed.

We fumbled for our bags by the low light in the cabin and stumbled down the little ladder to the ground. The air was dusty, but cool enough for me to suspect that we were quite high.

The sky was full of stars but, apart from that, all I saw was a patch of grass immediately surrounding the gyrocopter and lit by its floodlights, a barbed-wire fence and a vehicle track leading between two fenced paddocks.

Evi and Telaris led the way in that direction.

The gyrocopter took off, the *thud-thud-thud* of its blades fading until the only sounds left were the chirping of crickets and other creatures of the night.

After a short, brisk walk, we came to a farmhouse with an attached barn, most of it dark except for a faint glow of light from somewhere deep within. We walked around the side. A couple of low vehicles stood parked on a patch of dirt, visible because moonlight glinted on metallic roofs. They were military vehicles of the type that I'd seen used in desert patrols, mostly by private militias.

Evi opened a door into the barn and we followed him in, with straw underfoot that filled the air with its musty scent. Many of this area's farms were abandoned, because the main market—the city of Athens—had become cut off from producers unless they were with the large cooperatives that could export produce into the Exchange enclave. Most of these used to be goat farms, but artificial milk production had put them out of business.

It had been a long time since this barn had seen any goats, and the musty smell certainly confirmed that.

We went up two steps through another door into a pitch-dark room where the floor was tiled.

A voice called out elsewhere in the house.

"Coming," Sheydu said, in Coldi.

We entered a large kitchen, lit only by a battery-operated lamp on the table.

About five or six people sat around the table, all of them wearing Coldi-style armour and weapons. They were dressed in the featureless dark clothing that was so typical for Asto military when they went on missions.

It was normally hard to tell the difference between men and women in Coldi, but in this light, it was impossible.

The air was filled with the scent of Coldi bodies.

Every one of them got up and performed subservient greetings to my team and me. It would have been odd had I not known Coldi customs. I did not know these people.

"Sit down," a man who appeared to be the commanding officer said. "Have you eaten?"

When we said we had not, pans came out and one of the lower-ranked men set about cooking eggs for us.

The heavenly smell spread through the kitchen.

We had to finish the food before we could talk business. We were finishing off the last of the eggs and drinking coffee when the door opened and a senior officer came into the room. The lower-ranked officers got up from the table and left.

The man sat opposite me and nodded.

Damn that Coldi tendency to forego introductions. Meeting a total stranger could fire the *sheya* instinct for Coldi, and this could lead to embarrassing situations, like a fistfight. So you were supposed to have checked your reader to know the identity of people you met. My team would have already checked this group out and judged it safe, but I kept forgetting to do this because my human mind wasn't so afraid to meet people I hadn't interacted with before. It left me with no idea who this man was and no way to politely ask his name.

He spread a projection sheet out onto the table. It displayed a map with roads and the occasional village.

"The border is here," he said, indicating a line drawn across the map. "In the past few days, there has been a lot of activity just outside the enclave, especially on the west side of the road and the checkpoint. They've set up tents and occupied an old bunker. We guess that they're waiting for the bus to arrive, waiting for a good time to carry out their plans, whatever they are. Closing access to the Exchange, if they are ordered to do so."

"What have they done so far?" I asked.

"We've spotted them going on some patrols. We have established a camp here." He pointed. I couldn't see anything in the area where he held his finger. "It's also a bunker. Once we get confirmation that their satellite is out of action, we move the rest of the people up to this farmhouse. Seen from the camp, it's on the other side of a hill, although the hill doesn't show up very well in this image."

The bus was not expected at the checkpoint until tomorrow, and, for now, we should rest before going to the post closest to the checkpoint, while they waited for confirmation that the satellite was gone.

The house was really basic, and we were told to rest in the barn. The air smelled musty, but the hay was soft and we slept for a few hours while elsewhere in the world, and indeed in space, the wheels turned for us.

It was still light when I was wakened by someone walking through the barn. Another group of people had arrived. They had come with a number of trucks with Nations of Earth emblems on the side and contained yet more Coldi soldiers not in uniform.

I wondered where they had stolen the vehicles but was told that the emblems had been put on only yesterday. The vehicles even carried numbers on the roof, and apparently they represented valid numbers that belonged to decommissioned vehicles.

The kitchen provided a basic meal of some kind of heavy bread, taken standing up because there were about fifty people in the house now, and no room for everyone to sit. To be fair, they did offer me a seat, but I didn't take it, figuring that since there was a trip in the back of a truck ahead, I'd do enough sitting.

During this gathering the high-ranking officer whose name I still didn't know announced that the satellite was gone. Some people cheered at this.

While all of them were Coldi, I didn't think they were all off-Earth Asto military. There was a pair of women, for example—I judged them to be sisters—whose arms and necks were covered in tattoos. Their hair was cropped short and one had bleached it—Coldi hair tended to go purple if you did that—and the other had dyed it pink. There was no way that those were *Asto* military. They looked more like Zhori fighters.

But I hadn't wanted to know where Amarru got these people, and the less asked the better.

People who finished eating went outside and set about packing all our things into the trucks. There were seven trucks, and three of those were filled entirely with equipment. I spotted gun cases and communication equipment.

The team and I all went into the same truck. It was a basic personnel carrier with hard metal seats around the perimeter of the back compartment and a rack to store earth-style guns in the middle.

Our guns remained in their owners' arm brackets, except for

Evi's portable rocket launcher, which Sheydu rigged up sideways with the straps of the carry bag so it didn't go bouncing around the cabin.

Then we were off.

The convoy made its way over bumpy, dusty farm roads that went between abandoned farmhouses and collapsed sheds. Most of the paddocks no longer held animals and, certainly in summer, the ground was barren and rocky and almost devoid of vegetation. Here and there stood skeletons of dead trees. This was harsh, desolate country that had become too hot and dry even for goats.

We drove for perhaps an hour along bumpy tracks and sometimes straight through scrub and paddocks. Eventually we zigzagged up a hillside over a narrow and winding track, and came to a halt at the top.

Veyada, who sat next to the door, opened it and jumped out. He gestured for us all to come, so I followed Thayu and Sheydu down the little ladder.

We were on an inhospitable hillside, strewn with jagged boulders and leafless trees and shrubs. Some were dead, others probably only looked dead. The remains of a farmhouse stood at the end of the road, but the roof had collapsed and we clearly wouldn't be sleeping there.

A hot breeze blew dust over the parched terrain. I squinted into the low light. We were probably close to the checkpoint, but I couldn't see it. All around us were stony hills and more stony hills.

Several soldiers were unloading the trucks, carrying heavy equipment up a goat track that went up the ridge before disappearing down the other side.

We followed them.

The track first went up quite steeply before cresting the ridge and veering to the left.

A little distance along the hillside, around the corner, someone had built a shelter by digging into the hillside, with the dirt heaped against a rock wall so that it looked like an extension of the hill. With all of us filing into the shelter, it became quite crowded. It was perhaps two metres wide, with a ceiling made out of rusty concrete slabs that did not look like they would support the weight of soil on top. The back wall was taken up by plain timber benches—suffering a fair bit of dry rot—wide enough for someone to sleep on. There were even some half-eaten blankets. Also goat droppings, lots of those.

Narrow slits in the rough wall on the other side allowed us to look down into the valley.

A four-lane road ran through the valley, empty of traffic going in our direction, but with a line of waiting traffic going the other way.

A tall forbidding fence crossed the valley, with the only opening at the road, where a number of officers in Nations of Earth uniforms stood at a guard post and a gate. As we watched, the gate rolled aside to let through a small truck. The vehicle took about five minutes to cross a patch of no-man's-land to a second fence and gate where it stopped again.

This was the visual representation of the reality in which Athens had lived for the past twenty-five years. The outer fence was to stop people leaving Nations of Earth controlled territory, the inner fence controlled people entering the Exchange enclave. The outer border guards were Greek or from Nations of Earth. The inner ones were employed by the Exchange. They might be Coldi or Indrahui, or they might be natives of Athens. The same double checkpoints existed at the airport, only they didn't look half as threatening or ugly as they did there.

"It's busy," I said. I had been on that road, and remembered that there was always a queue, but couldn't remember having seen one this long.

"A lot of people arrived yesterday," the nameless mission commander said. "The news is getting out that there may be trouble."

"Where are these Cartel people?"

"They are camped on the other side." He handed me a pair of binoculars. They were Coldi-style, based on a projection rather than optics. They had a dial that allowed the user to change the ray frequency displayed on the inside of the eyepiece. Because it was still day, and the rocky landscape still warm from the sun, the infrared display was a mess, but I suspected it would become very useful in the dark.

I turned the display to visible light and dialled the magnification up.

Yes, I noticed a camp there, with a few vehicles and camouflaged tents. It was hard to see, because of the distance and because of the surrounding rocky outcrops and bushes.

"How many are here?" Sheydu asked.

"Four vehicles, probably about thirty or forty troops," said Evi, whose Indrahui eyes were much sharper than the rest of ours.

"Yes," the soldier confirmed. "We have counted three units of twelve each. Two are always on duty, one is off."

"What sort of backup do they have?" Sheydu asked.

"The closest base is over those mountains." He pointed. "It's not a straight road there, but if they fly, they can be here quickly. If we're going to do anything, we have to do it quickly, and then get out. If they fly, we'll have to take them down. That's the only option."

He went on to explain that Margarethe's bus would be here at about the same time tomorrow. He expected that the road would get busier, that more border guards would arrive and that units would arrive at the camp.

"They aren't really going to perform military action against their own *president*?" Veyada said.

For a Coldi, that was unthinkable.

"They'll say they didn't know she was in the bus," I said.

"Would they know?" Thayu asked.

"They probably do," the commander said.

"Can you intercept their communication?" Sheydu asked.

"They have some blocks which we are working to break. They don't communicate much. The camp doesn't even talk to the guards at the border post. We're not sure what is going on there."

But I thought I knew. The word *interesting* that Thayu loved to use did not spell *constitutional crisis*. It spelled *military coup*. The Pretoria Cartel was planning to increase its grip on the world.

Here were the players in front of us: the Nations of Earth guards at the border post who were probably unsuspecting, just doing their job, or knew about the camp and could not do anything because they were outnumbered by the Cartel militia people.

Nations of Earth was a victim as much as those people in Africa were, whose family members had gone missing. Only much of Nations of Earth was not aware of it yet. People like Piotr

Zbrowsky and Jarek Malicki were being used. And these guards here would soon find out the hard way, and when they did, the fact that this was a military coup in the making would become evident.

Margarethe was not going to Athens for talks with Amarru. She was going there for her safety.

Well shit. *That* should have been evident to me from the beginning.

I asked, "So if anyone tries to stop the bus at the border, we clear the way?"

The commander shook his head. "There is no if. We clear the path for the bus, once it's close enough that there is no time for either the guards or the camp to bring in reinforcements. We're not going to wait to find out what they're going to do."

22

I T WAS AMAZING HOW MUCH work was involved in
setting up a military action that would, with a bit of luck, last
less than five minutes. The soldiers discussed the best positions, the best weapons, a back-up plan and a whole lot of things
that left me with no idea what they were talking about.

I sat in on the meetings, but had almost nothing to say. A casual
observer might have thought I was there to provide a human
connection, in case I needed to speak to the border guards, but they
didn't plan on getting that close. I was there because ultimately, I
was in charge of the operation: it happened under my approval. As
groups went to perform tasks and peeled off from our camp in the
bunker, they faced me, they declared loyalty, and we shared a
moment of Coldi closeness before they went off.

There were guns to be calibrated and cleaned and tested, and
explosives to be set along the border fence. This happened at night
by people wearing full-body insulation suits so that they couldn't be
picked up on IR sensing.

Where had all their weaponry come from?

Sometimes I wondered who Nations of Earth thought they were
kidding when they thought they could stop the import of this kind
of material. If people wanted these weapons, they got them. And
there were already so many on Earth, I suspected that by now the
majority were made here, somewhere in Sudan probably.

While they were out, and Thayu had gone to sort out some communication thing, I shared a meal of rice cubes and sauce with Sheydu, who was monitoring the progress of her minions setting explosives along the fence. I mentioned that when we planned something with our team in Barresh, we would go in with much less preparation. We had a number of people who were decent with a gun and got the job done quickly.

"Yes, but we leave a lot of traces behind. If we perform an action, everyone will know we did it. I looked at that incident in this place called Ethiopia that everyone is talking about. Your signature is all over that. Evi and Telaris', too. I don't understand why Thayu let herself be roped into that project. She should have known better."

"We had no choice. There was no one to do all this stuff that you've been doing today. Even had there been, we had no time anyway."

"I think it had more to do with Thayu feeling insecure and not keen to toe the line after the treatment she received from some in the Inner Circle."

That was a story I was yet to hear. Why had Thayu decided to work for *gamra* while all the signs were that she was a very successful spy? Ezhya, clearly, trusted her, but some others might not have.

"She was on her own in a strange world. She had none of the help she needed."

I didn't like talking about Thayu behind her back, especially when she was only checking weapons on the other side of the hill.

"It was Taysha who compromised her position," Sheydu said.

He was the father of Thayu's son, who we had now lost contact with after his father's death.

"He wanted to use her to gain Ezhya's position. She had an opportunity to kill Taysha, and she didn't, because she considered that Ezhya should do this in order to cement his position. When she didn't kill him, a lot of people felt resentful towards her because they very much wanted Taysha out of the way, so Ezhya sent her as envoy to *gamra*. She felt that she was being dismissed, so she was not inclined to follow our procedures and protocol. That's why I think she tagged along with you without making sure that things were done properly."

I remembered how, when I first met her, Thayu had felt she needed to protect me from Ezhya's bodyguard, which contained Sheydu at that point.

"Yet you and Veyada fell under her when Ezhya's guard association fell apart."

"Of course we fell under her. She helped us. Thayu is very highly ranked."

These were things Thayu and I had not talked about. I'd never asked her rank when I first met her because it felt inappropriate. I'd never asked later because it felt like I should have asked much earlier and it made me feel inadequate as partner, not knowing this. And then I figured that it didn't make that much of a difference anyway because I didn't fit in their society. Until the time that I realised that I probably did.

"All right, if Thayu is ranked above most of Ezhya's old guard association, then why does Thayu think I am ranked above her?"

"I think you know that. You killed Taysha. If you were Coldi, your next step would have been to kill Ezhya when he turned up. Then you would have fought Asha for the position of Chief Coordinator."

"If I was Coldi. I'm not. I didn't like killing Taysha, but it was us or him. Now that it's all sorted, I have no inclination to harm any of those people."

"No. That's your problem." She pushed herself up and went to get some more tea which sat on a rickety wooden table in the corner of the bunker.

I looked at her back. "Seriously, Sheydu, would you want me to pick a fight with Ezhya and Asha?"

"It's not about wanting. What I want doesn't matter. It happens, that's the end of it."

It happened because of the *sheya* instinct, which I didn't have, a fact that put me in a very strange position. Then another disturbing thought. Veyada and Sheydu had come to me when Ezhya's guard association fell apart. I had always assumed that it was a severe demotion for both of them to be placed under Thayu, and hadn't understood why this had happened, but was it, really? When I asked why they had come, they had told me some story about wanting to learn and expand their knowledge. I had assumed that was an excuse, but come to think of it, Coldi rarely made such excuses.

Damn, the more I thought about this, the more it did my head in.

———

Thayu and the others came back later, reporting that they had placed all the bugs and triggers, and Sheydu went out to place more explosives.

The rest of us gathered in the dark on the shielded side of the ridge and drank tea. Some people stood guard; others went to sleep.

Thayu and I were directed to one of the vans where, on top of duffel bags and other equipment, they had made a surprisingly comfortable bed. The back door remained open, and a fluffy blanket kept us warm. It was a strange place to sleep, but I slept better than I would have expected, waking up only when the sky turned light.

The bus was getting closer, we heard at breakfast, and last minute preparations were made. I kept out of the way in the bunker, watching the growing line of vehicles wanting to enter the enclave on the main road. Was I imagining it or had more border guards arrived?

Our plan was that an explosion of a power station that stood by the side of the road would divert the attention away from the checkpoint and cause the civilian vehicles on the road to be evacu-ated. While the commotion was going on in the valley, we would take one of the armoured vehicles down the hill to the checkpoint and clear it, so that the bus could move through unhindered.

People in the communication hub were now talking to the bus, and it was expected at the checkpoint earlier than first thought. They had made good time.

But there was an issue that became clear as soon as the bus was about half an hour away: it was being shadowed by a gyrocopter. It was an unmarked craft that could belong to the Pretoria Cartel, or it could have been hired by journalists.

The members of our team were checking it out.

I could hear Reida's voice through the loudspeaker. ". . . Don't know who they are. They don't seem to be marked and they don't fly directly over us, so we can't get a clean reading on them."

"Have they tried speaking to you?"

"No. We've tried telling them to leave, but we've had no response."

The military communications team then tried to get readings from the gyrocopter.

They established that the craft had taken off from a nearby airport, but could not find out who was on board.

"It has all the signs that it involves Tamerians," Sheydu said to me while we watched the activities. She had been impatiently striding from one side of the shelter to the other, waiting for the action to start. Computers and radios were very much not her thing.

"We need to decide what to do about the craft," one of the soldiers said.

Everyone looked at me.

So, I was meant to make this call. Yes, Coldi would defer decision-making like this to their leader, but damn.

"Could it be forced down?" I asked.

"We could simulate an attack on it and scare it; absolutely," one of the soldiers said. "For obvious reasons, we prefer not to do this, since it would involve making us visible."

Fair enough. "Any alternatives?"

"We have the power to eliminate it. They're in range."

Shoot it down, of course, dumb Delegate. "Wouldn't that give away our location?"

"We'd move the launcher to a different location afterwards, but yes, it would give away that we're in the area."

Well, shit.

"I don't think that's a palatable option," Veyada said, and I was glad to have him on board to save my butt. "The way I understand this *referendum* business is that upsets are rarely good for the ruling faction, even more so when it comes out that the action was unjustified. We cannot establish with certainty that these are Tamerians—"

"But they probably are," said one of the soldiers.

"I agree, but we cannot be certain, so if we take out the craft and they turn out *not* to be Tamerians, then there will be trouble."

Credit Veyada with having grasped the situation so thoroughly.

"Taking out this craft is the only option?" I asked. "With the added risk that if we shoot, debris may fall on the road, on the bus or one of the vehicles that carry the president's security staff, or on a civilian vehicle."

"There is another option," Thayu said.

Everyone looked at her.

"These gyrocopters: if you fly a craft over the top of them, and engage the downward jets, their engines will have trouble coping. If you keep the camouflage on, no one will know that the craft is there."

They liked that idea, and I felt proud of Thayu. She was smart, and she didn't talk when she had nothing to say.

As it turned out, the group had an Asto-made craft with them which they kept powered, and as result it had been hidden so well in the middle of an open field that I hadn't seen it.

The small crew that boarded it a few minutes later seemed to step into oblivion when they climbed up the ladder. One moment they were there; the next, they were not.

By the time they were ready to go, the bus had come much closer.

Sheydu was nervous because she wanted the craft gone. It would interfere with the reception on her explosives, and they needed to go off when the bus was at a certain distance.

The craft took off. I could still barely see it.

Then Sheydu went to her control panel in the back of a van. It was time to go. We climbed into our allocated vehicles, taking everything with us. Once the explosion went off, this shelter wasn't safe anymore.

As I sat in the press of bodies in the back of one of the vehicles, waiting for the go sign, my heart was thudding.

Thayu, next to me, was calm and composed. She was checking her weapon, and glanced at me to do the same. I took the gun from its bracket.

We waited, silently.

My hands were sweaty.

Drops of sweat also ran over my chest.

It was so hot inside this vehicle, and everyone else looked so patient and calm.

And then a big thud made the ground shake, followed by another one. Those were Sheydu's explosions.

We were on.

The column of vehicles rolled down the hill. There was no track, and the ground in the paddock was bumpy. These all-terrain vehicles powered through any obstacles. They simply flattened the posts under their wheels, crunching over the remnants. We were being tossed and shaken in the back.

Then one of the solders climbed up onto the metal framework in the middle of the cargo area that I had assumed was for storing weapons but turned out to be for standing on. He opened the roof. Air laced with dust and acrid smoke came in. I hung onto my seat.

Another soldier climbed up as well. Thayu handed them the big gun out of the box. It took both of them to secure the weapon in a bracket that balanced on the edge of the roof opening. They turned it on, while the truck barrelled down the hill.

And then . . .

The soldier shouted, "Incoming!"

Both the soldiers ducked. Thayu grabbed my shoulder and pushed me down.

The truck swerved and slid sideways. Hit a rock. Almost tipped. A big thud made the air shake.

"What was that?" I asked Thayu.

"They have another gyrocopter. It fired at us."

The two soldiers had scrambled back into their position and pointed the gun up. Lights blinked on the weapon's panel. The charged plasma whirled in the chamber.

The thudding blades of the gyrocopter made the air vibrate. I held my breath. In my mind, I was taken back in time to that gyrocopter at the airport at Rotterdam as it had banked, and someone in the cargo hold had shot the jet that I had been due to board. I remembered Nicha pulling me along.

I'd been so lucky to have survived that adventure.

Someone yelled, "Live!"

Next, the big gun went off with a *foomp*, and again. The air was sucked out of my lungs. I bent over with my hands over my ears, as I'd been taught.

The truck swerved again. The safety harness bit into my shoulders.

Foomp, foomp.

I couldn't hear anything, couldn't see anything for the dust entering the cabin. I was faintly aware that if we stopped, if the truck was hit and we needed to get out, if we arrived at the checkpoint and that gyrocopter was still up there, I would need every skerrick of my rudimentary warfare skills to save my sorry butt. No, in preference to that, save Margarethe who was on that bus barrelling into this utter disaster.

Thayu moved next to me, handing another canister to the soldiers with the cannon.

There was a brief moment where the men opened the holder, dropped the empty canister on the floor with a loud clang and slotted in the new one.

Plasma whirled and they were ready again.

Foomp, foomp.

Then an ear-splitting crack, and groaning and creaking of metal, followed by a loud crash. Then dust whirled into the cabin.

The two soldiers clapped each other on the shoulder.

The truck kept going through a cloud of black smoke. As we passed, the back opening—the only way I could see out—offered a view of a burning pile of rubble on the hillside. The second gyrocopter, I guessed.

But now we were being fired on from ahead—or at least I thought the dull thuds against the vehicle were from bullets hitting the bulletproof glass. The two soldiers in the roof had turned their attention to the front of the vehicle.

"There is the bus," Thayu said.

"Road's free," one of the soldiers said.

Another was speaking into an earpiece. "The camp has been destroyed, but a number of vehicles are approaching so we need to make it quick."

The truck bumped and jumped over the rocky terrain and all of a sudden came to a screeching halt.

All other soldiers rose and jumped out the back. We followed, at a slightly slower pace into the dust.

We ran down a gully and then onto the empty road. A fake Nations of Earth truck with soldiers sheltered us. Somewhere in the distance I could still hear the *foomp, foomp* of discharges, but that soon stopped.

Smoke drifted over the road. Flames rose from the area of the militia camp, and on the hillside behind us, the gyrocopter was still burning. A small grass fire had started next to the road.

A single private truck driver who had been unable to shift his vehicle sat white-faced in the cabin with his hands up, whimpering.

The guards at the border post stood in the middle of the road, also with their hands raised.

The guardhouse had been reduced to a smouldering pile of rubble. Two of our other trucks had stopped there and Coldi soldiers checked in the rubble and surrounding land for danger. One gestured with his gun at the border guards to open the gate.

The man, wide-eyed, pressed a code on the locking mechanism.

Slowly, the gate rolled open.

I was glad that all the other members of my team were there, including Sheydu, her hair grey from dust, Evi and Telaris—both with huge guns slung over their shoulders—Deyu with a rocket launcher and Veyada carrying a backpack full of his mother's packets of explosives, remote detonators and other deadly items. He looked dusty, and the scratch on his face that he'd acquired vaulting the fence when fleeing the elephant had reopened, but he greeted me with a satisfied expression.

The black bus rolled up behind us, dark and menacing, and looking absurdly clean. The door opened.

Maya said, "It looks like the border patrol is not interested in seeing our documentation."

We climbed up the stairs, dusty and sweaty, into the bus' luxurious interior.

23

IT WAS LIKE ENTERING another world, one of sophistication, muted sounds and softly beeping equipment. Devlin sat at the main communication console, together with Reida and Eva and Alma, both looking at us with wide eyes. Lenka was with them, but she merely glanced up. I remembered her telling me that her husband was into boxing, so maybe some blood and dust didn't bother her. As an aside, I wondered why he wasn't here.

Margarethe sat on the other side of the aisle with her reader on her lap, where she had been writing something. She gestured me to the seat opposite her.

"Tea?"

"That would be great." When one had run through a dusty paddock, had been shot at and dodged explosions, tea was an awesome thing to have. "I'll make the seat dirty, though."

"If that's the worst we'll have to cope with, I'll be happy."

I sat down.

The other members of my team had all collapsed into the soft seats, taking off heavy equipment, but leaving their armour on.

The bus started moving, through the checkpoint, through the no-man's-land to the second checkpoint, where a couple of curious guards—two Coldi, one Greek—had already rolled the gate wide open.

Maya spoke to them briefly, but they were all smiles and let us and our newfound jumble of a military convoy through.

Phew. We had made it.

I sipped from the steaming hot tea and let the feeling of calm and safety wash over me.

Then I said, "Tell me this, honestly: your leaving Rotterdam was in effect the result of a coup?"

She didn't miss a beat.

"I wouldn't use that word, or if I wanted to use it, I would describe it as a very slow one—and unsuccessful, I should add, because Vice President Patel is firmly in control. I have spoken to him and most communication issues in Rotterdam have resolved."

That was only because someone up in space had, under my orders, destroyed a satellite.

We were now entering the outskirts of the city, the poorer suburbs populated by refugees, many of them African, who had made their lives in the enclave—most of them because they, or their parents, had gotten stuck here.

Athens was not, and had never been, a city as cleanly organised as some of the northern European ones. The main roads were wide, but they were busy and chaotic.

Our convoy attracted a fair bit of attention, since we came with six military vehicles, one of which had sustained some battle damage in the form of a shattered windscreen and dented roof. The Coldi soldiers sat triumphantly on the bent frame. What seatbelts?

A police vehicle tagged along, but didn't muster the courage to try to stop us. They were probably waiting for reinforcements.

By the time we had crawled a couple of blocks into the chaos, people were coming out of the apartment blocks that lined the streets, or appearing on balconies.

Some of them shouted, and I couldn't hear what they said.

Maya opened the window. The sound of many voices drifted into the cabin.

Margarethe stared at me. "They're chanting my name? No one has done that since the night I won the election."

A couple more police cars arrived, but instead of stopping us, they proceeded to clear the road. They knew where we were going:

not the city's centre, but the hillside suburb that housed the Exchange.

We arrived there not fifteen minutes later. The gates rolled aside at our approach, letting in the bus and the six military vehicles.

We went up the driveway. I told Maya to stop in front of the entrance under the overhang of the awning. When the door opened, Amarru stood at the entrance. I had *never* seen Amarru in the foyer of the building.

She had brought a bevy of Indrahui guards who lined up between the bus and the building. Evi and Telaris got out—Telaris had acquired a giant smudge on his back—and Reida and Deyu, both looking dark and menacing, and highly armed. Then the others.

I accompanied Margarethe, and we were followed by Eva and Alma, Karana with Ayshada on her arm, Nicha, Eirani, Lenka, Logan and Maya.

Amarru met Margarethe a few steps outside the building's glass doors. Two women, two worlds. Both were of similar age, both held considerable power, both wanted to see Earth join the only feasible future laid out for it.

They clasped hands, like equals, and they were, even in Coldi eyes.

Margarethe—being of northern European descent—was much taller than Amarru. "Well met," she said in Coldi.

"Well met," Amarru said in Isla. "We are honoured for you and your party to be our guests."

We went into the building.

Amarru's guards informed my association on the logistics of our stay, while I went with the two women in the lift to the familiar second-highest floor in the building, which was Amarru's inner sanctum.

Domestic staff bustled about bringing refreshments. Since it was now late afternoon, dinner would be forthcoming, or so I hoped, because my stomach was gurgling. Warfare made one hungry.

But while the staff were running around, Amarru took Margarethe into her communication hub and showed her the communication issues—and since I'd last seen the projection, it had gotten so much worse. On top of southern Africa, most of western

Africa was out, as well as southeast Asia, the American east coast and much of northern and western Europe. Proof that the satellite wasn't doing all that much and that the improved communication in Rotterdam was likely a relaxation from the Cartel's side so as not to draw too much attention to themselves.

I asked her how our campaign to hand-deliver voting cards was going.

"The reports say that it's been going well, but most of the affected voting stations are in the no-communication zone, so we don't know for sure. But the cards were printed and delivered, and are being distributed. We'll have to see what happens on the day."

And that day was only two days away.

One woman had the map with the election stations on the screen. Most of the countries in Africa showed red—meaning there was no communication—as did South East Asia, western Europe and the American east coast. But now also New Zealand was red. That meant that my father's vote wouldn't even count. I asked Amarru, "Voting cards went out to all these people?"

"Yes. If you were to go to the departure hall, you would see that it is virtually empty. We've engaged every craft we have."

"I bet there are lots of reports of illegal sightings of off-Earth craft, which our opponents can use to challenge the result."

"I haven't seen any yet, but there are bound to be. We'll have to weather that if it comes to the point where we have to face those questions."

Damn. I felt sick. So much hinged on this operation.

"Any news from Dharma?" Margarethe asked. As with Thayu and Isla, I knew that Margarethe had a working level of understanding of Coldi.

"He is likely to be in one of the regions where we do not have coverage," Amarru said.

"We need to talk about this coverage issue," I said.

Both women turned to me.

"I believe it would be hugely beneficial if we could issue a statement—a joint statement between you two—that acknowledges the existence of a Coldi network that uses Earth technology and that has been used in the past to spy on organisations and individuals."

Amarru gave me a sharp look. Margarethe's expression was more reserved. Margarethe didn't know what was at stake, she didn't know about my long-running problem with this issue. I'd failed to properly address it last time I was here, and all the previous times I'd come, because I believed—and I still did—that Amarru used the network for the good of the community. But that could easily change if someone else took her position. Also she *had* to be made to understand that humans in general did *not* appreciate being spied on. And that this would create serious problems in any future cooperation.

I *had* to resolve it, and now was as good a time as any.

I said in a slow and clear voice, "It is time that this is addressed. High time. Without exception, every opponent to Earth joining *gamra* I've spoken to in the past ten years has mentioned that they are worried about Coldi spying. They get their facts wrong. They confuse Coldi with *gamra*. They confuse Asto with Coldi. They confuse the Athens Exchange with Asto. Because no one has ever openly talked about this network, its history and its reach and function."

"Our existence depends on it," Amarru said in Coldi, and she didn't look at me.

"No, it doesn't, no longer."

She said nothing. Oh boy, I think she was angry. A number of people in the room looked from me to her and back. Thayu, who had been working at one of the workstations, watched with wide eyes. She half-rose from her seat, as if ready to spring.

My heart thudded. This was a confrontation I should have had years ago. I'd left it to the very last minute and this was probably not the right setting to have it.

Amarru remained silent, looking at the ground.

"Amarru, you have the register. You have regular Exchange coverage, which is both approved and tolerated by the local authorities. If there is one thing I've learned from this trip, it's that there is such a thing as native Coldi on Earth. They survive perfectly well without any spy network and have done so for many years. They don't even want it. It's a relic from a time past when the refugees from Asto came here. It's time to come clean about it, and cooperate, rather than exist in some kind of alternate universe where local laws don't apply to you. It *needs* to be resolved. I've brought you someone to talk to about this. Do it."

To be honest, she looked like she was about to kill me. I'd never confronted a Coldi person like this. They didn't *do* disagreements the same way humans did. At least not with people within their loyalty network. I didn't even know if Amarru *was* part of that loyalty network anymore.

Then she breathed out. Her hands—that she had held balled against her sides—relaxed. Her shoulders drooped. She bowed her head ever so slightly.

"Yes," she said, in a barely audible voice. "It will be done."

Thayu sat down, blowing out a breath.

Margarethe looked from me to Amarru, frowning. She had no idea what had just happened.

"Well, I'll leave you to discuss it, then." My heart was still hammering. "Make a joint statement about the network, about the next step in the agreement, about stages of disclosure. It would be hugely beneficial if we could have a statement that can go out with this afternoon's news cycle."

With that, I'd said what was on my mind, and went to the door. I was hungry and wanted to have a rest.

Walking next to me down the hallway, Thayu said, "That was one of the most subtle loyalty alignments I've seen."

I would have protested that it had nothing to do with loyalty alignments, that it was just something that needed to be said, but I knew she was right. As I continued to bumble my way through instincts I didn't have, I collected an increasing number of loyalty threads. "I've been wanting to have that confrontation for a while now. I've even been afraid of it."

"Well, you shouldn't have been. When he took you on, Ezhya should have made it clear that Amarru falls under you, not the other way around."

What she didn't say was that if I hadn't been afraid to have this conversation, I might have been able to prevent this precarious situation we found ourselves in today.

———

Amarru did talk to Margarethe. I didn't attend the discussion, but it went on for a long time. It was, as far as I could tell, fairly amicable.

All I knew was that at the end of it, they gave a joint statement in the presence of whatever journalists we could muster, where Margarethe declared that a formal agreement had been made to investigate the network, to make sure it didn't break any laws, and to coordinate the use of the system.

It was all very diplomatic, and much still needed to be sorted out, but it was a start, and news channels from around the world carried the story.

In between this and hoping that Dharma's work would pay off, we'd done as much as we could do.

The referendum started the next morning, and we had to trust on our plan, since the communication blocks showed no sign of lifting.

I joined up with my team and I spent a tense evening pacing about our accommodation. I spoke to my father and told him I wanted him to be prepared to come with me to Barresh if the no vote won.

He seemed relaxed about it, in his idyllic corner of the world. He said the sun was shining, he and Erith had gone out to vote already, there looked to be a good turnout and everything would be fine.

I wished I could share his optimism.

I went to speak to Eva, who was in the middle of a yelling match at her husband.

"No!" she was saying. "I've had enough of you and your friends. You can't tell me what to do anymore. I've *finished* with you—oh!"

She had noticed me.

"I'm sorry if I'm interrupting."

"You're not interrupting anything." She broke the connection and yanked off her earpiece, but when she looked at me next, her eyes glittered with tears.

"Look, I'm really sorry, for everything."

"No, Cory. You told me all those years ago, that I should study. And I did and I never understood why. And you told me that I should have opinions, and I thought that was strange. My parents just wanted me to get married so when you took off with Thayu, I was relieved, really, because I didn't want to get married. But then Jarek came along and he made my father happy, and when my father is unhappy, he just makes life unpleasant for everyone. So I married Jarek, but he was always a controlling jerk. And I understood what you meant. Because if I wanted to stand on my own, I needed to make a living that didn't depend on my family or my husband. So I learned to do things. I can stand on my own two feet, because I can do my own things now."

Her reader beeped. She looked at it, rolled her eyes and cut the beeping. "He's still trying to control my life. But you know what? He's being controlled as well. It's like a cult, with all the late-night meetings and the secrecy and the pledges to give money to worthy candidates. It has to stop."

Yes, it had to stop.

———

The morning of the referendum dawned bright and hot. We had a quick breakfast on the balcony of our apartment while that side of the building was still in the shade and the air was cool.

I didn't enjoy it as much as I normally would have. I'd slept badly, as my mind was going around in ever-diminishing circles.

But I was glad to have my association with me and they were all at the table: Nicha and Ayshada, Thayu, Deyu and Reida, Veyada and Sheydu, and of course Evi and Telaris. They had become my family and I would not go anywhere without them. If, after today, it turned out that I was no longer welcome on my home world, then that would be sad, but I knew I would always have them to help me.

Thayu touched my hand under the table: that Coldi gesture of solidarity.

She and the rest of the team had things planned for today that involved brushing up on skills and liaison with security personnel. They did not need to come with me to Amarru's communication hub to watch the nail-biting wait for election results. I had told them I didn't want to do that to them. Thayu accompanied me as far as the door to Amarru's office.

She touched me on the cheek. She didn't tell me not to worry, because she knew I would. She didn't tell me that she hoped that

Dharma would turn up, because we all hoped that, but he appeared to have fallen off a cliff, together with all the craft Amarru had sent out, all of which had gone into areas where we had no communication. War might have broken out there and we wouldn't know about it.

She didn't say anything about those things because we had talked about it at length last night. She just brushed my cheek and said, "Good luck."

I nodded, my mouth too dry to speak.

And she said, "I love you."

I pulled her briefly to me so that our foreheads touched. Coldi did not kiss, and she didn't find it particularly pleasant. But this, standing in each other's warmth and smelling each other's scent, that was intimacy to them.

Then I let her go and slid from that comfortable envelope of warmth and love. I waved to her at the door and watched her disappear into the lift before entering Amarru's office.

Whatever happened, we would continue with our efforts to have a family. We could try a few more things without having to resort to the surrogate option, and we would try them all.

In Amarru's communication hub, the action was in full swing.

In the semidarkness of the room, people flicked through screens, spoke to off-site people through earpieces, collected reports and scrolled through the news.

I went to the central bench, where Amarru sat with Margarethe. They both looked at me when I joined them. Margarethe looked like I felt: exhausted.

I asked, "Anything happening so far?"

I meant anything with the referendum, anything that would show that Dharma was alive or our huge action to distribute cards was having effect. I knew it was too early to see, but the uncertainty and tension ate at me.

"The news is full of speculation about why I'm not in Rotterdam," Margarethe said. "It seems the fact has finally reached the mainstream press, and they're asking questions. The right kind of questions, I think."

She showed me some headlines that wondered aloud whether certain factions in Nations of Earth had become too powerful. They did not mention the Pretoria Cartel outright, but mentioned "business interests" and "bought voters". As far as I could see, it was too little, too late, and wouldn't change the result today, but if the yes vote won—just if—it would be a good basis to build onto.

Shit. We were all in damage control mode.

The Pretoria Cartel and their hangers-on had succeeded in almost a complete take-over of the world by stealth. I was sure that had always been the plan.

For most of the day, we watched the news feeds with footage of people lining up to vote electronically, and of course this all happened in places where we knew there was still reliable coverage. We got a few messages from electoral offices outside the safe one, stating that their systems had not satisfied the parameters for reliable voting and that people in their region could choose to vote on paper. They said nothing about the arrival or not of hundreds of thousands of voting cards.

Voting was not compulsory, and people had been poring over the question of how low the percentage could be before the vote was no longer considered valid, but it didn't look like the regulations had considered that aspect. As long as the voting station's electronic systems returned uncompromised checks, people could vote. If only five percent voted, but those votes were valid, then that was accepted as a valid result. What about the people who wanted to vote but couldn't, I asked. But that, apparently, had never been a consideration. Nations of Earth only wanted to hear from people they approved of anyway: people who were educated and engaged in politics and probably lived in the major cities. This was something observers had been saying for as long as I remembered.

Once voting stations closed in Rotterdam, we needed to wait for the Americas. The day dragged on forever.

I went back to our accommodation where I found my association in discussion about training programs for all of us. At least some people were doing useful things.

After a short rest, I returned to the hub very early in the morning, because it was almost time for election results.

The big projection in the centre of the room with the map of the world and all the voting stations still showed a huge percentage of stations out of action.

I had somehow hoped against better knowledge that more would have come online.

No one had heard from Dharma.

The news—in a different projection—contained lots of hand wringing, and the news that the president was fine and watching the results from a safe location.

There was also news from the Nations of Earth court—almost all of them Cartel stooges—who stated smugly that the people would speak and that they had confidence that the people would make the decision that was right for Earth, with the underlying implication that this decision would be "no".

Watching the news feed made me so nervous I felt sick. There were a lot of reports from outside polling stations in Europe. Reporters asked people how they had voted, and mostly they had said no.

Then finally, the polls closed in the very last zone to vote: the pacific zone that included the islands and Hawaii. By now, it was light outside.

The map, that was fed directly from the electoral office at the Nations of Earth compound, went grey.

The first result popped up in Belgium. It was a red dot, meaning no. The second one was also red, also in Belgium.

New Zealand reported three green ones, and we cheered.

Belgium was the first country to fall, as only one area recorded a green majority. The area around Rotterdam followed quickly. Dots of green sprang up in South America. New Zealand remained mostly green, but the red stain spread from western Europe like blood. Except for Athens.

One by one, the areas reported. Northern Africa, mostly red; north-western America, whatever didn't remain grey went mostly red. Africa remained grey. Huge sections of Asia remained grey. South America became mostly green.

We watched, in horror as the counting and reporting slowed.

Red had the majority, but huge sections of the world remained grey. Margarethe was talking to Vice President Patel in Rotterdam. Her expression was dark.

I overheard snatches of the conversation. What could they do to make the result fairer? It looked like more than half the regions of the world had been unable to vote.

Amarru was busy, too, talking to someone in a serious voice. I was guessing she spoke to Ezhya or Asha, in orbit, ready to rescue us. I thought about Thayu, and how I wanted her with me, and my father and Erith and the farm and the boat and all the things he loved and I loved and didn't want to abandon.

But then a female operator shouted. "I got something. Putting it on loudspeaker now!"

A clear voice broke through the soft chatter of communications, "Coming in."

Amarru said, "Who's speaking?"

"Dharma Yuwono. We're coming in with a fleet."

24

A **HUGE CHEER BROKE OUT** in the room.

Amarru's staff quickly established that Dharma was aboard one of the larger cargo ships that Amarru had sent out, and it was right outside Athens, in the company of a fleet of cargo craft, trader craft, two "borrowed" gyrocopters and a few Sudanese solar gliders. They had struck a bit of trouble in some of the polling stations, because of Cartel militia trying to prevent counting, and in more than one case, trying to set fire to the boxes with voting cards.

Dharma said that he had made the executive decision to bring all cards and voting station personnel to Athens and he was sorry about the fuss that would create.

They were, Dharma said, followed by a number of gyrocopters of uncertain origin, which had been smart enough to keep their distance.

Then the hub downstairs reported that a whole fleet of ships was coming in. They could handle the Asto craft but what should they do with the craft that were obviously local?

They could land on the lawn, Amarru said, and then sent people to make sure said lawn was clear of people, because most of the local employees were arriving for work at this time of day.

The hub workers brought a live feed from the main arrival and departure hall downstairs. People were running around frantically on all of the levels, making preparations, which they would normally do much more spaced out over their shift.

Soon the first craft blasted out of the tunnel. It was a larger transport craft, not as silent as the smaller craft, and it would normally never be allowed to leave the Exchange enclave in any other direction than into orbit. You could see the air shimmering from the heat of the downward jets as it manoeuvred into its landing bay, directed by Exchange staff.

The door opened and a man came into the opening. He raised his fist. Everyone in the communication room cheered. It was Dharma.

He came down the ramp, followed by a couple of bewildered-looking *human* electoral observers dressed in Nations of Earth blue, pushing trolleys with stacks and stacks of boxes.

Exchange staff directed them out of the hall.

"Where are they going with those cards?" I asked.

"There is a hall in the town centre down the road," Margarethe said. "They have to be on neutral ground to authorise the boxes to be opened and votes to be counted."

Soon, the arrival hall was a sea of blue shirts and work overalls as all the boxes were arranged according to the region of origin and then transported out of the hall by Exchange workers.

Amarru directed them all to a line of vans outside the Exchange, and soon there was a steady stream of trucks, accompanied by security, that took the boxes of cards and the election workers out of the gates.

It took a while for the live feed to be set up in that hall.

First we saw the trucks arrive in the area—it looked like a sports hall—watched by some bemused locals. Then the trucks reversed to the entrance, guards arrived and the boxes went inside.

Amarru had the canteen bring down lunch so that we could keep watching it.

Local police came in for a look, and argued with the guards at the doors. Soon the first journalists arrived.

And boxes were still being brought in, stacked into huge piles according to region. Other people then carried those boxes to waiting vehicles, where they went to other hastily-set up counting stations across the city. There, groups of people in blue waited to tip the boxes out and begin counting, putting the cards into piles, which were then re-counted twice by others and placed in bundles of a hundred and then counted again, and restacked in boxes. More people in blue shirts arrived all the time. They either came with the craft, accompanying their own district's voting cards, or they arrived from within the enclave and even outside it, because they wanted to help.

I sat until after dark, watching transfixed as the people who valued a fair election in the world came together to help.

Slowly, results started to come in, first from Indonesia, where most of the districts voted yes. This was not surprising, because Dharma and Gusamo were from Indonesia and their treatment at the hands of the Cartel had received a lot of attention there.

Parts of central and southern Africa came in. A few voted no, but most of them yes. Most of the sparse red spots on the map turned green. Many of the grey areas turned green as well. Central and southern Africa fell almost entirely to the yes vote.

The percentage of districts that voted yes climbed, and climbed and climbed. Thirty-five percent, thirty-seven, forty, forty-two, forty-five. Then the count struck a patch of no votes.

I was a ball of nerves by that time.

Come on, come on, come on.

Forty-six.

Another two no districts in northern Africa.

Forty-seven.

A long time with no results.

Forty-eight.

Everyone around me was silent, staring, wide-eyed at the projection.

Then: forty-nine.

Two more red districts.

Fifty.

And fifty-one.

Someone yelled, "Look!"

Deyu was pointing at the projection.

Yes, I noticed it, too. Pretoria had gone green.

Everyone in the room went nuts.

"We won! We won!"

Some people jumped up and cheered and hugged, all very *human*. Many of these people had been here for generations. They belonged here, and now they would finally be acknowledged.

Amarru said, "Listen."

From somewhere outside the building came the sound of thumps and honking of horns. We sped to her office which overlooked the driveway and the hill, down into the city.

People on the lawn were cheering, the busses honking their horns. Somewhere out near the harbour, fireworks went up.

Thayu touched my shoulder from behind. "Hey. I guess this means we can keep coming here."

I hugged her, and the others came, too and I hugged them as well.

"I was afraid I would never be able to ride a horse again," Deyu said.

Because that was clearly all that mattered.

And I didn't care. I was tired, but didn't care to go to bed. We held an impromptu party in the canteen, which was fuller than I'd ever seen before. The roof almost lifted when Margarethe came in.

Everyone else was there: Dharma had come, and Eva, Alma and Maya. This place that had always been the domain of Coldi people would soon belong to everyone.

Margarethe told me the assembly was in shock. Vice President Patel was happy, but many others were not. She would need to replace many of the judges at the court, and insist that countries sent delegates who represented the country's overall vote. She said there would be inquiries into vote-buying and blackmailing of judges. There would be an investigation into tampering with communication by the Pretoria Cartel.

I spoke to Ezhya briefly. He seemed happy. "I must clearly prepare for an official visit."

As was typical for him, he invited himself.

He also wanted to know when I was coming back to Barresh, because he was keen to hear about the election.

Minke Kluysters sent Margarethe a personal letter of congratulations. She showed it to me.

"He's infuriatingly proper," she said. "You will never catch him doing anything against the law. He's very, very smart."

"He owns Sandowne Pharmaceuticals," I said. "They have been caught in this horrid affair of producing Tamerians. I'm sure that will come before a judge somewhere."

"The company, yes, but he will have some sort of excuse that lets him off the hook. He won't even need to appear in court. That's beneath him."

I wasn't so sure. Coldi lawyers were very good and they would now work with Nations of Earth.

————

We finally went to bed very early and were up again early the next day, because I wanted to return to New Zealand as soon as possible. But there were other things to be taken care of first.

Eva told me that she had elected to stay in Athens for the time being. While Alma had to return to work in Rotterdam, Eva felt that if she returned there, Jarek would try to talk her into staying with him. Her parents would tell her how bad she was, and she would just give in to them.

"I've had enough of doing what they said. Look where that got me."

I gave all her details to Amarru, who said that with her skills, Eva should have little trouble finding a job.

In the rush of people arranging things, I spotted Veyada with the Hedron lawyer Mereeni, vigorously arguing as they always had when we were at the court. I couldn't see any sign that they were attracted to each other, so I decided to bluntly ask Veyada about it while we were in the canteen.

He looked down. "I'm sorry."

"There is no need to be sorry about finding someone you like."

"I am sorry, because she doesn't fit in our association and I don't know what to do."

"What would you *like* to do?"

He laughed. "You know that you can ask the dumbest questions?"

I laughed, too. "Why don't you go and do it, then? Take her to a nice place and do whatever you do to a nice woman when you're together."

Veyada was always confident, sure of himself and clearly-spoken, but now he looked down, his cheeks red.

"It wouldn't be right."

"Why not?"

"Because she's from Hedron. Your association is loyal to Ezhya. I am loyal to Ezhya." Coldi from Hedron were mostly Ezmi, and they overwhelmingly didn't have the *sheya* instinct that led to the formation of rigid societal structures.

"But if she had the instinct, would you still have felt attracted to her?"

For a moment, it looked like he was going to say *I'm not attracted to her,* but then he blew a noisy breath out through his nose. "It's hard to say. I don't know where she stands on the subject of *sheya.*"

"Does she know herself?" Because *some* people from Hedron had the instinct. It was a genetic thing.

"I think she's been taken by surprise by it. She says it's why she constantly argues with me."

I had learned to interpret that as a sign that two people were equal in standing.

"Would she enjoy being taken somewhere by you where there is no one except the two of you?"

"Maybe, but it's irrelevant, because it won't happen." He looked at his knees.

"Veyada, I respect you very much, and I hate to see you unhappy. You've been unsettled and unhappy ever since you met her."

"That's because I've neglected to protect you properly. It has nothing to do with her."

"I think it does. What if I told you that I don't mind that she's from Hedron and I'd be happy if she came with us."

"I'd still tell you that my loyalty is with Ezhya and you."

"Does that mean that you can't see her? Whatever happened to the wide web of Coldi loyalties?"

"This is different."

"How? I can't see it."

He sighed again and let his shoulders sink.

"Or would it be that you're afraid she might refuse because of what you are and you're making up reasons not to be the first one to admit you're attracted to her so you can't be rejected?"

His eyes widened briefly.

Bingo.

"Go and talk to her. Ask her for dinner. Go into town. Stay in town, if you don't want any prying eyes or gossip."

He nodded and left the canteen.

I didn't see him for the rest of the day. I had no idea if he did as I told him. I asked Thayu and she didn't know, and I asked Sheydu and she didn't know for sure either.

But he was there the next morning when we were about to leave to return to New Zealand.

I didn't ask him any questions that might embarrass him. He had gotten very keen on doing ongoing security and fitness training, and kept talking about that, whether he wanted to do this to impress someone or not.

He seemed more relaxed, so whatever had happened or not happened, he had peace with it.

We spent another week relaxing with my father and Erith. We went to the beach, played with Fred, and went sailing and fishing. Veyada took part in everything. He played cricket and he went fishing and he made peace with my father's llamas.

Thayu and I spent some of the lazy nights by the fire talking about the impending fertility treatment. Since the injection of treated sperm hadn't worked, I now faced more invasive treatment, where Coldi genes were to be added to my existing cells. Lilona Shrakar in Barresh had explained that since the Coldi gene set attached to junk DNA as a piggyback spare set of genes, this came with a risk that the treatment would spread through my body as cells renewed.

We also heard about the many delegations from *gamra* that arrived in Athens, and it was with one of those that we went home a bit over a week later.

Nations of Earth had not yet dismantled the border checks in Athens, but that was sure to happen soon. I was merely happy that

my father could keep living on the farm and that I could keep visiting, and I was fully committed, next time Thayu and I visited, to
showing off our little boy or girl.

———

Thanks for reading Ambassador 7: The Last Frontier.

In *Ambassador 8: The Alabaster Army,* a scientist goes missing from
Barresh, a demand for ransom is made, and Cory is forced to finally
deal with the Tamerian problem.

ABOUT THE AUTHOR

Patty Jansen lives in Sydney, Australia, where she spends most of her time writing Science Fiction and Fantasy.

Her career started in earnest when her story *This Peaceful State of War* placed first in the second quarter of the Writers of the Future contest and was published in their 27th anthology. She has also sold fiction to genre magazines such as Analog Science Fiction and Fact, Redstone SF and Aurealis, before making the move to independent publishing.

Patty has written over fifty novels in both Science Fiction and Fantasy, including the *Icefire Trilogy* and the *Ambassador* series.

pattyjansen.com

BOOKS BY PATTY JANSEN

For a complete list of books, scan the image below with your phone.